Praise for Kerry Lonsdale

"Heartfelt and suspenseful, *Everything We Keep* beautifully navigates the deep waters of grief, and one woman's search to reconcile a past she can't release, and a future she wants to embrace. Lonsdale's writing is crisp and effortless and utterly irresistible—and her expertly layered exploration of the journey from loss to renewal is sure to make this a book club must-read. *Everything We Keep* drew me in from the first page and held me fast all the way to its deeply satisfying ending."

—Erika Marks, author of *The Last Treasure*

"In *Everything We Keep*, Kerry Lonsdale brilliantly explores the grief of loss, if we can really let go of our great loves, and if some secrets are better left buried. With a good dose of drama, a heart-wrenching love story, and the suspense of unanswered questions, Lonsdale's layered and engrossing debut is a captivating read."

—Karma Brown, bestselling author of *Come Away with Me*

"A stunning debut with a memorable twist, *Everything We Keep* effortlessly layers family secrets into a suspenseful story of grief, love, and art. This is a gem of a book."

—Barbara Claypole White, bestselling author of *The Perfect Son*

ALL
THE
BREAKING
WAVES

Also by Kerry Lonsdale

Everything We Keep

ALL
THE
BREAKING
WAVES

a novel

KERRY LONSDALE

LAKE UNION
PUBLISHING

Published by Lake Union Publishing, Seattle

www.apub.com

Amazon, the Amazon logo, and Lake Union Publishing are trademarks of Amazon.com, Inc., or its affiliates.

ISBN-13: 9781503941830
ISBN-10: 1503941833

Cover design by Damonza

Printed in the United States of America

For Evan and Brenna, for being you

Chapter 1

Growing up in Pacific Grove, a coastal town on the Monterey Peninsula in California, I had spent many Sunday mornings combing beaches, hunting for sea glass. I once believed the surf-tumbled glass had come from mermaids when the mythical creatures wept for sailors lost at sea, their tears hardened and washed ashore by the latest storm front.

Mermaid tears were treasure, meant to be guarded close to one's heart. They brought wishes of true love and kept you safe from those who meant harm.

But time taught me two valuable lessons: fairy tales and fables paled in comparison with real nightmares, and psychic abilities were a power the human body should not possess.

Chapter 2

Monday, before dawn

Burrowed under a down comforter and a silver blanket of light, I stared at the crescent moon outside my window and waited. The moon, looking like a tear in black silk, journeyed across the sky. The night grew older and the air colder. Still, I waited.

I inhaled deeply and scrunched my nose against the odor that was part of the house. Musty wood, damp towels, and molding leaves. We lived in San Luis Obispo in a small bungalow built before World War II, where over time the windows had been painted shut inside their frames. Brittle air stole through warped doors, and thin cracks webbed plaster walls. Black mildew spotted the baseboards where water had leaked into walls the landlord had shown no interest in repairing.

A dank, musty odor stung my nostrils with each breath. Pressure built in my sinus cavities as though I had an infection. Cassie had been sick, too, several times this past winter, but there were other reasons aside from our unhealthy environment that contributed to our colds. Lack of sleep, for one.

We needed to find a new place to live. Hopefully somewhere in the neighborhood so Cassie wouldn't have to relocate to another school.

I rolled to my side, pulling my knees to my stomach, and squinted at the clock's glowing digital numbers: 2:58 a.m.

The lease is up in June.

2:59

It's only April. I'll start looking for a rental next month.

3:00

I held my breath, listening, and counted. Five seconds. Ten. Pressure built in my chest. Twelve. Thirteen. Fourteen.

Cassie's sob whispered through the house. My ears pricked up. It drifted into my room, seventeen seconds after the hour. *Like clockwork,* I thought, exhaling in a whoosh. Rolling to my back, I coaxed my weary limbs to move, dreading what I knew would come next.

The scream pierced the air, a blade of noise that sliced down my spine. It tore through my chest. Cassie screamed again, the sound rattling my bones, jolting my legs into action. I leaped from the bed and stumbled to the floor, my foot caught in the sheet. I landed hard on my knee. Pain shot down my shin and up my thigh like a starburst.

"Cassie!"

I pushed to my feet, then limped-ran across the hall and into her room. In the dim glow of her night-light, she lay curled on her side under a pile of blankets, both hands clutching her head.

Cassie screamed, eyes squeezed shut. Her knees pushed farther into her chest, and she rocked onto her elbows, face pushed into her pillow, then flopped back to her side. She whimpered.

I rushed to the bed and shook her shoulder. "Cassie, wake up."

She rocked back and forth, fingers gripped like turkey prongs around her head. Tears leaked from the corners of her closed eyes. She groaned.

I gave her shoulder another shake. Tried prying her hands from her head. Her elbows were locked. "Cassie," I demanded. "Wake up."

Her eyelids fluttered open, and her hands eased away. She straightened her legs and rolled to her back, gazing at the ceiling with a blank expression.

"Jesus, honey. Wake up." I snapped my fingers several times, by her ear and in front of her eyes.

She blinked rapidly, drawing me into focus. "Mommy?" Tears sprang like water from a well and leaked across her temples into her matted blonde curls. She clutched her stuffed rabbit to her chest.

The alarm in her gaze reflected my own. "Same dream, Mermaid?" I crawled into bed with her. Her reaction to the night terrors scared me as much as they did her.

Cassie sniffled and nodded, bumping my chin. My heart still thumped wildly in my chest. We were on day four of the same dream, and it was the worst night by far. Tonight should be the last night for this particular nightmare. Thank God. Those screams of hers left an imprint. I'd be hearing them for months.

I inhaled deeply, coming down from my adrenalin rush. "Did you learn anything more about Grace?"

She nodded and rubbed the side of her head. Her dreams left behind echoes of pain in the exact spot where Grace would fracture her skull.

I smoothed Cassie's hair from her damp forehead and hummed, waiting for her sobs to subside. More than anything I wished to tell Cassie she'd be all right, that she'd grow out of her condition.

But she wouldn't. Her abilities were as much a part of her as the freckles on the bridge of her nose.

Cassie murmured a few words. I bent closer to her face. "What did you say?"

"I saw her skull. Her hair and skin were gone in one spot. And"— her breath hitched—"and there was blood on the ground."

I squeezed my eyes shut against the disturbing image Cassie's words put in my head. A broken young girl with the contorted metal of her bike in the street nearby. My stomach twisted like a knotty vine.

"The dreams are getting worse, Mommy."

"I know." I kissed Cassie's head, sniffed the innocence of her kiwi shampoo. God, she was too young to be having dreams like this. She was too young to see injuries of this kind. Like an untreated ailment, her premonitions were getting worse, more gruesome. The accidents she foresaw were followed by nightmares that recurred until the premonition came to pass.

I had no idea why, nor how to stop them. Since her toddler years, Cassie had had a heightened awareness when someone she cared about was injured, almost as though she hurt right along with them. Like a nurse, she'd flutter about them, trying to soothe their pain. Somehow, with the onset of her abilities, her visions tapped into her nurturing side. She only foresaw accidents, and always about someone she knew. And as soon as one premonition resolved, the next one followed not long after. A cycle that tormented us both, and I had to find a way to stop it.

"I told Grace a car will hit her," Cassie confessed in a whisper. "She doesn't listen to me and she doesn't believe me."

People never did.

"Do you remember what we've discussed?" I spoke the measured words against Cassie's head, ruffling her hair, and felt her hesitant nod under my chin. "Don't talk about your visions or your nightmares. Not with anyone. Your friends don't understand." No one understood.

Even I barely understood.

Cassie looked up at me with sad eyes. "But if I tell her, Grace will stay off her bike. I don't want her to ride her bike to school. She might die." Cassie rubbed her face against her stuffed rabbit. "I only want to help."

And I only wanted the visions to go away.

I rubbed Cassie's back as we stared wide-eyed at the ceiling. When it looked as though neither of us would fall back to sleep, I asked, "Do you want a glass of milk?"

"Yes, please." Cassie kicked off her blanket and I stood, holding out my hand. She clasped my fingers, and we padded down the hallway and into the kitchen. Her bare feet whispered across the cold floor. My heavier step found every squeaky board. She sat in her chair by the window, propping Bunny in her lap. The stuffed animal's plastic eye—the other eye had been lost in the sand at Avila Beach last summer—peered over the table. I poured two glasses and set one before Cassie.

The fridge hummed, and the house creaked as though shivering in the early-spring air. I watched Cassie offer Bunny a sip from her glass, tipping the rim until the liquid reached the worn fur, leaving behind a milk mustache. She used her nightgown sleeve to wipe Bunny clean.

I drank from my glass, allowing the milk to skim my upper lip. Cassie giggled when I showed off my milk mustache, and warmth radiated through me. I loved that sound. She hadn't laughed enough lately.

Cassie moved to the couch when she finished. I rinsed the glasses and turned on the TV, muting the sound. Then I sat down and snuggled with her.

The remainder of the night wasn't different from any other night since Thursday, and many other nights these last three months. Nestled against my side within the enclosure of my arm, Cassie watched the images play on the screen until she drifted to sleep. I remained awake and thought about the girl in Cassie's vision, her best friend. Poor thing. I did hope Grace survived the accident without brain damage. But I still prayed for the car to hit her.

The sooner her pain started, the sooner Cassie's would end, even if only for a short time.

Chapter 3

Monday, morning

I stopped at the curb in the school drop-off loop. As the Jeep Cherokee idled, Cassie watched a small group of girls huddled together like a soccer team before a game starts. There were five of them clustered by the open gate into the schoolyard, backpacks slung over shoulders and binders clutched against still-flat chests. They chatted among themselves until a lanky brunette pointed at my car with her chin. Four heads turned in unison toward us and ogled my daughter.

Vicious little monsters. Echoes of my own grammar school experiences vibrated through me. The taunting and jeers, then the cautious glances that eventually relegated me to the corner of the schoolyard. It was easier to play the role of social outcast than to explain the odd things I saw or seemed to make other people do.

I twisted around in my seat to look at Cassie.

She turned to me, bags heavy and dark under her blue eyes. "I don't want to go to school today."

The corners of my mouth turned downward in understanding. But I had an art history class to teach at the community college, and no one was available to stay home with her. "I have to work this morning, Cassie. And I have a meeting with a client this afternoon." A beachwear boutique downtown wanted to see selections from my summer line of wire-wrapped sea glass jewelry. Otherwise, we'd have both remained home and taken a long morning nap.

She massaged Bunny's ear and turned back to the window. "Grace's accident is supposed to be today. I hope she didn't ride her bike this morning."

"If she didn't and she's here, don't say anything. Promise me you won't talk about your vision." I reached behind the seat and gently squeezed her knee.

"I promise." She popped open the door. Leaving Bunny behind, sprawled on the backseat, she slid outside.

"I'll be here when the bell rings," I said before she slammed the door.

Cassie made her way toward the schoolyard, chin tucked as she cut a wide berth around the girls. Their gazes followed, and after she walked through the gate, they tucked their heads together. I was sure they gossiped about Cassie.

Warmth danced along my spine, and electricity tingled my mouth. Power simmered below my surface of control.

I tightened my grip on the steering wheel. "Think happy thoughts, Molly," I mumbled to myself. Happy thoughts.

Flexing my fingers, I sighed. It turned into a yawn. Coffee. I needed some desperately. Shifting into gear, I left the parking lot and headed to the café up the street, my thoughts drifting back to Cassie.

Her abilities had only recently manifested, and I worried she was already a social outcast. If only she'd learn not to talk about them at school. Then again, I hadn't listened to my father, I acknowledged with a heavy weight of guilt and a pang of unease. Why should I expect Cassie to listen to me?

A short time later, coffee in hand, I was returning to my car when a call came in. Juggling keys and coffee, I dug out my phone from the bottom of my purse.

"Hello?"

"Ms. Brennan? This is Bev Marsh from the school office. Cassie is okay, but Principal Harrison has requested to meet with you. Are you available this morning?"

My heart clenched. Thoughts about any number of scenarios barreled through my mind. The girls I saw earlier pushing Cassie on the ground, tugging her hair, or mocking her with their words.

I glanced at my watch. One hour before my class started. "I can come right now if that's all right with you."

"Thank you, Ms. Brennan. I'll let Principal Harrison know."

The school's office smelled of instant coffee and printer ink. Along the rear wall, a copier thumped. Papers steadily piled on the output tray. Late arrivals lined up to collect tardy slips, their disgruntled, sleepy faces a telltale sign they'd overslept.

I rested my damp palms on the high countertop. "I'm here to see Principal Harrison," I told the woman sitting behind the counter.

"Ms. Brennan?"

"Yes."

"One moment. I'll let Principal Harrison know you're here." She picked up the phone. "Why don't you have a seat while you wait?"

I turned toward the waiting area. Cassie sat alone, swinging her legs, face downturned as she fiddled with a bracelet on her wrist. Her backpack took up the space by her feet. I went over and knelt in front of her.

"Cassie, darling, what are you doing here?" I felt her legs, her arms, and cupped her face, making sure she was all right, that all her bones were intact. I held her hands.

She lifted her face and shrugged her shoulders. "I don't know. Right after the bell rang, Mrs. Pierce told me to get my backpack and go to the office."

That didn't sound good. I sat in the chair beside her and smoothed her hair, wondering what had happened to have the principal calling us both in. "Principal Harrison wants to meet with me. Anything you think I should know, or that you want to tell me?"

Cassie shook her head and dropped her chin again. She clasped her hands in her lap, and the bracelet slipped from her sleeve, drawing my gaze. Embedded in a thin weave of frayed twine was a triangular piece of pale-blue sea glass. A memory surfaced, like the rising tide. It sparkled with a distinct clarity and took my breath away. I saw myself as a young girl several years older than Cassie, holding out my hand to receive the pitted glass, found in the sand by a boy I once knew. Owen. I wanted to linger on the memory, get lost in the rush of sensations it brought forth like water surging toward shore. A mix of longing and regret. Heartache.

I took a deep breath, realizing I'd been holding the pendant I wore around my neck. Another long-ago gift from Owen. It'd been a long time since I'd thought of him so clearly, and a long time since I'd left him.

Adjusting the bracelet on Cassie's wrist, I asked, "Where did you get this?"

"Found it." Cassie tugged her sleeve, hiding the glass.

"Cassie," I prodded. "Were you digging through my jewelry box again?"

She popped a shoulder. "I liked the color."

Aside from a collection of expensive necklaces and earrings I had designed, there were a few delicate pieces that had belonged to my mother. And a few special trinkets from Owen, like the bracelet Cassie wore.

I was about to remind her not to play with my jewelry when Bev called my name.

"Ms. Harrison will see you now."

I stood quickly, and my shoulder bag dropped to the floor. The thud echoed through the office. I picked up the bag and coaxed Cassie to her feet with a word of encouragement.

Bev's gaze jumped from Cassie back to me. "I'm sorry, just you, Ms. Brennan. Cassie, you can wait here until your mom's done."

Cassie flopped back into her chair.

I bent until my eyes were level with hers. "I won't be long." I angled my head toward the bookcase under the bulletin board. "Go find a book to read."

Cassie moistened her lips and walked over to the bookcase. She flipped through the books, selecting one with a kitten on the cover, and returned to her chair. Cassie loved cats, had even asked for a kitten from a litter up for adoption outside the corner grocery mart. One day, I had told her. Caring for an animal was too much when it seemed lately I could barely care for my own daughter.

I straightened and followed Bev down a hallway. Jane's door was open. Bev rapped her knuckles on the doorframe. "Principal Harrison, Ms. Brennan is here." She pointed at the two chairs in front of the desk. "Have a seat."

I murmured my thanks and took the seat closest to the door. Bev left us alone.

"Give me one sec to finish this e-mail." Jane typed on the keyboard, her back to me. Sunlight poked through the blinds, spilling across the soft-blue walls in diagonal lines. A calming color. Voices filtered from the hallway.

Jane punched a key, turned off the monitor, and swiveled in the chair. She gave me a considering look through magenta-framed glasses, her eyes tired, like she hadn't slept much last night.

Join the club.

A smile, appearing more forced than genuine, stretched Jane's tinted lips. She clasped her hands and dropped them on the desktop.

Bracelet beads rattled and clicked on the wood. "Thanks for coming in on such short notice."

"Of course."

I had known Jane Harrison since she'd taught Cassie in first grade. Last year she had been promoted to vice principal and had assumed the role of principal this year after Deidre Whitmore retired. Jane was a fair principal and interacted well with students. I guessed we were about the same age, but Jane was married with no children. She had once confided that she and her husband, Quinn, were planning a family. That had been almost three years ago.

Jane straightened pencils already neatly aligned on the desk and frowned. A shadow fell across her face, and I sensed her mind drifting. I gripped the armrests, irritated and impatient. From deep within me I felt a rush of electricity. The desire to redirect her thoughts back inside the room rippled up my spine. To coax her to spit out whatever it was that had Cassie sitting in the waiting area and me across from Jane. I turned my gaze inward and let my eyelids fall closed for a moment. I took one deep inhale and felt my body relax, my mind ease, as I regained control.

Better, I thought, with another rise and fall of my chest. My eyes snapped open, and I plastered on a pleasant smile.

Jane's fingers twitched, causing a pencil to roll out of formation. She pushed it back and clasped her hands again.

"I would have contacted you on Friday, but an emergency came up and I had to leave early."

"The emergency doesn't have to do with Cassie, does it?"

She shook her head. An onyx curl bounced over her glasses frame. "Cassie is a different matter. An incident between Cassie and her friend Grace that occurred Thursday afternoon was brought to my attention. Grace's mother, Alice Kaling, called me Friday morning. I've spoken with the girls and their stories match, as do other witnesses."

"What exactly happened?"

"Cassie was berating Grace about her bike helmet. She insisted Grace get a new helmet or not ride her bike to school."

"And what's wrong with that? Cassie only wants her friend to be safe."

"Cassie told Grace she was going to get hit by a car and that her blood would be all over the street and her head cracked open. That she'd be asleep in the hospital for a long time. Cassie said she had a vision about this." Jane leaned forward. "She screamed this during lunch period, and it was witnessed by a lot of kids. Cassie really spooked them, especially when she chased Grace into the bathroom and cornered her in a stall. Grace stood on the toilet bowl calling for help. She slipped and fell."

I pressed my back into the chair. My eyes burned as my heart went out to my daughter. I needed to get help, and not the kind found under a doctor's care.

"I'm afraid, effective immediately, Cassie is on suspension."

I straightened. "Suspension?"

Jane regarded me for a moment. "We have a zero-tolerance policy for bullying, you know that. And this wasn't Cassie's first infraction."

"She was only trying to help Ethan," I defended in reference to Cassie's other offense.

"If you say so." Jane picked up a pencil, rolled it between her fingers. She frowned. "Odd how he broke his leg exactly how Cassie said he would."

Something shifted inside my stomach. "What are you implying?"

"Nothing. But I do wonder if Ethan saw her harassment as a challenge. He might not have swung so high and jumped from the swing, otherwise."

"Interesting theory." I shouldered my bag, itchy to leave. "But it's my understanding from Cassie that Ethan runs around with a group of boys who push one another to do daring stunts in the play yard. Perhaps you need better recess monitors."

Jane pursed her lips and set down the pencil. "The suspension is only a week. But if there is one more incident—"

"I know, I know," I interrupted with a loose nod. Cassie would be expelled.

Jane's face softened. "Cassie's a wonderful girl, and a gifted student. She used to be well behaved inside the classroom and out in the school yard. Now, though"—Jane turned her palms upward—"she seems more withdrawn, unless the other students don't listen to her, which makes her extremely upset. Her stories are quite colorful and disturbing. They scare the other kids. Is everything all right at home?"

"She hasn't been sleeping well," I said, leaving it at that.

Jane scribbled on a notepad. "There's a child psychologist I recommend here in town." She ripped off the paper and handed it to me. "Give her a call. She might be able to help."

If only. But I doubted a local child psychologist had expertise dealing with Cassie's abnormalities. I slid the note into the front pocket of my purse without looking at it.

"How's Grace?" I asked.

"Aside from a bruised elbow, she was fine when I saw her last Friday. I'm sure Cassie will be fine, too," she added hastily. "The suspension is only a week. Maybe the time away will be good. She can catch up on her sleep. But do get some help for her. I'd hate for us to reach the next step. We'd miss her."

"Yes, that would be unfortunate," I agreed, resigned to what I had to do next. There was only one person I knew who could possibly help Cassie.

Jane glanced at the wall clock. "Unless you have any more questions, I have another appointment." Without waiting for my answer, Jane pushed away from her desk and stood.

I did the same, straightening my skirt with damp palms. I would miss my class today, and then I would have to convince Admin I'd need the rest of the week off, even though I was already maxed on sick time.

It'd been a rough few months with Cassie, and I'd put off the inevitable long enough.

Jane directed me into the hallway as she thanked me for my time. Her gaze then shifted, caught by something happening behind me.

I turned around. Bev was rushing down the hallway toward us.

"Principal Harrison? Mrs. Kaling phoned."

"Put it through to my office. Ms. Brennan and I just finished."

"She left a message with me." Bev shifted her feet, her eyes avoiding mine.

"What is it?" Jane asked.

Bev leaned in and whispered in her ear. Jane's gaze swung in my direction. Bev gave me a fleeting glance, then hastily walked away.

A chill rippled over my skin. "What's wrong?"

"It's Grace," Jane replied in a strained voice. "There's been an accident. She's in the hospital."

My stomach lurched.

"It happened exactly like Cassie said it would," Jane whispered.

She looked behind me and turned two shades paler than fair. "Oh my." She backed into her office and closed the door.

"She's afraid of me."

I turned around and looked down at Cassie. A lone tear dripped over her cheek, and my heart dropped with it to the floor.

Chapter 4

Monday, midmorning

She's not afraid of you, I wanted to object. *Just confused, and maybe shocked.* But we both knew that wasn't the truth. We'd seen Jane's expression.

I crouched in front of Cassie. "How's your head?"

"Better," she whispered. It would be, now that her premonition had been fulfilled.

"Guess what? You have the whole week off school," I said, wanting to get her mind off Grace. "Let's go get a doughnut."

A sad smile pulled up her lips. She reached for my hand.

We left the school office and walked to our car. I called in to work and made up the excuse that Cassie was home sick. Then I rescheduled my afternoon appointment to the following week.

I was exhausted from worry and lack of sleep. The urge to lose myself in my studio at home was overwhelming. To have my mind coast into sanding and shaping glass, into framing the material in looping swirls of sterling silver wire. To fulfill the promise of transforming what had once been trash into stunning pieces of art despite the natural flaws. Imperfections made the glass beautiful and unique. I visualized drop-hook earrings and a necklace with glass clusters embedded in silver casings, olive with amber, pine with plum.

Maybe later, when Cassie napped. I glanced at her through the rearview mirror. Purple semicircles propped up her eyes. She yawned, coaxing a yawn from me.

Creativity would have to wait.

The effects of Cassie's visions were apparent from her behavior at school. Slipping grades, deteriorating friendships, and countless hours of lost sleep. Her face had a pallid cast and was punctuated by sunken eyes and concave cheeks. Her appetite had diminished, and I couldn't imagine the psychological damage the nightmares were doing to her young mind.

What had I been thinking? I shouldn't have waited this long. Cassie needed help, and I thought I could be the one to give it to her. But teaching an eight-year-old to meditate and calm her thoughts was easier said than done. I also hadn't expected the visions to become so horrific.

"Why are you sad, Mommy?" Cassie asked from the rear seat. It wasn't my expression she read, or the slight bow of my shoulders she saw, but the ribbons of blue in my aura. For Cassie, seeing colors came as naturally as breathing.

I made eye contact with her and watched her face fall apart.

"I'm sad," she admitted before I could reply.

"Are you thinking about Grace?"

Cassie nodded. She wiped her eyes and nose.

I stopped at a red light. "I'm worried, too."

Cassie fiddled with the zipper on her sweatshirt, sliding the tab up and down the metal teeth.

"How about two doughnuts this morning?"

A watery grin curved Cassie's lips. She held up both thumbs.

We picked out our pastries at a café on Monterey Boulevard and ate them on the grass in front of Mission San Luis Obispo de Tolosa in the heart of downtown.

Cassie ate half of one doughnut before the fountain lured her to its side. Two bear cub statues were poised in play at its edge. She splashed the bears, then rubbed water over one of them, pretending to give it a bath.

"Don't forget to scrub behind the ears," I suggested, searching the bottom of my purse for my phone.

While Cassie scrubbed vigorously behind the cub's ears, I brought up Nana Mary's number. She picked up after the second ring.

"Hello?" she said, sounding winded.

"Chasing the birds from your garden again?" I surmised. I hadn't seen her garden in two years, but she loved to complain about her daily battles with the feathered pests.

"No, not today. I'm just a little tired, that's all. How are you, Molly dear?"

Cassie scooped water in her hands and pretended to have the bear statues drink.

"I'm doing all right," I answered, watching my daughter. I popped a large bite of doughnut in my mouth. She waved and I waved back. "Any chance you can visit? Perhaps stay a few days?" I asked around the food in my mouth.

"Isn't Cassie in school?"

I chewed, swallowed. "Well, that's why I'm calling. She . . ." I frowned, my voice stalling. Cassie had stopped playing in the fountain and was staring, unfocused, at me.

"I'm not quite up to the trip. It's a bit long of a drive and my week is pretty full."

Pacific Grove was only two and a half hours from here. Far enough away that it wasn't convenient to visit regularly but close enough to travel there and back in a day.

"You're welcome to come here," she was saying.

I put Cassie's half-eaten doughnut back into the white bakery bag and took another bite of mine. "You know I don't like sleeping in that house."

Nana clucked her tongue. "Molly girl, that was a long time ago. One day, this house will—"

"Hold on a second, Nana," I interrupted. Cassie was looking at me with an odd expression, tugging at her sweatshirt zipper.

I covered the phone's mic. "Everything okay, Cassie?"

Before she could answer, a switch popped in an electrical panel nearby. Black nozzles rose out of the ground like missiles in silos, followed by the rush and whir of spraying water, nailing me in the chest and face.

I squealed, shoved the remaining third of my old-fashioned doughnut in my mouth, and snatched up my purse, dashing to dry land.

I swallowed, my hand pressing against my sternum, then laughed. "Whoa." I pushed wet hair off my forehead. Water dripped from my chin and plastered my blouse to my skin. "I didn't see that coming." I glanced back over my shoulder, noticing the bakery bag hadn't fared so well either. And I wasn't inclined to dash back through the sprinklers to get it.

Later—like when the sprinkler cycle ended, I decided. I wiped the wet phone screen against my hip, which disconnected my call.

"Great," I grumbled. At least the phone had survived. I launched the screen to redial Nana and pressed it against my ear. I looked over at Cassie, and my breath caught in my throat.

She stood frozen, her eyes moonlike circles as she stared at me. Her face paled.

My heart lurched. I knew that look and swore under my breath. Not another premonition. Give the girl a break.

Cassie shrieked and I jerked. The phone slipped from my fingers. She screamed again, high-pitched, curdling my blood.

What had she seen? Who had she seen?

I glanced around the park. There wasn't anyone we knew. She always knew the people in her visions.

"Mommy!" She ran to me and slammed into my stomach. She pounded me with her fists, still screaming my name.

This was a bad one, the worst one yet. I couldn't imagine the nightmares she'd have this time. Her premonitions always returned as dreams for four solid nights in a row, revealing a little more information each time. The cycle didn't stop until the fifth day—the day the premonition was fulfilled.

"Cassie, calm down," I yelled when her fist packed a solid punch into my hip bone. I grabbed her flailing arms and lowered to my knees. "Focus, honey. Focus on my voice or you're going to hurt yourself."

"Don't leave me!" She clawed my soaked shirt, her face blotchy and purple. "Don't leave, don't leave, don't leave!" She shrieked, a piercing scream that stabbed my eardrums and had the fine hairs on the back of my neck rising to attention. Several heads turned in our direction.

I clasped Cassie's cheeks and forced her to look at me. "Calm down," I repeated. "I'm right here. Relax. Look at me."

Cassie pounded my shoulders. The impact vibrated my toes. "Cassidy," I admonished. My fingers dug deep into her upper arms. "Look. At. Me."

She squeezed her eyes shut and shook her head. "Don't leave. Don't leave. Don't leave," she whimpered.

Each plea was a tear straight through me. "Sweetheart." I held her against my chest. "It'll be okay," I soothed. "We'll fix this. Nana will help us fix this."

The sprinklers shut off with a whoosh, and the fountain bubbled nearby. Flat sheets of clouds moved overhead, dimming the sunlight. Rain was imminent. I rested my chin on Cassie's head, wishing I could protect her from the violent images brewing in her mind.

"Stay with me, Mommy."

"I'm right here, honey."

She shook her head and cried. "You're going to leave me."

"Never. I'm not going anywhere."

She squirmed in my arms and exploded. "You don't believe me!" She pounded my shoulders, my chest. "You're just like everyone else! You don't listen to me! You have to listen! YOU HAVE TO BELIEVE ME!"

I roughly gripped her shoulders. "Believe *what*?"

She screamed. Her arms flailed. I fought to restrain her. She slipped out of reach. Her chest heaved, arms falling limp against her sides, and her eyes shimmered behind a curtain of tears. She looked at me like I'd betrayed her.

Air shuttled from my chest. I fell back on my heels. What had I done? My hands started shaking. This premonition seemed different from the others. Something was off.

"What did you see?" I asked in a strained whisper.

Cassie's lower lip quivered. Tears flowed like waterfalls. "You couldn't breathe. I saw you die."

Chapter 5

Monday, midmorning

Passersby were stopping to stare, their looks curious, even accusatory. I didn't want them to question why Cassie was screaming, and I didn't want them to hear what she was saying. They wouldn't understand. So I did the only thing I seemed capable of doing, given the circumstances. I scooped her up, along with my purse and phone, and speed-walked to the car, leaving the gawkers to do just that, gawk.

On the drive home I called the community college and explained that there'd been an emergency and that I had to leave town. I also left a message with Cassie's school. I didn't give a date for when I'd return, but I did give them my grandmother's number. I called her next.

"We're coming," I said, surprised at how calm I sounded.

"Oh?" she asked. "When?"

"Now. We'll be there in a few hours." I hung up.

As I pulled into the driveway, the weight of Cassie's premonition settled on my chest. It left me gasping in the driver's seat while Cassie watched with a terrified expression.

Move, Molly. Do something.

I got out of the car, urging Cassie to follow, and left her standing alone in the foyer as I raced through the house, grabbing toiletries and clothes, dumping everything into our suitcases. Short breaths exploded from my lungs, my face hot and my neck clammy as I packed.

I hurried down the hallway to my studio, where I popped lids on plastic bins of sea glass, wires, and tools, topping off the pile with my portfolio. Then I did a mental check that my students' tests were still in the car for me to grade. I don't know why I thought I needed all this. Maybe doing ordinary tasks would convince both of us that life would carry on normally. Or maybe I just wanted to pretend Cassie's premonition wasn't true.

"I'm not going to die." I lifted the bins and moved into the hallway, nearly running into Cassie.

She whimpered, kneading Bunny's ear. Tears glazed her cheeks, giving her a porcelain-doll appearance under the fluorescent ceiling light.

"Cassie," I exclaimed, and dropped the bins to the side. They landed with a thud. I sank to my knees. "Don't cry, Mermaid. Please don't cry."

"Don't leave me." Fresh tears flowed like a wave pushed ashore.

"I'm not going anywhere, I promise," I said as soothingly as I could.

"But, I saw—"

"What *did* you see?" I asked when her voice stalled. "Do you know why I couldn't breathe?"

Her mouth turned into a grimace, and she shrugged both shoulders.

Cassie once said her visions played like a music video. Images flickered at rocket speed, so fast she initially had only an idea as to what would happen. But something similar to the actual incident usually triggered the premonition. As my damp shirt chilled my skin, I replayed what I'd been doing right before Cassie had freaked out. The sprinklers had popped on, soaking my face, hair, and shirt. I'd been wet. *Still am,* I thought, shivering as realization dawned.

My gaze shifted to the bins of sea glass. *Of course,* I thought with a tidal wave of sadness that burned my lungs and the backs of my eyes. The ocean. My second home.

"Do you think—" I started, my breath catching. My eyes sheened, and I pushed down the sand-dollar-size lump in my throat. "Do you think I drown, Cassie? Maybe that's why I can't breathe."

"I don't know," she said in a hesitant voice. Her gaze turned inward, and after a moment her eyes lit up like bioluminescence, sparkling in the dim hallway. She nodded rapidly. "Yes, yes, that's it. I think you drown."

"All right, then. I believe that's what you saw. I really do. But, Cassie, sweetie." My hands flitted over her, touching her arms, her shoulders. I cupped her cheeks. "Your abilities are new. You've only had a few visions, and just because what you've seen so far has happened, doesn't mean they'll all come true."

She twisted Bunny's ear and sucked in her lower lip.

"Remember how you thought telling Grace about her bike accident might stop her from riding her bike to school? That way there wouldn't be an accident and she wouldn't be hurt? I'll just stay away from water; that way I won't drown. How's that sound?"

"Oh"—she hiccupped—"kay."

"Listen to me. I'm not going to die."

I couldn't die. I had to take care of her—I was the only one who could. Nana Mary was too old to worry about raising a child. She'd had my own mother in her late twenties and was now in her seventies. My friend Phoebe, Cassie's godmother, was no longer an option either. She'd divorced last year and, after her parents' passing, had been living off her small inheritance and her ex-husband's alimony to feed five mouths. She had just enough money to scrape by for the next few years until all four kids were in school and she could go back to work.

As for Cassie's father, she'd never known him, God rest his reckless soul.

I pulled Cassie into my arms and hugged her tight. "We'll be all right. Everything will be all right. Now"—I leaned back to look at her, brushing aside the curls that clung to the dampness on her cheeks—"why don't you and Bunny go to your room and pick out what you want to bring to Nana's house. Perhaps a coloring book and crayons?"

"Okay." She kissed my cheek and reluctantly left my arms.

I lowered my face into my hands. *Holy crap, what am I going to do?*

Avoid the water, just like I'd told Cassie. Sighing, I rose to my feet, gathered up the bins, and took them to the car.

A half hour later, bags packed and loaded into the Jeep, we drove north. We hadn't visited in two years. Between Cassie's school and my teaching schedule, which went through the summer months, it was just easier for Nana to come to us. But she hadn't visited since the holidays, which was before Cassie's abilities had manifested.

It started to rain as I pulled onto the freeway. Cassie yawned loudly, and within moments the hum of tires rolling on pavement and the rhythmic swish of wipers across the windshield lulled her to sleep.

She slept for most of the two-and-a-half-hour drive, waking as we drove through town. Art studios and cafés framed in striped awnings that billowed in the sea breeze passed outside the car's windows. We drove by retail stores and antique shops offering a sense of familiarity but no sense of belonging. I hadn't considered Pacific Grove home since the day I'd left to attend the Jewelry Arts & Design College in Los Angeles, and I didn't intend to call it home again. Returning to Pacific Grove always roused the fears and doubts I had about my own abilities. And remaining in Pacific Grove risked the life of the one person I'd once cared for the most.

Guilt and regret swirled inside my belly, rippling my muscles. Forcing the feeling aside, I concentrated on our immediate needs: getting help for Cassie . . . and keeping me alive.

In the rearview mirror, I saw Cassie glance around, taking in everything outside the windows. I opened mine and breathed in the salt-filled air. The rain had stopped. Roads glistened in the early-afternoon sunlight breaking through the clouds as we turned onto Nana's street, where the deep-blue bay stretched to the horizon. Pulling to the curb behind Nana's faded-blue Volkswagen Beetle, I stopped in front of what used to be her rickety, old, threatening-to-crumble 1911 Victorian. In its place stood a remodeled Victorian cottage painted a vibrant purple. The image of a giant Easter egg popped into my head.

"Nana fixed her house. It's pretty," Cassie said.

"It's purple."

I gawked. Nana had mentioned once or twice that she was having a bit of work done on the house. What I was looking at was not a *bit* of work.

The house was beautiful, though. Nothing like the one I'd grown up in. Lush lavender sprigs poked through a distressed wooden fence, which was new but fashioned to appear aged. Creeping rose vines heavy with pink blooms clung to the trellised garden entrance.

The front door opened, and Nana stood on the porch, arms spread wide. Cassie flew from the car. "Nana!"

She was bawling when she reached Nana, who scooped her up. Cassie hid her face in the folds of her great-grandmother's sweater. Nana looked at me, alarmed. Cassie's shoulders shook, and my eyes watered.

I slid from the car and turned directly toward the ocean at the end of the street. I froze. My hands flew to cover my mouth. *What the heck am I doing here?* Driving straight to Nana, who lived by the beach, was the worst thing I could have done, considering Cassie's premonition.

Deep-blue waves rippled behind the fir trees that lined Ocean View Boulevard, the road intersecting Nana's. Usually the sight, combined with the scent of salt and seaweed, gave me a rush of anticipation. I'd drop everything and race for the shore, drawn to the beach like my father had been to alcohol, to hunt for rough and tumbled shards of glass. The ocean was my addiction, the place I loved most.

But not anymore, I thought, looking toward waters of the bay that kissed my favorite cove. Lovers Beach. Was that where I'd drown?

Dammit, Molly, you're not going to drown. I slammed the car door. Avoid the beach, that was the plan. Easy-peasy. I popped open the rear hatch and unpacked the car, lining up our suitcases and my plastic bins on the sidewalk.

Straightening, I rubbed my lower back and caught a glimpse of the house next door. A vintage Camaro, its hood propped up and toolbox opened nearby, was parked on the driveway. A rush of excitement pushed through me, tumbling me back to my high school days. Back when I spent hours watching Owen tighten bolts and hoses on his '67 Mustang GT. Nana mentioned several years ago Owen's parents had retired to the Florida Keys. I wondered who was now living there. They'd fixed up the place with new landscaping, paint, and windows.

As for Owen, I hadn't seen him in twelve years.

"Molly."

I tensed and swung around. Nana stood beside me on the curb. A daisy rested over her ear, poking from her chin-length, honey-blonde hair, tinted to hide the gray. A faint, powdery aroma, Nana's perfume, tickled my nose. It masked a sour odor whose source I couldn't determine. Her eyes shimmered with tears.

A sharp burn stung behind my eyes and pierced my chest. "Cassie told you."

Nana's mouth twisted into an upside-down smile.

"She's like Mom," I whispered with regret.

Nana rested a hand on her chest and her eyes closed. She took a moment before asking, "How long?"

I angled my head down and stared at my heels. In my rush to get on the road, I hadn't changed out of my soiled clothes. My blouse was still damp. I shivered.

"Five days." I explained what I knew of the premonition cycle. "Something always triggers the premonition, and it's usually similar to what will happen. She saw one boy swinging too high on the swing and had a vision about him jumping and shattering his tibia. She saw her friend Grace riding her bike, and with me, I was doused this morning by the sprinklers. My soaked clothes and hair triggered Cassie's premonition. The visions then return as dreams. Well, nightmares, actually. The more nights she dreams about what she saw, the clearer the image gets. I'll know a little bit more as to how and where it happens tomorrow."

Nana made an impatient noise and sliced her hand in the space between us. "Cassie looks sick. How long has she had her abilities?"

I folded my arms over my chest. "About three months."

"And you never told me," she accused, then shook her head. Disappointment marred her face. "I should have known to ask if she was showing any signs. Your abilities manifested around the same age. As did your mother's. They usually do with the women in our family fortunate enough to have them. Why didn't you call?"

Because I'd have to come here. Just like I am here now.

"Her visions weren't bad like this in the beginning," I defended. "They've gotten worse, and I thought I could manage on my own. I thought I could—"

"Teach her to shut everything down and ignore her gifts," she finished.

"They aren't gifts." They were lethal abnormalities. "Besides, I don't know how to teach her."

Nana gave me a sympathetic look. "That's no fault of yours. I shouldn't have let your father talk me or your mother out of teaching you. You never had the chance to hone your skills."

I felt a thickness in my throat and glanced toward the bay.

"Does Cassie know what you can do?" Nana asked.

I quickly turned back to her. "No. And she never will."

"Has she tried reaching out to you with her mind?"

"I block her. The same way you block me," I added glibly.

Nana pursed her lips, admonishing me with one stern expression. Behind her, I noticed Cassie wandering in the front yard, looking through bushes.

"What other abilities, aside from precognition and telepathy, has she shown?"

"Just one." Thank God. "She's clairvoyant only in the sense that she sees auras."

"Like you."

"Yes . . . like me."

"Well, then," she mused, scratching the back of her head with one fingernail, "we have our work cut out for us. I'll train Cassie—"

"To not use her abilities. She needs to know how to 'turn them off.'" I air-quoted. "She experiences physical pain with the nightmares, and that scares me more than her premonition that I'll drown."

"I'll do what I can. Meanwhile, you must figure out what's going to happen if—"

"Kitty!"

Nana and I jolted. A shorthair tabby squeezed under the rustic fence and scampered down the sidewalk, belly low to the concrete.

Cassie squealed. "More kitties!"

I followed Nana through the arbor and into the front yard, which was divided by raised planter boxes overflowing with herbs and flowering shrubs. Camellias, English roses, and star jasmine perfumed the air.

Walking paths edged the yard and weaved between planters. A furry face popped from a bush. Wide amber eyes stared back. Dirt speckled the feline's nose. A twig of greenery was clamped in its mouth.

"Is that—?"

"Catnip," Nana explained. "They love it."

An orange tabby crawled from another bush. Frankie. I added up the cats. "Four." I gawked at Nana. "You're the Neighborhood Cat Lady."

She flinched. "Only Frankie is mine. And they stopped fighting when I planted the 'nip. Now they all get along."

"Because they're stoned." I winced at the bite in my tone. I didn't like the idea of being back here. I didn't want to sleep in my old room with the echo of memories best forgotten. It put me on edge.

Cassie picked up a tuxedo cat. It squirmed in her arms. Nana waved Cassie over. "Support the back feet, dear." She positioned Cassie's hand under the cat, but the wiggly feline was quicker, planting its feet against Cassie's chest. The cat launched from her arms and ran, clawing up and over the fence and into the backyard.

Cassie started to chase after the cat but stopped. She looked at me with big eyes, then shuffled to my side. She clasped my hand and leaned against me.

"Help me bring our things inside," I suggested, hoping to keep her mind occupied on things other than her vision.

"All will be better soon," Nana reassured. She winced and rubbed her forehead.

"Headache?"

"Don't you worry about me." She extended an arm toward Cassie. "Come inside. Lunch is ready. And so is your new room. I can't wait for you to see it."

The side gate to Nana's backyard slammed and so did my heart. My breath left in a hard rush as I watched the man approaching us.

He was tall with dark hair. Several days' growth dusted his face. He didn't smile, but his gray eyes were fixed on me.

Breathe, Molly.

Cassie made a noise, and I forced myself to look at her. Her eyes were huge when she glanced at me, then at the man. He strode across the yard, his work boots heavy on the gravel pathway, and stopped directly in front of me.

"Hey, Lollipop."

My pulse pounded in my ear. I pushed out a breath. "Owen."

"Mommy." Cassie tugged my hand. "He has the same colors. You match."

Chapter 6

Owen hooked his thumbs in his front pockets. "That's right, our auras are the same shade," he said, nodding slowly.

I wanted to cringe. I couldn't believe Cassie had blurted that, after all the times we'd discussed her *not* calling attention to her abilities around other people, whether or not they knew we had them, which Owen did. At least, he knew about me and what I could do. But that wasn't the point, because to Cassie, Owen was a stranger. And he was here, filling the space right in front of me.

An unexpected surge raced over me, rippling my skin, making me dizzy. It curled inside me, digging deep into the crevices of my heart where I'd buried all those gut-wrenching sensations I hadn't allowed myself to feel for the past twelve years.

Owen watched the play of emotions on my face. Joy, happiness, longing. Love. Because I had once loved him something fierce. His gaze pierced mine, and I knew he picked up on every nuance. My hitched breath. Fingers twisting in the tails of my damp blouse. The shuffle of my feet as though I might bolt. And I wanted to run. From the ocean, from Cassie's premonition, and from Owen. For in his expression, I saw the turmoil and despair I'd caused him.

As if realizing his face was an open book, he shook his head and schooled his expression. "What do you think it means, us being the same color and all?" he asked with a touch of cynicism.

I frowned, my lips parting. "You know exactly what it means," I whispered. I'd told him on numerous occasions. It meant we were more than compatible. We were soul mates, if one believed in that sort of thing. We both had at one time, but thanks to me, I doubted Owen trusted that explanation anymore.

A cloud darkened his gaze, and he glanced away.

"Owen." Nana climbed the porch steps. "Do you mind helping Molly with her luggage?"

"Sure thing," he said over his shoulder.

"You don't have to do that for me," I objected.

"I'm not." He gave me a tight-lipped smile.

He was doing it for Nana Mary.

Inhaling deeply, holding the air inside, I lifted my hands in a suit-yourself gesture. As much as I deserved the bite in his tone, it hurt.

"Join us for lunch when you're done," Nana said to him.

He opened his mouth, hesitated, then nodded. "All right."

Nana smiled over at us before slowly walking into the house, hand-in-hand with Cassie. I frowned at how cautiously she moved.

Owen waited until they'd disappeared through the front door. "It's been a long time, Molly. How are you?"

Dread moved through me like a passing storm. Dark and ominous. My daughter had been suspended from school for reasons I hesitated to divulge. Nana was upset with me, because I'd not told her Cassie's abilities had manifested. I might die by the end of the week. And, to top it off, Owen was here, talking to me. Sort of. "I'm fine," I said in a flat monotone. "You?"

"Fine," he answered in the same tone.

I shifted uneasily toward the house, toward Nana and Cassie. But the part of me that secretly never stopped caring about Owen was curious.

I angled my head toward his old house. "When did you move back?"

"About eighteen months ago. I bought it from my parents and have been slowly remodeling it over the past year."

"Year?" Nana hadn't mentioned that he'd returned.

"It's been slow going because I worked on it during my free time. Mary's house was the priority." He gestured toward the front door.

Nana hadn't mentioned that either.

"You did this?" I circled my hand to encompass the house, following the structure's lines with a sense of wonder. By outside appearances, his craftsmanship was exceptional. I studied him closely as he nodded. He rubbed the back of his neck, as though my admiration made him uncomfortable. Turning toward the street, I noticed the truck parked in front of his house, the signage on the passenger door. TORRES CONSTRUCTION. REMODELING AND RENOVATION. He'd done it, just like he'd planned. After two years in Mexico building homes through an organization with his church, he'd returned to get his degree in construction management so he could remodel homes. Like me with sea glass, he converted the old and worn-down into something new and beautiful.

A jolt of jealousy burned the inside of my stomach, twisting with a regret I didn't anticipate. All those years of his life I'd missed, no thanks to me. We'd been apart for more years than we'd been together, either as childhood friends or teenage lovers. I knew in my gut if I hadn't been forced to make the choices I had, we'd still be together. We'd probably have kids.

But then I wouldn't have Cassie.

I pointed toward the house, overwhelmed with more emotion than I'd ever imagined dealing with today. Cassie's suspension. Her premonition. My possible demise. And Owen. I needed to get away before I fell apart. "I'm going to—"

A noise from the side yanked Owen's attention in the direction of his house. I followed his line of sight.

Frankie scrambled up a fence post and strutted along the top. The orange tabby settled and, tail swishing, gloated at whatever was in Owen's yard.

Loud barks ricocheted between the two homes. Owen whistled an order, which was ignored. A dog slammed against the fence. The tabby dug its claws into the wood. The barking grew incessant.

My eyes widened. "How many dogs do you have?"

"Two." He held up his middle and index fingers.

"Sounds like twenty," I yelled over the noise.

The corner of his mouth twitched up, then one of the dogs leaped against the fence. Nails scratched the wood and a head popped above the ledge. Frankie arched his back and scrambled off, crawling under the bushes. Owen's smile faded. He swore and hollered at the dogs. They whined.

"Come meet them." He motioned for me to follow.

I shook my head and loosely pointed with an upturned hand at my luggage on the curb. "Later perhaps?" I needed to get inside. I wanted to change clothes and to eat. And I wanted to be with Cassie and talk with Nana. I also wanted to put some distance between me and Owen. Seeing him again hurt more than I imagined it would.

"Come on." He gestured with his arm. "It'll be quick, and then I'll help you with your stuff."

I hesitated, then relented. "All right." The sooner I could get him to help with the luggage, the sooner I could get away from him.

He grinned, and I followed him to his gate.

The dogs whined. A brown paw scratched the wood, and another poked out from underneath.

"Trust me, they're harmless," Owen said, and released the latch.

Two chocolate Labradors shimmied their way through the opening. They squirmed around Owen's legs, seeking his attention. Then they saw me. Wet noses nudged my legs and hands. A laugh erupted from my chest. I dropped to my knees, momentarily forgetting my horrible morning. Large tongues slathered my cheeks and neck. "Oh!" I squeaked.

Both scooted closer, tails thumping the ground. The larger of the two nudged between my knees, knocking me off balance.

"Oomph." I landed hard on my hip. Both dogs fought for lap space as I struggled to keep my skirt down.

"Crazy-ass dogs." Owen grabbed them by their collars. "Sit."

Two furry rumps dropped to the ground. Front paws pranced, and bodies quivered with restrained excitement.

Owen clasped my hand, assisting me to my feet. A current shot up my arm, sparked my skin, and kicked my pulse rate up a notch. Owen's chest rose sharply, and I knew he felt it, too. That connection. It was still there.

We let go at the same time. Owen tucked his hand into his back pocket. I brushed off my skirt. Dog slobber smeared the front.

"Sorry about that."

"No worries. It'll wash out." I wrung my hands. My palm still tingled.

Owen pointed to the larger dog on the left. "That's Mudd."

The dog's tail thumped harder at the sound of his name. Tongue lolling, he seemed to grin up at us.

"And that's Dirt." Owen pointed to the other dog, who whined.

A slight smile curved my lips. "Nice names."

"Fits them. You should see what they look like after a run on the beach."

I watched how they remained at Owen's side. He'd always been good with dogs. "They seem well behaved now."

He grunted. "Don't let them fool you. They're escape artists."

"Really? How?"

"No idea." Owen rattled the gate latch. "I'm trying to figure that out." He nodded toward the beach. "They love the water. I seem to remember you love it, too."

My mood darkened at the mention of water. I twisted my fingers.

Owen regarded me, his look penetrating, gray eyes brightening with flecks of blue. "How are you, for real?"

My gaze dropped to Mudd. I patted his head. "I'm fine."

His brows bunched. He didn't buy it, but he didn't push further. "Your daughter is beautiful."

I nodded, lips pressed tight. My beautiful daughter might lose me.

Owen petted Mudd. "What's her name?"

"Cassidy. She's eight."

"She reminds me of you."

"In a good way, I hope."

A slight smile touched his face. "Of course." Then he glanced away. He stroked Mudd's head a few times, his gaze easing from me to the dog and back. "Is she like you?" he asked quietly, almost hesitant.

I sucked in a sharp breath and looked toward the ocean. Storm clouds were moving inland. Owen knew about me, and the abilities the women in my family possessed. But he wasn't a father and wouldn't understand the burden Cassidy carried.

Then again, he could be married and have several kids.

"Do you have children?" *A wife? A lover?*

He stiffened. He shook his head and ordered the dogs into the backyard. He closed the gate behind them and turned around. "Mary's waiting. Let's get your luggage inside." His voice sounded thick.

I watched him walk to the Jeep, his back rigid, and I wondered what about my question had upset him. Or maybe it was just me.

When he lifted both roller bags, I jogged after him, grabbing one of the bins with my jewelry and supplies. Owen nodded at the other items on the sidewalk. "Go ahead. I'll come back for those."

He led the way up Nana's porch, then set down one of the rollers and held open the door, allowing me to pass. I stopped abruptly in the foyer, greeted by the aroma of spices, beef, and potatoes. Nana's and Cassie's voices drifted from the kitchen down the hallway, which had been updated with paint, lighting fixtures, and door hardware. The interior renovation looked exquisite and extensive, but Nana's cooking smelled the same. My stomach rumbled.

"I think lunch is ready." Owen tilted his head toward my midriff.

"Funny." I grimaced but caught the twitch of his mouth from the corner of my eye as he set down the bags.

I turned full circle, ignoring the burn of the weight in my arms. Dad's recliner with the permanent indent in the cushion was gone, as were the front window's heavy drapes. My father had preferred to drink his beer while watching TV in the dark.

Natural light from the large bay window flooded the front parlor. New built-in shelves framed the fireplace. The wall between the parlor and dining room had been knocked out. It opened the space, allowing for more light. The rooms were cozy, and the furniture—in warm earth tones—was minimal. Pops of color appeared in pillows and wall hangings.

There weren't many reminders of the previous house left. It was harder to visualize ghosts of long-ago events lurking behind doors that didn't look like the doors in my memories.

So much of the house had changed, and all so suddenly, too. Where had Nana gotten the money to do this? And why now?

As I studied the improvements, the usual sourness I felt in the pit of my stomach while under this roof didn't appear. Though that could be because I had other, more pressing issues to contend with.

I turned to Owen. "Nana had you do all this?"

"Me and my crew." He rapped the hallway wall with his knuckles. "Most of these interior walls are load-bearing, otherwise I'd have opened the space more."

"I like it just the way you did it. Your work is wonderful."

"Thanks." He held my gaze for a moment, and my skin prickled with a familiar awareness.

"I'll take these to your room," he said, picking up the bags.

He jogged up the staircase, carrying the luggage as though it weighed nothing, and walked past my bedroom door.

I frowned, skipping up the steps after him. I passed my old bedroom, then my parents' room. An old memory appeared like an apparition, and my steps faltered. Dad, sitting on the edge of their bed holding Mom, her lithe body bowed across his lap like a dancer in mid-dip.

I gasped and picked up the pace, trailing Owen to Nana's room, the master suite at the end of the hall.

He deposited the bags beside the chest at the end of the bed and stood in the center of the room, hands on hips.

I stopped at the threshold. "This isn't my room."

"It is now. Mary wanted you here."

I glanced over my shoulder, back down the hallway.

"She took your parents' room," he explained, sensing my confusion.

She'd done it so Cassie and I wouldn't have to sleep there, I surmised.

I set down the bin next to the suitcases and glanced around. The room was furnished simply, with linens in natural hues but still feminine. Against one wall was a slim desk and chair, and in the far corner was a chaise draped in knit blankets. I recognized Nana's weave. The bed was queen-size and positioned under a bay window. Without looking, I knew I would see the ocean through the left-side pane.

I trailed my fingers over the down comforter, stopping at the end of the bed, then hugged the bedpost. Owen watched me, studying my reaction.

"I like it."

His posture relaxed, and he dipped his chin in a barely perceptible nod. Then his face shuttered. "I'll get the rest of your things." He left the room before I had the chance to thank him.

Chapter 7

Monday, early afternoon

After Owen left, I unpacked, then walked into the adjoining bathroom, which had been enlarged. Owen must have knocked out the wall to the walk-in closet in the spare room. The fixtures were new, and the rickety porcelain toilet that had tilted off its base when you sat down too hard had been replaced. So had the claw-foot iron tub.

Like the sea glass bracelet Cassie was wearing, that old tub brought thoughts of Owen.

My first friend, first love, and first heartbreak, though the latter was no fault of his. The blame rested solely on me.

We'd met when I'd first moved here. Despite the two-year age difference, which is huge when you're eight and ten, we'd become fast friends. And he'd learned of the abilities that ran in my family almost as quickly. My mother had told Mrs. Torres one morning to be extra cautious while driving to work. Stay in the right lane while on the highway, she warned. Sure enough, the delivery truck barreling down the highway only sideswiped her car. Had Mrs. Torres driven in the left lane like she preferred, her car would have been crushed between the delivery truck behind her and the moving van at a dead stop in traffic in front of her.

Owen had asked whether I was special like my mom. It was the first time someone other than Mom had referred to my abilities in that way. He'd never asked me to show him—he'd just believed. Knowing what my mother could do was proof enough. Besides, friends guarded one another's secrets. They didn't lie. But he'd heard about the incidents at school in those early years, the things I'd done when I hadn't had much control. As my classmates had gradually shunned me, Owen had drawn closer. Always accepting, always loving, always asking nothing of me in return but for me to love him. In the end, I'd shunned him. Pushed him out of my life.

His image from moments ago appeared before me. His steely gaze and tight jaw. The fists he'd clench and either force to relax or hide in his pockets. He had every right to hate me, and I was sure he did.

I skimmed my fingers along the oil-rubbed bronze faucet of the new tub, and a memory of Owen adjusting the old tub's handles came to mind. I had been seventeen at the time, watching him from the doorway, arms crossed and shivering, antsy to strip off my soaked clothes. A rogue wave had caught me while hunting for glass. My skin itched from the salt water.

Owen stuffed a wrench into his back pocket, which tugged the faded jeans he wore farther down his lean hips. He held his fingers in the running water to check the temperature. He didn't want my skin to burn. I didn't want him to move away.

When he straightened, he smiled a crooked grin that exposed the small chip in his incisor. A ripple of excitement twirled inside me. My skin heated.

"You need a wetsuit."

I unfolded my arms and his gaze lowered.

"You definitely need a wetsuit."

He excused himself from the bathroom and went to move past me. I raised my hand to stop him, my palm hovering above his chest. "Stay."

We both knew the meaning of the word went further than him staying while I showered.

"I can't. Your father—"

"—isn't home."

"He will be."

Owen's eyes were intense. He gently touched my cheek. "I won't let him use me as an excuse to punish you." His thumb stroked my cheek, then he left.

Now I cautiously eyed the new tub. It was deep and had jets.

A shiver tiptoed up my spine. The fine hairs across my skin rose as the impact of Cassie's premonition hit me again.

I slowly turned away from the tub and peeled off my soiled blouse. The bath was beautiful. It was a shame I'd never use it.

Would I ever allow myself to take a bath again?

I'd fallen asleep in the tub before, so it could happen again. I could just drift off, slip under the surface, and then I'd be gone, even if I were sitting in a tub the size of the one behind me.

My throat rippled over a knot of bile, and I dropped my skirt. I changed into jeans and a wool sweater. It might be spring, but April on the central coast was still wet and cool.

Dirty clothes in hand, I returned to the bedroom the same moment as Owen. My breath hitched at the sight of him. He stopped just inside the doorway, setting another plastic bin on the floor.

"I put Cassie's suitcase in her room. Your old bedroom." He angled his head toward the front of the house.

He stood there, unmoving, as though he wanted to ask a question. I didn't move either, and I didn't know what to say to him. What could I say? *Sorry I broke up with you even though I still loved you?* Scratch that. I'd still been *in love* with him. And seeing him again had completely caught me off guard. I wondered whether he felt the same.

Then again, he'd probably known I was coming. He'd at least had a couple of hours more than me to prepare for the sight of me.

My fingers clutched the pile of soiled clothes in my arms. I raised a brow, inviting him to say something first, do anything but stand there with that wary look on his face.

He broke eye contact, suddenly interested in the doorknob he clutched. "Mary wanted me to remind you lunch is ready." He closed the door.

I stood where I was, listening to the thump of his boots down the stairs, and when he reached the first floor, I released the breath I'd been holding.

Cassie, Owen, and Nana were eating by the time I made my way downstairs.

"Smells wonderful," I said, entering the kitchen. Celery, parsnips, and sautéed onions. My stomach rumbled, and I pressed a hand to my midriff. "Forgot how hungry I was."

Nana stood and tapped the seat back of an empty chair beside Cassie and across from Owen. "Sit, sit." She removed a dish from the cupboard.

I sat and looked around. The large dining area from before had been divided into a breakfast nook and an intimate seating area before a fireplace. A flat-screen television hung on the wall above the mantel. Nana's knitting basket was stowed at the foot of an armchair. Frankie lounged on the seat cushion.

Like those in the rest of the house, the windows looking out to the backyard had been widened. Gray clouds billowed above neighboring rooftops. Another storm would be overhead within the next few hours. A gust of wind pushed against the glass as though testing its strength.

Beside me, Cassie mutilated her shepherd's pie. Her spoon clacked against the bowl with each pea she pushed aside. She didn't like peas, and neither did Bunny, according to her. The stuffed animal was perched as usual on Cassie's lap. She'd stopped crying and, for the moment, seemed to be happy. *A good thing, too,* I thought. She'd been through so much lately. I worried her abilities might break her carefree spirit.

Nana returned with my food. She placed the bowl in front of me and cleared her own. Steam heated my face. I murmured my thanks before she went to the sink and rinsed the dishes.

"Thanks for lunch, Mary." Owen finished his meal and dropped his napkin on the table. Just like old times. Nana used to pay Owen with a meal whenever he assisted around the house, so seeing him seated across the table from me was not an unfamiliar sight. Rather almost too familiar.

"Of course, Owen. Anytime." She smiled, glancing from him to me before returning to her task at the sink.

Owen nodded with his chin. "That's a nice color on you. Matches your eyes."

My cheeks heated. I tugged the neckline of my green, cable-knit sweater. "Thanks," I murmured.

Cassie tapped Owen's arm. He looked over, and she pointed with her spoon at the pea pyramid on her plate. His brows arched. "Impressive."

Cassie shoveled food into her mouth. "Nana cooks better than you, Mommy."

"Eat your peas, Cass."

She made a yuck-face and pushed the pile farther to the edge of her plate.

Owen chuckled. Cassie laughed and made another yuck-face, tongue out, eyes crossed.

"Cass," I warned.

She sighed and toppled the pea pyramid.

"I'm going to help Nana in the garden," Cassie announced.

"Oh." Shepherd's pie dropped in my stomach. I looked over at Nana washing dishes. What had happened to her offer to work with

Cassie? She needed to start right away—time was of the essence. *My time* was of the essence. "Why are you gardening now?" I asked Nana, unable to keep my tone from rising with the question.

"We're making tea," Cassie answered.

"Cassie's going to help me select herbs." Nana scrubbed a dish.

"Is there a purpose for this tea?" *Or is this a sit-by-the-fire-and-let's-chat tea*, I thought, feeling somewhat anxious.

"There's always a purpose for everything." Nana's gaze drifted briefly to Owen.

I frowned at him, and he shrugged a shoulder, probably just as confused as I was.

Nana shut off the water and dried her hands. "Molly, dear, will you finish the dishes? I want to pick the herbs before it starts raining again."

"Sure," I said, cupping my hand over my mouth full of food. I forced it down my throat, anxious to finish lunch, and gulped down some water.

Nana walked to the back door. "Come along, Cassidy."

Cassie held Bunny toward Owen. "Will you watch Bunny for me?"

My jaw dropped, the water glass clutched in my hand midair.

Owen took the stuffed animal. "I'll take good care of him."

Cassie looked disgruntled. "Bunny's a girl."

He cleared his throat. "My apologies, Miss Bunny," he said to the rabbit.

Cassie propped fists on her hips. "She accepts your apology."

"I'll take good care of *her*," Owen said.

I set down my glass a little too hard. Water sloshed inside. "Are you sure?" I asked Cassie. She didn't even know Owen.

"I'm positive. He has nice colors." Her fingers fluttered around Owen's head before she ran out the door Nana held open.

Owen stared at the stuffed toy in his hand. He blinked a few times.

"She never lets anyone watch over Bunny," I said. "Not even me."

Owen didn't look at me. He tucked the bunny on his lap.

Nana started to close the back door. "Before I forget, Molly, will you take my dress in for a rush cleaning? Tomorrow is poker night. And go to the cleaner's on the corner next to my attorney's office. You know the one." She snapped her fingers, trying to bring up the name.

"Monarch?" I supplied.

"Yes, that one. Central Dry Cleaners always scratched my buttons from pushing the press too hard. I stopped going there years ago."

"Which dress and where is it? Upstairs?"

"It's the one with the blue-and-green pattern stitched on the hem. I brought it downstairs to remind me to take it in. You'll find it next to my coat inside the hall closet," Nana said, then shut the door.

I blanched. I hated that closet.

Mudd and Dirt barked outside, exuberantly greeting Nana and Cassie from their side of the fence. Inside, silence as thick and heavy as the rain clouds outside descended over the table. I picked up my spoon, only to set it back down.

Owen looked steadily at me. "You okay?"

No, I wasn't, but I nodded tightly, wiping my hands on the napkin in my lap. I let my gaze wander to the hallway.

"Thanks for doing Nana's remodel," I said to get my mind off the closet.

He made a noise of acknowledgment in his throat. "We just finished last week."

I caught an undercurrent in his tone. "You've been watching out for her."

"Mary takes care of herself."

"I worry about her."

He rubbed the back of his neck. "Mary is a little older and a little slower since I left for Mexico. Aside from her frequent headaches, she's made of good stock."

My brows bunched. "What headaches?"

"You'll have to ask her. I've tried. She won't tell me."

"All right," I agreed, skidding my spoon through the pot pie. I blew on the chicken and carrots, then took another bite.

"I called you."

I hesitated, my spoon halfway to my mouth.

"Several times. Right after you moved away." He rubbed his hands on his thighs. "Actually, I called you a lot."

"I know," I said, keeping my eyes glued to my bowl, too ashamed to look at him and see the hurt reflecting back at me.

When I'd left Pacific Grove for college, just a few short weeks before Owen moved to Mexico for a two-year program building houses, I'd told him I didn't want to be with him anymore. He'd argued for us to stay together despite what had happened to my parents. It shouldn't have affected us. But losing them had shattered me. So I'd done what I had to do. I'd lied and had told him I no longer loved him.

"You changed your number."

So I wouldn't be tempted to answer his calls. He would have broken down my resistance, and then I'd have had to confess why I'd left him. And that I'd been terribly afraid of myself. I couldn't risk harming him the way I had—

"I came to see you."

My jaw fell open. "What?"

He averted his gaze, preferring to stare out the back window. "It was your last year of college." He cleared his throat. "And you were pregnant."

Oh God. My spoon clattered inside my bowl.

I could only imagine how Owen had felt when he'd seen me. The same way I'd probably react had I seen him with a wife and child. Livid, and envious that we hadn't had that together. Starting a family had been one of our dreams, and I'd taken that from him.

"I didn't know."

"I know," he said. "I didn't want you to. But I wanted to see you. You looked beautiful."

His admission made my head spin. "Owen—" I stopped, unable to find the right words. What would I say? What could I say?

Mudd and Dirt barked again. Owen glanced at the window behind me. "I need to check on the dogs." He excused himself from the table and stood, picking up his plate.

I slowly rose to my feet. The chair scraped over hardwood, loud in a kitchen that had grown quiet after Nana and Cassie had gone outside. "I'll take that." I reached for Owen's plate and noticed my hand shook.

So did he. He lifted his eyes to mine. They were heavy and bruised with unspoken declarations and apologies.

"Please," I snapped, motioning for the plate before I broke.

He gave it to me, then tucked Bunny under his arm. "I'll keep her close."

I nodded and went to the sink, turning on the water. Over the spray, I heard Owen's footsteps cross the kitchen. They stopped at the doorway.

"Molly."

I stilled, a soapy dish in one hand, sponge in the other.

"Welcome home."

He didn't wait for my reply. His boots echoed through the narrow hallway to the front door. The latch clicked and I fell apart, letting the tears that had been threatening to spill all day fall. And the day was only half-over. When I finished the dishes, I left the kitchen and stopped at the hall closet. Hanging on the doorknob was Nana's dress.

Damn you, Owen.

After all these years he still understood me better than anyone.

With a vicious yank, I snagged the dress and left the house.

I found a parking space a half block down from Monarch Cleaners. Grabbing Nana's dress, I briskly walked toward the shop, anxious to complete the errand and get back to Nana's. We had to discuss how she planned to help Cassie. Was there a way to change the outcome in Cassie's vision? Could she help Cassie see more details without the nightmares? I also wondered whether all of Mom's premonitions had come true. Had they been as violent and disturbing as Cassie's?

Gold lettering caught my eye. My stride slowed as I passed a bank of windows. I stopped and read the lettering on the glass.

Spencer Martin, Esq.

Attorney at Law

Family Law—Estate Planning

Adoptions—Child Custody—Divorce

I shifted the dress to my other arm as a quickening stirred inside me. There'd been more to Nana's request for a dry-cleaning run. The mention of her attorney's firm I suspected had been intentional.

Sneaky Nana. She was right, though. I always figured I'd have time to make a will. I was young and healthy, and still paying off a car loan.

I peered through the window. Inside were several desks. A man dressed in a suit and tie sat behind one and talked on the phone. Otherwise the office seemed empty.

Turning away from the window, I went into the dry cleaner's. The door sensor announced my arrival with a sharp beep. I fell in line behind two other patrons, and while I waited, I formulated a plan to swing by the attorney's office afterward to see whether I could get a rush appointment with Mr. Spencer Martin, Esq.

The door sensor beeped again, and someone moved into line behind me. Fabric rustled and a child whined, complaining about wanting to watch a TV show.

A fingernail grazed my neck, then flicked my earring. I flinched and turned, gaping at the woman standing behind me. Recognition set in. "Phoebe!" I gasped, surprised.

"Your earrings are gorgeous, *Mol-lee.*" She put a hard emphasis on both syllables of my name. "I knew it was you. What the heck are you doing here?"

I blinked at my best friend and fought back a wave of emotion. "I just got here an hour or so ago."

"You drove all this way to drop off dry cleaning?" She cocked her head at me, brows up.

"Ha. No. This is my grandmother's dress."

She pouted. "I can't believe you didn't call me."

"I'm sorry. It was a last-minute decision."

Pouting turned to concern. "Everything okay?"

I opened my mouth to reply when three-year-old Kurt appeared from behind her. Phoebe glanced down at her son, who clung to her sweatshirt hem, sucking his thumb.

Remnants of breakfast were a work of art across the front of his Buzz Lightyear shirt. He stared up at me under a tousled head of auburn curls and pointed at my ear. "Purty." He mumbled the word around his thumb.

"Look at you, Kurt! You're so big." The last time I'd seen him had been in August, when Phoebe had visited with the kids for a few days. I lowered to Kurt's level and gave him a little wave. He shrank back. I looked up at Phoebe. "He doesn't remember me," I said, a little disappointed.

"Probably not. He's three. His world revolves around food, demolishing my house, and TV."

I smiled at Kurt. "Well, I remember you and how much fun we had when you visited me."

His eyes grew big with uncertainty. He scooted behind his mother and wrapped an arm around her leg. I straightened. "Attachment phase?"

"Major attachment. I'm thinking to change his name to Velcro."

"Where are the others?" Phoebe had four kids—Jeff, Dale, Kurt, and Danica—all named after NASCAR drivers, thanks to her racing-fanatic ex-husband's obsession. She and Vince had been divorced for almost a year.

"Jeff and Dale are at school. I'm on my way to pick them up. Danica's in the car. Shit." Her eyes darted around the dry cleaner's. "Hopefully no one heard," she said in a loud whisper. "The way my luck's been going, some paranoid Betty will report me to the authorities."

"You are the least negligent mom on the planet, even though you are breaking the law," I whispered dramatically from the corner of my mouth.

"Shh-shh-shh." She waved her hand in a lower-the-volume motion. "I can see her. She's right there." Phoebe pointed out the storefront window. "She's passed out in the car seat. Little bugger. Screamed all freaking morning and crashed the moment I rolled out of the driveway. God, if I could leave her in the car with the motor running all day I would." She sighed heavily. "I'm kidding, you know."

"That bad?"

"She's the most temperamental of them all. I thought the more kids you had the easier it got," she griped. "Apparently not."

I gave Phoebe a commiserating look, and she answered with a tight smile. "I swear to God I'm happy," she said through gritted teeth, pointing at her stiff grin with both index fingers. Her lips stretched wider. "See?"

"Aw, Phoebe."

She blew air through pursed lips, and her back bowed. "Hell, who am I kidding? I'm freaking fried. And my first date in eons was a disaster."

"You started dating?" She hadn't mentioned wanting to date when we'd chatted last week.

"My neighbor's been wanting to set me up with her little brother. He's gorgeous. I mean, G-O-R-G-E-O-U-S gorgeous. I finally said yes to get her off my case. And I really, really wanted to get out and just have some fun." She held up the dress in her hands. Dark stains dotted the bodice. "It's my first date since King Asshole ditched me, and this little bozo"—she jiggled her sweatpants-clad leg to shake her clinging kid—"spills grape juice down my chest before I set foot from the house. My one dress that still fit! I was totally looking forward to the night out. I even cleaned the cobwebs in my crevices."

"Pheebs!"

The lady in front of us gawked.

"Of course I had nothing else nice to wear and spent the evening with the most gorgeous guy ever in a flower blouse that would have looked better as wallpaper than a shirt on me."

Her shoulders rose and fell as she sighed loudly. Then she tugged down the waist of the sweatshirt stretched tightly across her chest. She'd put on weight since August, and her usually thick and wavy hair was knotted in a messy bun, the chestnut strands dull and brittle.

She nudged my arm. "I'm really miffed you didn't call me this morning. Why are you here?"

"Oh." I sighed the word. "Just visiting." I didn't want to worry her with the truth, but I did want to talk with her about Cassie.

"Yeah, uh-huh. I call bull, missy." She jabbed my sternum with her index finger. "You can make it up to me tomorrow. Coffee at my place. Then you can tell me the *real* reason that got your sorry ass back to PG."

"All right." She grinned, and I smiled back. Despite the circumstances that had brought me to Pacific Grove, it was good to see her. "Owen's here," I blurted.

Her mouth fell open for a beat, then her eyes lit up. "Really?"

"You didn't know?"

She pointed down at Kurt. "I don't get out much. So"—she nudged me—"what's it like seeing him again?"

"Amazing and scary and sad and weird."

"All that?"

And then some. "I never imagined seeing him again. Well, I did, but I never expected it would actually happen. He bought his parents' house when they moved."

She sighed. "I bet he looks hotter now than he did when he moved away."

I hugged Nana's dress to my chest. "He does," I admitted.

Phoebe beamed. "Called it." She licked the tip of her index finger and dotted the air, making a sizzle sound. "So, what time should I expect you tomorrow?"

The patron in front of me left, and the shop owner gestured me forward. "Does nine work?" That would give her time to drop off her two older kids at school.

"Nine's perfect." She pointed at my ear. "Will you bring me a pair of earrings like the ones you're wearing?"

My fingers captured an earring, the sensory memory reminding me of the color and material. Key-lime sea glass dangling from sterling silver ear wires.

"Take these." I slipped off the jewelry and watched them drop into Phoebe's palm as though in slow motion.

She lifted one of the whimsical pieces to the light and whistled. "Beautiful." She swapped her pearl studs with the dangles. I watched them swing on her lobes. They were ordinary pieces of glass. I had plenty like this pair. But there was a real possibility I would never see those specific pieces of glass again. Just like I might not see Cassie after Friday.

My daughter might lose her mother.

Just as I'd lost mine.

Chapter 8

Twenty-two years ago

Mom had met Dad after she'd graduated from high school, while visiting a friend at the University of Minnesota. He was twenty-six at the time and worked in the administrative office. Mom decided to move to Minnesota despite my grandparents' discouragement. She hardly knew my father well enough to make such a big move, but she loved him and wanted to give the relationship a chance. Within four months, my parents married. I arrived fourteen months after that.

At first, my parents were happy. They had dreams and plans, which included my father's aspirations to one day be the university's dean of administration. Dad worked while Mom stayed home and cared for me, until the day he lost his administrator job. It was the first time I'd heard the words *downsizing* and *budget cuts*.

From then on, Dad had difficulty staying employed. He always found a reason to quit. He blamed the people he worked with and the tasks he had to perform. It just wasn't the same as what he'd had at the university.

Depression set in, and soon he turned to alcohol. That was when he started blaming Mom, for she'd had a premonition about the layoff and my father's slide into the bottle. In the way one does who doesn't take responsibility for his actions, Dad eventually had Mom convinced she was at fault. Had she not foreseen and told him what would happen, perhaps my father would not have ended up as an alcoholic who couldn't hold a job. Maybe it was the vision that had set his downfall into motion, for my father couldn't see any other outcome other than the one Mom had foretold. Mom's abilities became his excuse for failure.

So Mom stopped using her abilities, or at least she tried to.

During the days when Dad was between jobs, Mom worked while I was in school. But for the hours she could work, because she didn't want me home alone with Dad, she didn't make enough money to support us and Dad's drinking. When they couldn't make their rent payments and the landlord threatened to evict us, Mom suggested we move in with her mother. Grandpa had recently passed, and Nana was lonely. It would only be temporary, Mom proposed. There were plenty of opportunities for my father to consider at the local schools and colleges. Life would be better for them. We packed our belongings and headed west.

On the long drive from Minnesota to California, we stopped for breakfast in Idaho. I remember an advertisement of fluffy white eggs and brown bacon had been painted on the diner's large glass windows. EGG SCRAMBLE SPECIAL $2.99. The highway stretched in both directions until the road fell off the edge of the earth. Corn grew everywhere I looked. Stalks leaned and bowed in the breeze like enormous grass blades worshipping the sun.

The parking lot was full. Four Idaho State Police cars were parked by the road. Dad gave them a cursory glance as he locked our Honda Civic. He adjusted his pants, wrinkled from sitting in the driver's seat, and tucked in his shirt, shoving a hand deep into his trousers. "Place looks crowded. Let's make it quick, ladies. I want to get to California before midnight."

I climbed from the car, clutching my teddy bear's left paw. Mom held my hand, and we followed Dad into the diner. He was right: the place was packed and buzzed with urgency. Something was amiss. I looked up at Mom, and she shook her head. She pressed her index finger against her lips and angled her head toward Dad. No mind-talking. That was our agreement if we wanted to live with Nana. So I listened to the conversation to figure out what was wrong.

I picked up bits and pieces, fervent murmurs, as the hostess showed us our table.

Missing for forty-eight hours.

He's only nine. He must be afraid.

Mike is taking it hard. He blames himself.

Who was Mike? He must be the boy's dad, I reasoned, scooting into the booth. I propped my bear beside me in front of its own paper placemat. The hostess had seated us near the police officers, who huddled over their table, deep in conversation. They studied a map that had been unfolded and spread across the table.

We ordered quickly: egg scramble special for Dad and French toast for me. A bowl of oatmeal for Mom. While we waited for our meal, and then as we ate, Dad read the job listings in the newspaper Nana Mary had mailed him. I devoured my French toast and licked my fingers. They were sticky. Mom ignored her oatmeal. I thought it was because it looked like paste and smelled like paint, but she didn't seem interested in eating. She kept looking past my shoulder toward the police.

I turned around. A man had joined them. He stood beside the table. His eyes were bloodshot, and the skin around them red. It looked as though he'd been rubbing them, or crying. Yes, definitely crying. He was the lost boy's father, and I didn't need to read his mind. It was written all over his face.

I turned around to tell Mom. She gripped the spoon. Her face had lost its color.

Dad was watching Mom. He swore. He knew that look; he remarked on it often. "Sheila . . ."

Mom shot to her feet, bumping the table. Glasses wobbled. I grabbed my orange juice.

"I'm sorry, Brad," Mom told Dad. "I have to do something."

Dad fisted the newspaper pages. His stern gaze followed Mom.

She walked to the police officers' table. The crying man stood aside to make room for her. They exchanged a few words.

"I know where your boy is," I heard her tell him.

The fervent energy I'd felt when we first arrived increased. Voices rose from the table where Mom stood. One officer laughed. Another swore, said something about "crazy carnie psychics." But the crying man gripped Mom's shoulder. "Where?"

"He's in a cement ditch. He's hungry and scared."

The man's eyes jumped around Mom's face.

"Don't listen to her, Mike," said an overweight officer with a thick beard. "She just wants money. Stan, here, has another lead." The officer thumbed at the man sitting beside him.

Mike looked at the officers, then back at Mom. "Show me."

Mom nodded. She pointed out the window. "We have the Honda out there. Let me tell my family. You can follow us."

Mom returned to our table, but she didn't sit down. "We have to go."

Dad pressed his lips flat. He slowly folded the paper.

"There's a young boy, Molly's age. He's lost. I know where he is."

"Why not just tell them?" Dad tucked the paper under his arm.

Mom twisted her fingers. "They don't believe me."

"They didn't say nice things to her," I said about the police officers.

"They never do," Dad grumbled. "But your mom asks for it. It's her fault. You remember that, Molly Poppy. Your mind ability is odd, and it makes people lose their jobs." He gave Mom a penetrating look.

Mom wiped her hands on the sides of her skirt. "I sense where the boy is, but you know how difficult it is for me to describe what I see," she continued. "I have to show them. Please, Brad. We have to help. I have to save him."

Dad ground his jaw. Mom pushed on. "If we don't help, he might die, and his death will be on us."

Dad stood. "No, Sheila. His death will be on the people who lost him." He tugged his belt, adjusting his pants, and glanced at Mike, who was waiting for us by the diner's door. The man looked desperate.

Dad shook his finger at Mom. "This is it, Sheila. Last time." He waved his finger from Mom to me. "You promised no mind tricks from either of you if I agreed to move in with your mother. Sheesh, what kind of man lives with his mother-in-law because he can't support his family? Let's go."

After Dad paid for breakfast, we drove away from the main highway and deeper into the cornfields with Dad behind the wheel and Mom telling him where to go. We turned onto a dirt road. Mike followed in his truck, tailed by four police cars.

Within a few moments Mom told Dad to pull over. "Wait here," she said, and got out of the car.

I watched her walk up a slight embankment. Wind ruffled her white skirt, and dust swirled around her ankles. Her long platinum hair was loose. It fanned her shoulders. She disappeared over the embankment. Mike followed her down.

"I don't like this," Dad grumbled. He got out of the car and walked around the hood. He waited like the officers did. Shifty and uncertain.

A few moments later Mom appeared over the ridge. She looked over her shoulder, and I saw Mike behind her. He carried his son. He was filthy, his hair matted with twigs. Tear tracks drew lines on his dirty face. He waved good-bye to Mom, then hugged his dad's neck, tucking his head against his dad's shoulder.

I looked at Mom, who was speaking with the police. They talked with her a long time, taking her statement, she later told me. I was proud of Mom. She'd saved the little boy.

Mom and Dad returned to the car at the same time.

"Get into the car, Molly. I need to talk with your mother."

I crawled into the backseat and shut the door. Dad grabbed Mom's upper arm and tugged her around the front of the car so that the car was between them and the police officers. He turned to Mom and clamped a hand where her shoulder curved into her neck. He spoke to her in a hushed tone; I couldn't hear what he said through the open windows. He was angry, though, his face growing tomato red. When he finished, Mom nodded, her forehead dipped toward the ground, and he pointed for her to get into the car.

They sat at the same time. Dad slammed his door; Mom gently closed hers, the latch barely audible. Dad took a deep breath and looked over at Mom. "I do love you, Sheila, very much."

"I love you, too," Mom whispered, her posture rigid.

Dad leaned over the center console, waiting. When Mom didn't look at him, he said, "Give me a kiss."

Mom slowly eased over. Dad grasped the back of her head and gave her a quick, deep kiss. He pulled away and started the engine. "I assume we have an understanding."

Mom folded her hands in her lap. "Yes."

"I want everyone in Monterey to see us as a normal family. No mind tricks. That goes for your mother, too." Dad narrowed his eyes at Mom.

I stared wide-eyed at her. My heart pounded in my throat. Mom always mind-talked with me. She read me stories that way. She told me she loved me that way. And Dad was taking that away.

Tell him no, Mom. I sent her the message. She didn't answer.

"Did you give those cops your real name?" Dad asked after a moment.

Mom shook her head. "I gave them a fake one, like you asked. Same with the phone number."

Mom?

"Good." Dad nodded. "I don't want to deal with them calling us, treating us like freaks." He made a U-turn, and we headed back toward the highway.

Mom!

Again she didn't answer. And she didn't look at me. She kept her face forward and her hands folded in her lap.

Tears welled in the rims of my eyes. I didn't understand what was wrong with us. Mom told me we were special. Why couldn't Dad see that? Why did he hate that part of us so much?

Propping my chin on the door ledge, I watched the world speed by outside the window. I didn't want to go to California. I wanted to go home. And I wanted us to be the family we used to be, when Dad had a job, my parents had loved each other, and we had laughed.

We hadn't laughed in a long time.

Chapter 9

Monday, midafternoon

After I checked in the dress under Nana's name and confirmed with Phoebe that I'd see her in the morning, I made my way to the law firm next door. A sign had been posted on the door.

GONE TO COURT.

I exhaled slowly, cheeks puffing. I pulled out my phone, swiped aside a few text notifications from my students wondering when their test grades would be posted, and snapped a photo of the firm's phone number. I'd call Mr. Martin later.

As I drove back to Nana's house, a call came in. Principal Harrison's name lit the screen. I looked out the front window, then back at the phone. *She's afraid of me.* Cassie's words twisted inside me.

Pulling into a graveled parking area alongside the beach, I answered the call.

"Grace is still in the hospital. They're running tests." Jane made the announcement after her greeting.

My heart slipped into my stomach. I visualized Grace in a coma, a breathing mask covering her delicate face and tubes stuck in arms that had just been steering a bike. Shifting the car into park, I left the motor running.

"Cassie sensed the accident," Jane surmised, "like she did when Ethan broke his leg. And that other little girl who slipped on the cafeteria floor and cracked her elbow. She knew that would happen, too."

I stared at the surf outside my window. Waves hammered the rocks. Dark clouds piled overhead. "Yes."

"There have been others I don't know about, haven't there?"

My blood ran cold. "Why do you ask?"

There was a clicking sound like a ballpoint pen on Jane's end of the line.

"Can you bring Cassidy by my office tomorrow?"

"We're out of town."

"You are?" She was quiet for a few beats. "When will you return?"

"Soon. Why?" I wondered whether she'd changed her mind about Cassie's suspension. "Is everything okay?"

"Ah . . . yes." She cleared her throat. "Everything's fine. I can wait . . . I mean, it can wait until you return. How's Cassie doing?"

"She's doing fine." I kept the response generic. "How about Grace?"

"She's good."

I straightened in my seat. "She is?" I asked, surprised. I'd feared the worst. Cassie had seen Grace in a coma, her little body bruised and broken.

"Grace is doing quite well, considering," Jane was saying. "Cassie should call her. I'm sure Grace would love to hear from her."

My grip tightened on the phone. I felt light-headed. "How . . . how's this possible?"

"I don't agree with your daughter's tactics, but Cassie can be quite convincing. Alice Kaling bought Grace a new helmet, one that fit properly. It saved Grace's life. She survived the accident. The driver went through a red light. His car tagged her rear tire.

"Molly, if it weren't for Cass—" Jane's voice broke. I heard a noise through the phone and imagined her swiveling in the office chair, looking out the window at the same cloud-shrouded sky above me. She took a moment to collect her thoughts.

"Molly," she began again, her voice heavy with emotion, "Cassidy saved Grace. I doubt Grace would have said anything to her parents if Cassidy hadn't nagged her. And the Kalings never would have known Grace took her helmet off when she rode her bike. I guess the helmet hurt Grace's head; that's what Alice told me. She thought Grace was making excuses so she didn't have to wear it. But thanks to Cassidy, the Kalings purchased a new one. Do you know what this means?"

I suspected the question was rhetorical, but I knew exactly what it meant. Alice had changed her daughter's fate, altering the outcome of the event Cassie had foreseen.

And I could do the same.

I felt giddy. I wanted to run laps across the sand.

"You have a very special daughter," Jane said.

"Yes, I do."

I said good-bye and disconnected the call, then slipped the phone into my purse. My entire body relaxed, melting into the seat. I was going to change my fate, especially now that I had proof Cassie's premonitions didn't have to end the way she'd seen them.

Wind knocked the window; waves slammed the shore. Thick clouds marched overhead, a solid front moving inland. They hadn't released the rain yet, but precipitation hovered thickly in the air. I still had time.

I intended to have lots and lots of time.

The shoreline beckoned. Bursting with excitement, I itched to hunt. Turning off the motor, I got out of the car. Salt-heavy wind whipped my clothes. Hair lashed my cheeks. I turned my face into the wind and wrapped my arms around my thick, cable-knit sweater. Following the frothing edge of the tide, I walked the length of the beach.

Sea glass was scarce today. Amateur hunters must have picked through the sand over the weekend. I'd probably have better luck a few feet within the surf, wetsuit on and net in hand, searching the strip of stones and shells where the waves broke. But not today. I still had to stay out of the water as I looked for the glass shards. I moved farther up the beach, away from the tide.

For as long as I remembered, I had loved the hunt. Every sea-tumbled piece discovered meant a better one was out there. And the desire to find those broken bottles and vases worn by waves and recycled by the sea was too great to ignore.

Through the years I had covered countless miles on beaches across California. I handpicked the glass in my jewelry. But the mecca of beach-tumbled glass was right here in Pacific Grove, among the pebbles, flotsam, and shells, close to the house where I'd been raised.

Over one hundred years ago, horse-drawn carriages loaded with garbage had been dumped into the ocean at Lovers Point. And later, several miles up the coastline, a public dump had opened. Locals had disposed of and burned their garbage on the bluffs. Ashes, wind-blown trash, and broken bottles had made their way into the ocean.

Despite littering and recycling laws, and the increased use of plastics, worn glass still made it to shore, though not as abundantly as in past decades, which made a well-tumbled shard with a frosty surface a true find. Trash turned into treasure.

Like the glass I kept close to my heart.

A memory surfaced, and I saw my hand, the hand of a twelve-year-old girl, held out to receive a piece of pitted glass Owen had found in the sand. He'd often joined me on the hunt after his parents returned from church. His father hadn't bothered driving straight home. Rather, he'd pulled to the side of the road, where Owen had leaped from the car, waving good-bye as he tugged off his shoes, rolled up his one good pair of khaki pants, and sprinted across the sand to where I paced in my sea glass quest.

It had been such a day when he'd discovered the glass that I still wore, tucked safely underneath my sweater, between my breasts. He'd shown me the glass, a crescent-shaped shard of jade green, when I'd shown him the treasure I'd dug up.

The minuscule pieces in my cupped palm had paled in comparison with the gem he'd held between his thumb and forefinger, letting the sunlight shine through. It had glowed.

My breath left in a rush. "It's beautiful."

He fisted the glass, making it disappear. I pouted, pretending disappointment.

He extended his hand and opened his palm, revealing the glass where it rested. "For you."

"Really?" I gingerly took the glass, holding it up to the sun. "It's stunning." The best piece of glass I'd seen.

The wind whipped my hair into my face. Strands stuck to my lips. Owen smoothed the hair aside. "So are you," he murmured, his eyes widening as though the declaration surprised him. Then his expression changed into a look of determination and something else I couldn't quite make out. It sent my pulse racing. His hand curved around my nape, holding back my hair.

I blinked and stared at him, my eyes planet-size as he pulled my face toward his. Gently, and ever so slowly, he pressed his lips against mine. Our first kiss, at twelve and fourteen, and completely unexpected, just like the glass he'd discovered. His lips moved over mine as a floating fuzziness moved through me.

He pulled away first, his face inches from mine. His thumb skimmed my chin. "Hi."

"Hi," I said with a shy smile.

"I hope you don't mind I kissed you." The words rushed from him with nervous excitement. "I've been wanting to for a really long time."

Lightness flowed outward from my chest, sending an exhilarating rush to my toes and fingers. "You have?" I gasped.

He nodded vigorously, biting into his lower lip. He'd then kissed me again.

Shimmers in the sand caught my attention, jerking me back to the present. I bent low and scratched aside coarse granules to reveal a frost-white shard. It was a common color, but the crescent-moon shape was unusual, like the one I'd worn for years. I visualized the piece encased in silver wire, resting against black linen, and tucked the find into my jeans pocket.

Behind me the restless ocean slapped the sand. Another glimmer. On my knees, I scooted across the sand, catching the piece before it was lost in the water-darkened shore. Two feet away, a piece winked at me. I snatched the glass before it disappeared in the tide. I knelt in the sand and studied the sea foam–blue shard shaped like a teardrop.

Mermaid tears.

Folklore tells of sea maidens who tamed the raging ocean to allow their sailors safe passage. But for those sailors they had loved and then lost at sea, never to be seen again, they eternally wept. When their tears hit the seawater, they turned to glass. And to this day, their tears washed ashore as gleaming, colorful treasures. Remnants of true love. Like the shard in my pendant and the piece in the bracelet Cassie wore. *Cassie.*

What the heck was I doing?

Clouds broke overhead, releasing their package. Rain splattered, creating divots in the sand. Seawater snaked around my knees and rose quickly to my thighs. I froze.

Holy shit.

I bounded to my feet, backpedaling up the shore. Waves clawed toward me like death hunting me down. My pulse thundered in my ears. I swore. God forbid fate sneak up on me as quickly as the tide.

My legs were drenched, chilled to the bone. I shivered. Sharp edges bit into my palm. I opened my hand and stared at the sea glass. What had I been thinking?

I hadn't.

I'd been stupid and foolish.

The glass fell to the sand. I looked at my palm. Tiny drops of blood smeared across my hand and washed away in the rain.

I gritted my teeth and gripped the steering wheel, shaking it. *Dumb, dumb, dumb.* I smacked the steering wheel. Then I collapsed against the back of the seat and cried.

I don't want to die.

I cried for Cassie, for the burden of knowledge she carried. And for Owen. Seeing him had thrown me for a loop. I couldn't let him inside again; I just couldn't. I cried for my mother, her life cut short too soon. *Oh, Mom.* I pressed the heel of my palm to my heart. I'd been motherless for twelve years. Thanks to my stupidity, Cassie could be motherless within several days.

When was I going to learn that every mistake I make could have devastating repercussions? I'd almost made my last mistake.

Eventually I left the beach and parked in front of Nana's house. I found Cassie in front of Owen's, pouring buckets of dirty water into the gutter. Owen was rolling up the hose. They both looked up when my car door slammed. Owen waved me over.

"What are you two doing out in the rain?" I asked, walking toward them.

"Cassie helped me wash my car." He sounded irritated and glanced at the sky. "Rain started sooner than I expected."

I turned to Cassie, and my step faltered. Her face paled to sheet white. She trembled violently. Her mouth worked, but no sound came out.

"Cassie?" Fingers of panic grasped me.

"You went to the beach." She sucked in a large gulp of air, her rib cage expanding. She exploded. "YOU WENT TO THE BEACH!" She snatched a dirty sponge off the ground and slapped Owen's Camaro. "WHY?" *Slap.* "Why, why, why?" She punctuated each word with a smack of the sponge. Gravel lodged inside the sponge scraped the car's surface.

Owen hissed. "Cass—"

She let out a shrill scream. "Why?" She burst into tears.

I felt sick. "I'm sorry, Cassie. I—I was collecting sea glass. See?" I dug into my front pocket and opened my hand. Five pieces nested in my palm.

Cassie slapped the back of my hand with the sponge. The glass tumbled to the ground. "You don't listen!" She stomped the ground. "Stay away from the beach! You have to stay away!"

"I—I was perfectly fine," I tried to reason.

"No! Your colors are all wrong."

"I stayed out of the water."

"LIAR!" Cassie stabbed a finger at my dirty pants and sandy shoes. "You lie!" She threw the sponge at me. It bounced off my chest, leaving a soapy oval on my sweater.

Cassie's gaze bounced to Owen. Her lips quivered, eyes wide. She looked scared. I wanted to scoop her up and tell her everything would be all right, but I had royally screwed up.

"You're going to die!" she cried, and I died a little bit inside. "You're going to leave me! I don't want to lose you."

I reached for her, and she pushed away my hands. She ran off to Nana's house. The front door slammed behind her. I started after her and stopped. There was no way I could reason with her while she was this fired up.

"God, I screwed up." I buried my face in my hands.

Owen moved to stand in front of me. He pulled my hands down and gently peeled wet hair off my damp face. Rainwater dripped down my neck. "I'm sorry." I motioned toward his car. "I'll pay for any damage."

He picked up the sponge and tossed it in a bucket. Mudd and Dirt whined from behind the gate.

"You didn't answer me earlier."

I met Owen's gaze. "About what?"

The fence creaked, wood bowing as one dog pushed his weight against the gate. A paw poked from underneath.

"Is Cassidy like you?"

I stiffened. Owen's eyes flared. He had his answer.

"She obviously sees energy fields. What else? Is she empathic? Intuitive? Clairvoyant?" Owen's voice rose over the dogs' persistence to escape from the backyard. He ignored them. "Or is she like you, an influencer?"

"She's nothing like me!" I bellowed. Lightning flashed overhead. "She's good and innocent."

"So were you."

Good old Owen. He'd never judged me or my abilities. Just accepted them as part of me. Too bad I couldn't do the same. "What I did was vile." I backed away.

"What *did* you do, Molly?"

Owen advanced, not waiting for an answer. "Is that why you pushed me away, whatever it was you did? Because for the life of me, I've never been able to figure out where we went wrong, or why you didn't want to be with me anymore. Your parents died, you shut me out, and suddenly"—he snapped his fingers—"it's like the life in you left, too."

"Don't you dare lecture me."

"It's not a lecture."

Another flash of lightning.

"Fine. Stop the interrogation. Back off." My life was already dangling on a cliff. I didn't need Owen adding weight to push me over the ledge.

Thunder echoed over the rooftops. The dogs howled. Rain poured. My teeth chattered.

Owen gave me a hard look. "What happened to you?"

I opened my mouth to fire a retort, and the gate burst open. It banged against the side of the house. Mudd and Dirt barreled down the driveway and sideswiped me. My arms flailed. Owen dragged me into his chest.

Barking madly, the dogs charged down the sidewalk and across Ocean View Boulevard. An SUV screeched to a halt, narrowly missing Mudd's rear legs.

Owen swore and stepped away. He locked eyes with me. Emotions tumbled between us.

"We *are* going to talk."

He didn't wait for my reply and took off at a full run.

Chapter 10

Monday, late afternoon

I stood in the entryway of Nana's house. Cassie's muffled cries traveled down the steep, narrow staircase. My hand fluttered to the wood rail, and my foot rested on the bottom step. Cassie deserved an apology from me, but she also needed the cry, like I had broken down earlier in the car.

Moving away from the staircase, I went to the kitchen, where I found Nana Mary grinding herbs. She crushed leaves, measured, and added the flakes to a boiling pot of water. She glanced over her shoulder at me before turning back to the stove. The ceiling's canned lighting shimmered on her cheeks. She'd been crying.

"You hurt her."

Nana's tone was more a statement than an accusation, but I still felt defensive. "It wasn't intentional."

Her eyes roamed down my sodden pants. I'd left my shoes on the porch. They were wet and sandy. My socks were damp, making my feet cold. I shivered, and Nana shook her head. She folded a dish towel, and her gaze caught mine. Cassie's pain, raw and deep, reflected in Nana's expression.

Nana was empathic, and her heightened senses had picked up Cassie's emotions as they undulated through the house with her cries. I saw everything Cassie felt in Nana's face. My betrayal looked right back at me.

I turned away, going over to the fireplace. Frankie lay curled on the rug at my feet. He peered up at me through one eye before stretching his body and rolling over, exposing his stomach to the fire. I held my palms toward the flames. The heat chased the chills.

"Cassidy's scared," Nana said from behind me.

"Me, too." I rubbed my upper arms. Flames danced, and I moved closer, seeking their warmth. "Did she tell you about her friend Grace?"

"She mentioned her vision came true. She's worried about the girl."

I heard Nana sit in the chair behind me. A weary sigh escaped as she settled and picked up her knitting needles. The metal rods clacked together, the sound rhythmic. White noise that induced memories from my youth. We'd spent many evenings side by side, she knitting a blanket for a new patient at the hospital while I read.

"I spoke with Principal Harrison earlier. She said Grace's injuries aren't severe, nothing like what Cassie had predicted. She believes Cassie saved Grace."

Behind me the click-clack of Nana's needles continued.

"Cassie will want to save me." I hugged my chest.

"And what's wrong with that?"

"She could get hurt. What if, despite everything I do to avoid water, I still find myself in a lake, or the ocean, like what happened today." I guiltily pointed at my wet pants. "What if she's there and sees me drowning and runs into the water in an attempt to save me? She could drown, too." I couldn't risk that chance.

Nana hummed. I couldn't tell whether she agreed with me.

"Do you remember the first day you arrived here with your parents?" she asked after a moment. "You were timid."

Because Dad was intimidating.

"I hadn't seen you since you were a baby," Nana explained. "Your parents were in love at the time."

I barely remembered them being in love. They hid their troubles well from the outside world. But Nana would have sensed the turmoil, which may have been why Mom had invited her to visit only once, right after I'd been born. Aside from that, Mom hadn't visited Nana the first eight years of my life, except the time Nana had flown her home before Grandfather passed.

"Your mother had grown frail since I last saw her. And Brad—" Nana paused. She pulled her eyes from the fireplace, looked down at the project in her lap. She worked the needles. "He'd changed."

"Alcohol does that to people." I sank into the armchair beside Nana. The window behind me rattled. Raindrops pelted the panes.

"But you"—she pointed a needle at me—"you were special. I felt how special you were the moment you walked in the door. Squeezing that ratty, old teddy bear in your arms. Your green eyes so big and hair blonder than Cassidy's. You had the look of your mother. Still do," she said with a note of melancholy.

Mom's eyes had been blue like Cassidy's. I stared into the fire, picturing their shade. Looking at Cassidy, watching her grow, was like seeing my mother's face again. My heart ached for her.

"While your parents settled in," Nana was saying, "you and I drank hot cocoa right here in the kitchen. Your manners were impeccable, but you kept fidgeting with your shirt. Do you remember that shirt? I do. It had pretty ruffles on the collar and sleeves. The color was a soft orange, like peaches during summertime. You told me it was your favorite color. Do you remember why?"

I shook my head, sinking deeper in the chair.

Nana's unadorned lips curved into a smile. She knitted a row. "It matched your aura color and I told you so." Her hands rapidly wove the yarn. "Your mouth fell open, like this." She opened her mouth wide.

Her brows arched high. "My, oh my, your eyes were huge. Then I asked if you could see my colors." She hummed. "The look on your face."

Wind gusts picked up outside, slapping a wall of rain against the kitchen window over the sink. Water dripped like tears down the glass. Nana's weathered hands kept up a steady rhythm, weaving the blanket in tune with her tale.

"That's when I figured out why I felt fear from you. My questions scared you. Our abilities scared you. It made me sad your mother hadn't been training you."

"Dad didn't let her."

She pressed her lips flat and shook her head as though dismayed by the past. "You'd told me your daddy didn't like you talking about people's colors."

The memory was hazy, a lifetime ago. Nana's hot chocolate came to mind. It had been the best I'd tasted. The marshmallows had been large and square, plumper than the ones at the grocery store. She had made them from scratch. I'd pushed the marshmallows deeper into the chocolate and watched them bob inside the mug.

Nana had leaned closer and whispered. "In my house, you can talk about colors all you want." She pressed a finger against her lips. "Your daddy doesn't have to know. It'll be our little secret."

"Okay." I swung my legs, sipping chocolate. "Your color is yellow. It's pretty."

"That's right. Very good." Nana patted my hand. "Your mommy tells me you're special." She emphasized the last word.

I stared inside the mug.

"I'm special, too."

I poked at the marshmallows.

Nana's voice dropped to just above a whisper. "I can share my memories. Can I show you one?"

I slowly nodded.

"Give me your hand." Nana clasped my hand in hers and pushed into my head. It felt like a fingernail scratching my forehead, and then a video played inside my mind. I saw Mom holding a baby. I felt Mom's love for the baby.

I gasped and stared at Nana. "Is that me?"

"You've gotten so big. That was the last time I saw you. I'm happy you've come to live with me." She squeezed my fingers. "Show me what you can do."

I pulled my hand from hers. "Mine isn't nice like yours."

Nana frowned. She studied me. "Is that what your daddy told you?"

I peeked down the hallway before returning my gaze to the tabletop. I didn't like talking about the things I could do. It angered Dad, and I didn't want him to punish me.

"Don't be afraid."

I didn't want to be. I wanted to be brave. "I can make people do things."

Nana watched me with a curious glint in her eyes. I dipped my head, fascinated with the loose thread on my shirt hem. I tried to yank it off. The fiber sliced into my skin.

"Show me."

I lifted my head and stared at Nana.

"I won't tell your daddy. I promise. But I'm curious. Show me."

I chewed my lower lip.

Nana patted my hand. "No one will know but us."

"Promise?" When she nodded, heat flashed up my spine. The roof of my mouth prickled. *"POUR OUT YOUR COCOA."*

Nana gasped. She watched her hand, trembling violently, grasp the mug's handle and flip it over. Hot chocolate spilled onto the hardwood floor.

"Oh no!" My hands slapped my cheeks. I leaped to my feet. I'd forgotten to tell her to pour out the cocoa *in the sink*. "I'm sorry! I'm sorry!" I started shaking. Tears fell down my face. Grabbing a dish towel, I dropped to the floor and mopped the mess.

When Nana hadn't moved, I stopped cleaning and slowly looked up, afraid she would be frozen, holding the mug in the air. But she wasn't. She was laughing.

She whistled and shook her head. "My, oh my. That's some gift you have, dear. Have you ever tried it on your father?"

I nodded.

"What did you make him do?"

I wrung the dish towel.

Nana placed a hand on my shoulder. "You can tell me. It'll be our little secret, remember?" She cupped my chin. "What did you make your daddy do?"

I kept my gaze angled down toward my lap. "I make him throw away his beer. But I only do it when I'm really mad at him."

She sharply inhaled. "And?"

I fell back on my heels. "He gets angry at me because he knows I force him to do it and he can't stop himself from pouring them out. He says I cost him a lot of money."

Her brows lowered. "What happens when your daddy drinks, Molly?"

I tugged the corner of the dish towel. "He yells at Mommy. Sometimes he hurts her. It makes her feel sad."

Another gust of wind shoved the house, pulling me out of the past. Nana twisted around and faced the large window behind me.

"Why are we talking about this?" I asked, irritated she'd stirred up old memories like silt at the bottom of a pail of stagnant water.

She looked pointedly at me. "You and Cassidy are very much alike. From the first moment you stepped foot inside this house until the day you lost your parents, you wanted nothing more than to save your mom from your father. There had been no stopping you. Do you think Cassidy will act any differently?"

No, I didn't.

Wind tumbled over the house. Tree branches scraped metal gutters. Frankie hissed, ears back. Hair stood along his spine. Nana shot a glance at the window as though questioning its strength. "More storms are coming," she said.

I shivered, as much from the dampness of my clothes as the memories Nana's tale stirred.

"I've been thinking, Molly." Nana's needles clicked as she ended a row. "Cassie could use her mother right now."

"I'll go see her in a moment. I was giving her a chance to calm down."

"That's not what I mean. Show Cassie what you can do. Speak inside her mind. She might not feel so alone and scared."

As Nana spoke, the slight chill I felt a moment ago hardened to ice, stiffening my limbs so that I gripped the arms of the chair, my fingernails digging into the woven fibers. I'd kept my abilities locked tight in the far reaches of my mind, which was what I wanted Nana to teach Cassie. Apparently my attempts hadn't worked. The techniques I'd taught myself didn't work on her. But if I opened my mind to her and showed her my abilities, as rusty as I knew they would be, the results could be disastrous. I wouldn't risk that again.

"Cassie doesn't need me. She needs my mother. Cassie's more like her."

Nana's gaze flitted to the right, then down into her lap. She set aside the needles and blanket she was knitting.

A door slammed upstairs. It slammed again. Nana and I looked at the ceiling. Another slam. *Boom, boom, boom.*

I cringed. "That's Cassie. She does that when she's mad." I stood and glanced at my dirty jeans. "I'll check on her, then go change."

Nana didn't respond. She gazed into the fire, her stare distant. Frankie slinked across the floor and hid underneath Nana's chair.

After dinner, I assisted Nana in cleaning the dishes. Cassie went upstairs to get ready for bed. She had finally calmed after I'd promised a gazillion times I'd stay away from the beach for the remainder of our stay in Pacific Grove. Tonight, assuming this premonition followed a similar pattern, the vision would return in her dreams, shedding more light on the how and where of my drowning. Then all I had to do was avoid getting into that situation. Like, for the rest of my life. I had no proof of whether avoiding the situation prolonged the premonition and Cassie's nightmares, but I guessed I would find out. Hopefully they'd cease once the cycle of days passed and the events didn't transpire.

A knock sounded on the front door. Nana and I paused with the dishwashing. She nudged me with her elbow. "It's Owen."

I popped a brow. "Is he a regular at this hour?"

"Go answer it."

I groaned, drying my hands, and went to answer the door. Owen stood on the dimly lit porch. Rain fell in sheets behind him. He held up Cassie's stuffed toy. "Some bunny misses Cassie."

My pulse jumped at the sight of him. Nervous excitement skittered around my belly. I took the toy. "Thanks."

He stepped closer and leaned a shoulder against the doorframe, his face inches from mine. I smelled the mint on his breath, which came in swirling puffs, chilled by the night air. He didn't ask to be invited inside, but he didn't seem eager to leave, which I found surprising considering our strained run-ins today.

"How is she?" His voice was low, meant only for me.

"Mad. She's getting ready for bed right now." I gave the rabbit a stern look. "You came home in the nick of time," I said. Nerves, as well as motherly goofiness with my daughter's toy, pitched my voice higher. My cheeks warmed, and I cleared my throat.

Owen's mouth twitched. He looped his thumbs in his front pockets and chin-nodded toward Bunny. "I tried convincing her to come earlier. She was having too much fun leering at the dogs from her perch. Dirt finally had enough of their stare-down and thought she'd make a great chew toy. Bunny quickly changed her mind."

"Yikes. That wouldn't have ended well." For Bunny or Cassie. She would have been devastated to lose her favorite toy. "Thanks for coming to Bunny's rescue."

Feet shuffled behind me. I glanced over my shoulder. Nana stood halfway down the hall. She held a glass of amber liquid. "For heaven's sake, Molly, it's storming. Let the man inside."

Wind rolled across the porch. Raindrops scattered, dotting my face.

I wasn't inclined to sit and socialize, but manners dictated I open the door wider. "Do you want a drink?"

His mouth pulled up at the corner, his eyes warm in the cold night. "I'd love one." He straightened. "But not tonight. Your daughter needs you, and you need time with Mary. She's wanted you to visit for a long time. I can wait." He stepped back from the door. "'Night, Lollipop." He flashed a grin, flipped up his jacket collar, and bounded off the porch.

Damn, Owen. Why do you have to act so nice?

He was not making it easy for me to ignore the baggage between us, waiting to be unpacked and dealt with. I shut the door with more force than intended. Windows rattled.

Upstairs, Cassie lay tucked in bed under the glow of her nightstand lamp. Light refracted through the plastic crystal lampshade and danced across sea moss–painted walls, giving the room the appearance of being underwater. Eyelet curtains hugged the paned window overlooking the street. Owen and Nana had designed a beautiful oasis for Cassie, perfect for a young child who loved the ocean as much as her mother.

"Hey, Mermaid." I sat on the bedside and held up the stuffed rabbit. "Missing anything?"

"Bunny!" Cassie snatched the toy and flattened it against her chest. Bunny's beady eye bulged over Cassie's arm.

I scooted up the full-size bed and sat beside Cassie. A book rested on Cassie's bent knees.

"What are we reading tonight?"

She closed the book and showed me the cover.

"Hmm. *The Velveteen Rabbit*." I took the book from her. "We haven't read this in what? Three days?"

Cassie giggled. "Bunny told me this morning she wanted to hear the story tonight." She positioned the stuffed animal between us with an unobstructed view of the pages.

Floorboards creaked, and I looked up. Nana came into the room cradling a fancy teacup. A red hummingbird fluttering over periwinkle flowers decorated the cup. Steam spiraled from inside, and I felt the warm moisture against my chin and cheek when Nana leaned across me and handed Cassie the tea.

"Careful, dear," Nana advised as Cassie took the first sip. "It's hot."

Cassie grimaced. "Bleh."

"Drink up and you'll have princess dreams, with fairies and magic and—"

"Bunnies?"

Nana gave a little snort. "Lots of bunnies. You'll have a good night's sleep."

On her way out she stopped in the doorway. "I almost forgot, Molly. I spoke with Ophelia this afternoon."

I frowned, the name sounding somewhat familiar.

"She's the owner of Ocean's Artistry in Carmel."

Mom's favorite jewelry store. "What about her?"

"I told her about your work and that you were visiting. She'd love to see some of your pieces. Give her a call. She has time on Wednesday."

"All right," I agreed for the sole reason of pleasing Nana.

She blew Cassie a kiss, then told me she'd be downstairs knitting by the fire.

Cassie reluctantly finished her tea and set the cup aside. She burrowed deeper in the covers, resting her head against my upper arm, and I began to read. Her breath came in short puffs, her lashes a dark crescent fringe against peachy cheeks. She didn't move or ask a single question through the entire story, one she'd heard dozens of times. As I neared the end, I wondered whether she'd fallen asleep. Then she asked a question she never had before.

"Am I sick, Mommy?"

I frowned and looked down at the top of her head. Her hair part zigzagged, messy from a windy day. "No, honey, you're not sick."

"The kids at school tell me I'm crazy. They say I should live in a hospital for mental people."

I sucked in a breath and held her tighter. Unfortunately, her troubles at school were all too familiar. Kids were as vicious today as they'd been decades ago.

"I know I'm different, but I can't help what I see. I've tried super-hard, but the dreams don't go away. I can't make them stop and people get hurt. Will the doctors throw Bunny away?"

Like the stuffed rabbit in the story, tossed in the trash when the little boy was diagnosed with scarlet fever. My heart ached for Cassie.

Her chest rattled as she inhaled. She rubbed her face in Bunny's fur. "I don't want you to die."

"I'm not planning to die, Cassie."

"But the vision . . ."

"I'll figure something out. I promise."

Fair skin bunched between her brows. "I can take care of Bunny, but who will take care of me if something happens to you?"

My pulse jumped. A walnut-size lump stretched my throat. The words "I'll take care of you!" sizzled on my tongue. I wanted to speak them, promise everything would be all right. But what if I messed up again like I had this afternoon? What if I couldn't find a solution?

What if, no matter how hard I tried, I couldn't escape my fate?

Not an option, I reasoned, feeling determined, and scooted lower on the bed. Cassie snuggled against my side. "I spoke with Principal Harrison today."

She stiffened.

"She wanted us to know Grace is awake and doing well."

She sat upright and gawked. "Really?"

"Know what else Principal Harrison told me?"

She shook her head.

"You saved Grace."

Her brows curved high. "I did?"

"Mrs. Kaling bought Grace a new helmet because of you. The helmet protected her head." I tipped Cassie's chin. "You saved her life."

Cassie's mouth formed a small circle. "I saved her," she whispered, awed, and shimmied back under the covers.

I stood and kissed the tip of her nose. She lay back against the pillows and yawned.

"Good night, Cassie."

"Night-night, Mommy."

I clicked off the lamp and turned to leave.

"Mommy?" Cassie called as I reached the door. "I'm going to save you, too."

My fingers tightened on the doorknob. I briefly closed my eyes, my mind harassing me with images of Cassie struggling in the water, trying to drag me out. The conviction in her voice scared me almost as much as the idea of dying.

I shook off the images and blew her a kiss.

"Good night, Mermaid. See you in the morning."

Chapter 11

Monday, night

When I returned downstairs, Nana was sleeping in the chair under the blanket she'd finished knitting. Slender metal needles rested on the end table by the empty brandy glass. Frankie lay curled on her lap. He kneaded the blanket. I scratched his head. "Guess my chat with Nana will have to wait until tomorrow." He purred and pushed his paws deeper into the yarn.

Nana's head listed to the side. Her brows twitched, bunching the skin between them. Was she dreaming, or did she have a headache like earlier? Owen had mentioned she had them frequently.

I smoothed aside the short tresses draping her forehead. She looked so much older than I remembered, her skin almost translucent with age. A longing I hadn't felt since I was a teenager moved through me, the urge to reach out and touch her mind almost irresistible. For so many years I'd had to be strong on my own, and then I'd had to be strong for Cassie. The realization that I had to face what Cassie had foreseen and somehow come out alive was enough to make me want to curl into

Nana's lap, where she could bathe me in the warmth and security of her thoughts.

But she'd closed herself off to me, and it'd been that way since the day I'd lost my mother two weeks before I'd graduated from high school.

∽

I had stood at the bottom of the stairs, watching the coroner officers bring down my mother in a body bag. Every hope for her happiness had been zipped up tight in the bag along with her. My heart had shattered, like the tiny pieces of glass I treasured.

The officers moved past me, and I took a wide step backward, slamming up against the wall. My hands flew to my face, cupping my mouth and nose, and I crumpled to the floor. Large, hoarse sobs tore through my throat. Movement on the second floor caught my eye. I looked up the staircase at Nana, her face ashen and eyes unfocused.

I extended an arm up to her and my mind followed, reaching out. *Nana?*

Waves of pain and sorrow and guilt assaulted my senses, ripping another sob from my lungs. It only lasted a couple of seconds, then it was gone, as though Nana had unplugged an appliance. Confused, I reached out again and found . . . nothing. Just empty space.

My gaze met hers. She dipped her chin, slowly turned, and walked away to her room.

Loud, booming steps hit the front porch. "Molly!"

Owen burst into the entryway. "Molly!" he yelled again, coming to a sudden stop when he saw me crouched on the floor. He dropped to his knees in front of me, his face broken. "Molly. Sweetheart. I just got home and saw the ambulance out front. I'm sorry. I'm so, so sorry." He reached for my hands.

"She's dead, Owen. She's dead," I cried.

"Baby."

"She's dead. She's dead."

"Shh-shh-shh." Owen tugged me forward, trying to pull me in his arms.

I didn't want to be there, inside the house. I had to get out.

I shoved Owen away, knocking him off balance. His hand flew out to catch himself as he landed on his hip. I took off through the front door.

"Molly!" he shouted behind me.

I ran and ran. The wind ripped through my hair, and salt air tore down my throat, bursting into my lungs. My legs and arms pumped. I flew across Ocean View Boulevard and down the cement steps to Lovers Beach, where I screamed. I screamed and screamed until I collapsed to my knees and fell back on my heels. My chin dropped to my chest, and tears dripped onto my lap.

Dad had been the wave in which Mom tumbled. He wore her down, leaving her spirit pitted and discarded like sea glass. Now my beautiful, fragile mother was gone.

"She's all right, she's all right," I heard Owen tell someone. "She's with me. I've got her."

He eased down into the sand beside me, hugging his bent legs. He didn't touch me, and he didn't ask questions. He just stayed with me until I, exhausted, cold, and alone, leaned over and rested my head on his shoulder.

"She's gone."

"I know, baby. I'm sorry." He wrapped his arm around my back and kissed my temple. "I love you," he whispered against my skin.

After a few moments, he eased away from me. "We should go check on your grandmother, and then you can stay at my house. You can both come over." He stood and reached down for my hand.

We walked slowly back to the house, where I saw Nana standing on the sidewalk, talking to two police officers.

"Why are the cops back?" I asked. The two officers there now were not the same ones who had left as the coroner officers finished up.

"I don't know," Owen murmured. His grip tightened around my hand.

They looked up as we approached, and Nana turned fully to face me. "Molly." Her voice held a note of disbelief.

My gaze jumped from her to the officers and back. My heart thumped hard in my chest. "What is it? What's going on?"

"Your father . . . ," she started.

"What about him?" My voice sounded thin.

"There's been an accident. He's dead. He was killed by a hit-and-run driver."

My head lolled, and I swayed on my feet, my eyes blinking rapidly.

"Molly?" Owen sounded so far away. "Molly!"

I crumpled, the world going dark.

Frankie meowed, and I blinked. The cat was looking up at me with wide eyes. He stretched out a paw, claws splayed, seeking attention. I gave him a quick scratch under the chin and Nana one more look before I left the room.

I walked down the hall, and I kept walking, right out the front door, stopping only when I reached the sidewalk. Then I headed toward the beach. Like before, I had to get out of that house, away from the ghosts of memories even an extensive remodel couldn't purge. Standing here, in the dark and the pouring rain, I could breathe. Energy pulsed through me with the rise and fall of my chest. I tilted my face to the sky and let the rain cleanse it, hoping it would calm my mind.

Over the downpour came the thundering roar of waves pummeling the shoreline. Rain sparkled under streetlamps. Color shimmered on the edges of my vision.

I'd stopped at the end of Owen's walkway. The light from his den cast a pale glow on his porch. Inside, I could see him hunched over a desk, brow furrowed.

He glanced up and stared out the window. I held my breath, even knowing he couldn't see me, not that well. It was darker outside than in. He pushed away from the desk, stood, and left the room, turning off the light. I exhaled, feeling slightly disappointed. For a moment I watched muddy rivulets weave over the sidewalk and pour into the gutter, then I turned to leave.

Owen's front door opened. Light from inside spilled onto the porch. "Molly?"

His eyes glittered, ghostly white in the night. He flipped on the porch light, and my gaze met his across the yard. He stepped off the porch and into the rain. He held a hand over his head to keep the water out of his eyes. "What are you doing out here?"

"Uh . . ." I glanced back at Nana's house.

"Come inside." He waved me forward. "You're soaked, and I'm getting soaked." He looked down at his sock-clad feet and grimaced.

I glanced down at my feet, which were also shoeless. My brain registered my chilled toes. I shivered.

His jaw firmed. "As much as it pains me to say this because of all the work I did, I know why you're out here. That house bothers you." He gestured toward Nana's Victorian. "So that leaves us two choices. We can talk out here and freeze our asses off or we can go inside."

"What if I don't want to talk?"

Owen tossed out his arms, let them fall back to his side. "Fine, then. We'll have that drink you offered me."

My teeth chattered. I hopped from one soggy foot to another.

"Suit yourself," he acquiesced. He turned to go inside.

"Wait." He was right. I didn't want to go back inside that house. At least not until my mind calmed. "All right. One drink." That should be enough to still the chaos in my head.

He led the way into the house. I shivered again, my fingertips and toes slightly numb. I glanced at our feet and rolled my eyes. We looked pathetic. We both had soggy wool socks. Owen bent over to yank his off.

Mudd and Dirt skidded into the foyer. Wet noses nuzzled my hands. Tails wagged. Dirt bumped my thigh, pushing me into Owen. Still bent over with one sock half-off, Owen collapsed against the wall. He swore and ordered the dogs into the other room. Sulking, they left, heads bowed, tails tucked.

"Wait here." He bounded upstairs.

The house was dark, aside from the dim light overhead and a soft glow coming from the main room. A light flashed on in the hallway upstairs. I tugged off my socks. Owen returned a moment later wearing a dry shirt. He'd slipped off his jeans and into gray sweatpants. He handed me a towel and a flannel shirt, then pointed toward the bathroom. "You can change in there."

I scooted down the hallway, teeth chattering, and after I'd dried and changed, I followed the light into the main part of the house. Owen stood at a sideboard, his back to the room. The dogs lay curled on giant cushions before the fire. Tails thumped and heads lifted when I entered the room.

Owen opened a bottle of liquor and poured. Ice crackled inside two lowballs.

I settled onto a leather couch and tucked my bare legs underneath, tugging the shirttails over my knees. Magazines were fanned on the coffee table. *Camaro Performers, Architectural Digest, Blue Water Sailing.* Small car parts were aligned on a grease-stained white towel. It was too dark to see the room's details, but he'd done some work. The carpet was new, plusher. Vases filled with seashells and sea glass decorated the mantel. Without looking inside, I knew they were the ones we'd collected over the years.

My hand fluttered to the sea glass pendant resting on my breastbone. We both had kept them all.

Owen moved to stand before me, drawing my gaze upward. "Here."

"Thanks." I sniffed inside the glass. Bourbon. "You've been hanging around Nana. You two and your hard liquor."

His mouth quirked. He sank to the coffee table and faced me. "Did you talk?" He sounded worried.

I shook my head. "She fell asleep. Why?"

He leaned forward, elbows on knees, glass clasped between his hands. "You were standing outside in the pouring rain. You had that same look on your face you used to get when you're ready to run."

As in run away. I sagged into the couch.

"You used to run to the beach like that when you were upset."

I blinked, shocked he remembered. And that he still seemed to care, judging by his tone. I looked down at the untouched glass in my hand. A sharp tang filled my nose as I inhaled. I didn't like hard alcohol; the taste and the smell reminded me of my father. It also weakened my resistance. I'd see colors.

Owen sipped his drink. "What's bothering you?" When I didn't immediately answer him, he knocked his knee against mine.

I flinched and tucked my knees in closer. His nearness overwhelmed me.

"You're right," I acknowledged. "It's the house." *And my possible imminent demise,* I thought grimly.

My gaze remained fixed on the glass in my hand. Screw it. Today had been a day from hell. I tossed back the bourbon. A fire blazed down my throat, exploded in my stomach. Air blasted from my lungs. I considered the empty glass. "That's strong shit."

Owen continued to study me, and I shrugged my shoulders, an apologetic gesture. He'd put so much work into the house, and I felt bad. I tapped my forehead. "Bad memories. I needed air."

"Anything you want to talk about?"

I shook my head, and he rubbed his thumb along his chin. "Do you mind if I ask you a question then?"

I clasped the pendant, sliding the glass back and forth on its delicate chain. "All right." I drew out the last word so it came out as one long syllable.

His face grew serious, and I tensed. Nerves fluttered in my stomach like paper windmills. Other than the snap of flames in the fireplace, the room seemed to grow quieter.

"Why did you end us?"

I blinked at his bluntness, my lips parting. The pendant dropped to my chest. The sorrow in his tone shot straight into my heart. It ached, reminding me how much I'd lost over the years because of one moment I'd been out of control.

Owen had been right earlier. After my parents died, I had graduated from high school and crawled into myself, virtually shutting him out. I shut out everyone because I didn't want to feel anymore. When I didn't feel, the anger and guilt and self-loathing dissipated. I could breathe again, whereas throughout that summer I'd been suffocating.

Two days before I left for school, I'd broken up with Owen. He fought for us, laid out all the reasons why we should stay together. Now more than ever, especially since I'd lost my parents and we were both moving away from home. We needed each other. He almost broke down my defenses, almost had me telling him exactly what had snuffed the life from me. I couldn't risk that, so I told him I no longer loved him.

He didn't believe me. Just tossed up his hands and told me to go chill at school for a few weeks. I would realize soon enough how wrong I was.

We went our separate ways. I didn't call him, and I didn't e-mail him. But a few weeks later he started calling. He left long voicemail messages I could barely listen to. He told me about his day, about the great work they were doing for an orphanage, and about how much he missed me. He kept calling and e-mailing, and over time I felt myself wavering.

So I changed my phone number and deleted my e-mail account. Because I didn't want Owen to hate me should he learn the truth.

In the end, I'd done exactly what I set out not to do, I thought wryly. By breaking up with him, I'd made him hate me.

Moistening my lips, I took a deep breath. "We weren't compatible." A partial truth. Those summer months had been rough between us.

His gaze dropped to my neck. He lifted the pendant, and I inhaled sharply at the brush of his fingers against my skin. My stomach fluttered with an old awareness.

Owen studied the sea glass he'd given me all those years ago, then let it fall gently against my breastbone. His eyes met mine. There was a hardness around his that sent my pulse racing.

"I don't believe you."

I grasped the pendant. "Believe what you want, but I told you I didn't love you anymore."

He flinched. "I didn't believe you then, and I still don't."

"Just because I'm wearing a necklace you gave me doesn't mean—" I stopped, because I wore the necklace to keep something of him close to my heart, since I wouldn't allow myself to have him. I shifted restlessly on the couch. "Look, Owen, I just didn't want to be with you anymore."

"I know when you're lying to me. You can't look me in the eye and you get all shifty."

I stilled.

"You were my best friend. I think after all the years we spent together I deserve to know the truth." He leaned forward, forcing me to sink deeper into the couch. "Why the hell did you break it off? Because for the life of me, I could never figure it out. I kept replaying scenarios in my head, wondering what I'd done to make you push me away. I loved you. And goddammit, seeing you again . . ."

Brings all those feelings back. The thought formed in an instant when he didn't finish his sentence. As though we'd been thinking the same thing.

Tears burned the rims of my eyes. One escaped the corner, and I quickly wiped it away.

Owen inhaled deeply through his nose. He dropped his head, and I knew he was taking a moment to gather his wits.

"I told myself I wasn't going to ask you," he said, blowing air through his nose, a sound of self-disgust. He parked an elbow on his thigh and gripped the back of his neck. "I wanted to give you time so that you'd get used to being around me again. Maybe you'd remember how good it used to be between us."

I trained my gaze on the glass I held in my lap. Did he expect us to pick things up where we'd left off? Even after the way I'd treated him? Guilt swirled in my gut like birds taking wing on air currents. I didn't deserve a second chance at love. I didn't plan to be around for a second chance. Cassie and I had to leave town. I needed to put distance between myself and the ocean.

"I used to tell myself I didn't need you," he said quietly. "Why would I want someone who didn't want me? I kept asking myself that so that I would stay away. Except that one time nine years ago when I just had to see you, even from a distance.

"Molly." The tone in his voice, full of longing and regret, drew my gaze back to him. The vulnerability in his gray eyes floored me. "Why?" he asked simply.

My breaths shortened, building pressure underneath the guilt and shame and, when it came right down to it, self-loathing until I could no longer withhold the admission. "I thought you weren't safe around me." He still wasn't.

He shrank back. He stared at me, incredulous. "What the hell does that mean?"

I shook my head, silently willing him not to ask. I'd have to explain what happened the day my parents died. And to this day I'd told no one.

Owen sipped his bourbon, his face a portrait of disappointment in me.

I glanced away and took inventory of the framed pictures displayed on the built-in shelves visible above his right shoulder. "How are your parents?" I asked, searching for a lighter subject.

Owen's eye twitched with irritation. "They're fine. Living in the Keys. Where's Cassie's father?"

A wave of sadness pushed me to my feet. Time to get off today's emotional roller coaster.

He followed me up. "Who is he?" His throat rippled as he waited for my reply.

"He's dead, Owen."

"Jeez, Molly, I'm—"

"It's okay." I raised my hand. "We dated only for a few weeks and spent one night together. He died before I could tell him about Cassie. I never regretted having her. She's my world."

"Did you love him?" His voice came out strained. I knew that no matter how I answered his question, it would hurt him.

"Yes," I said, and a breath shuddered from Owen. "I loved Steve not because of what we had together, but for the sole fact that he's Cassie's father. What we did have together was nothing like . . ."

Owen inched closer, our bodies almost touching. "Like what?"

I looked pointedly at him. "Us." I whispered the admission.

Where Steve had been comfortable, Owen and I had been white-hot and electric in between those comfortable moments. He'd left such an imprint on me that no one else could come close to matching what we'd once had together.

He shot me a look from under the hood of his eyelids. "I'm going to sound like an ass no matter how I say this, so I just am. I'm glad you're unattached." He lifted damp curls off my forehead, tucked them behind my ear. Warm shivers raced through me. "I'm glad you're back."

Orange hues radiated from him. I ducked my head, overcome with emotions I hadn't expected to feel, or the colors I hadn't seen in so long.

Wow, they're beautiful. Like the rays of the setting sun, the way they shot across the ocean right before the sun dipped below the horizon.

I slammed the doors in my head. Stupid alcohol.

"What about you?" I asked, turning the conversation back on him. "Any past loves?"

He shook his head. "I dated here and there. Nothing long-term. There wasn't, well . . ." He gave me a half grin. "Those relationships paled in comparison with us."

"I thought for sure you'd be saddled with a wife and kids by now."

A dark shadow crossed his face. "Nope. It's just me."

"And the dogs."

He looked disgruntled. "They are more of a handful than kids," he said, then smiled.

I returned his smile, and my heart took an unexpected tumble. The fire burned lower, and the room dimmed. The hour suddenly seemed very late. "I should go." I set the glass on the coffee table.

He walked me to the door. "Hey," he said, turning around, hand gripping the knob. "Anytime you have to get away, work things out"— he tapped his head—"or just talk, come here. Like you used to. I'm here if you need me. All right?"

"All right," I agreed, somewhat wary, as though waiting for him to press for us to talk further. Set a date and time. When he didn't say anything more, only looked at me expectantly, I tugged the cuff of the shirt he lent. "I'll bring it back tomorrow."

"Keep it. I like thinking of you wearing it."

My face heated. "Geez, Owen." I grimaced, and he grinned.

"By the way." His expression turned serious. "Have you asked Mary about those headaches of hers?"

I frowned. "Not yet, why?"

"I think she's sicker than she's letting on. I'm worried she might be dying."

Chapter 12

Tuesday, after midnight

Nana was dying?

No, she couldn't.

After leaving Owen and then showering, I paced the hallway from Cassie's room to Nana's, finally pausing outside Nana's door. My thoughts churned like sea glass tumbling in waves. Owen believed she was dying. She was old but not that old. She should have years left, and I thought we'd have many more together.

All those years I'd come up with excuses to stay away were nothing but lost time. And I had no time to make it up with her.

God, Cassie could lose us both. Who would care for her?

Perspiration bloomed across my chest and down my back. My breaths quickened as I returned to my room, thinking of Phoebe. I had to talk with her about this tomorrow.

Needing to keep my mind occupied, I opened the plastic bins I'd brought with me. Sea glass winked a dull, tarnished glow as though lit from within.

The desk lamp didn't provide ample light, so I moved one of the bedside lamps to the floor and spread out my tools.

Rain pattered the roof and the heater hummed. Warm air disturbed the room, caressed the back of my neck as I hunched over my pliers and wire. Within a few moments of twisting and shaping, my shoulders relaxed, and the turmoil brewing inside my head eased as I focused on my craft.

Then at two thirty a.m., I packed my supplies and went to Cassie's room, where I counted down the minutes, just as I had many other nights since late January. I didn't know why the nightmares came at this time. Perhaps it was when she entered the dream phase of sleep. But I could rely on them being consistent.

The digital numbers on Cassie's nightstand clock changed again. 2:50. *Almost time.*

She breathed steadily. Light snores wrinkled the room's silence. 2:55 came and went. 2:59. 3:00. I pushed away from the door and came into the room. 3:01.

Cassie snorted. A soft sigh escaped. I frowned. Was she still asleep? Cassie never slept past three after a vision.

I compared the nightstand clock with my phone. 3:04.

She stirred, rolling to her side. She kicked Bunny off the bed. I picked up the stuffed toy and watched Cassie. Her lips were parted slightly, her lashes dark smiles on her face. If she dreamed, it wasn't about me. She slept too peacefully.

I looked at the clock. 3:05. I looked at Cassie, still asleep. I looked at my hands, and Bunny's beady eye stared up at me. Cassie wasn't dreaming.

Don't panic.

Since the day her abilities had manifested, I'd wanted my daughter's nightmares to end. For weeks I'd longed for the visions to stop. And for countless nights I'd wished for a normal night's rest. But not tonight.

I needed her nightmares. She had to tell me where I drowned. *How* I drowned.

I squeezed Bunny. Why had the dreams stopped now? What was different? My mind cranked through the day's events up to the final moments before bedtime. I'd talked with Owen on the porch, then tucked Cassie into bed. Read her a story. Nana had brought tea.

The tea.

I snatched the cup on the nightstand and sniffed the leaves at the bottom of the cup. Dirty socks, dried sweat. I scrunched my nose. No wonder the tea had grossed Cassie out. What herbs had Nana used?

Drink up and you'll have princess dreams.

No nightmares.

I returned the cup to its saucer and tucked Bunny under the covers. Cassie stirred and mumbled in her sleep. I shook her shoulder. "Cass."

Her lashes fluttered, eyes popped open. She looked around the room, disoriented, then saw me leaning over her. "Mommy?"

"Hi."

She frowned. "Is it morning?"

I sat on the bed. "No, honey, it's still nighttime. You didn't wake up." She yawned. "I'm tired."

"Did you dream?"

Her eyelids drifted close. "No," she mumbled.

No.

My hands started shaking.

I stood and stared down at her. Cassie sucked in a breath. "I'm sorry."

Oh . . . shit.

I circled the room, hands steepled over my mouth. What was I supposed to do? There had to be other options aside from simply avoiding the beach, because yesterday's escapade had shown I couldn't even do that. What if I ended up in the water, despite how hard I tried to avoid it?

I returned to Cassie's side. "Can you tell me anything more about what you saw yesterday?"

She sat upright and hugged Bunny. She shook her head.

"Was it dark or sunny?"

She shrugged.

"Day or night? The beach or a pool? Were you with me or was I alone? Any idea *how*?"

"I don't know." Her lip quivered.

"Dammit, Cassidy. I might die. I have to know how to stop it from happening."

I paced the room, once, twice, and turned back to Cassidy. Tears marred her face, glistening spider trails across her cheeks. She roughly kneaded Bunny's ear. "I don't know," she whimpered.

Heat blazed up my spine. Words crackled in my mouth. "You have to know something. Give me something! Anything, dammit! Think! *THINK!*"

"I am, I am, I am," she cried. "There's water all around your head. You can't breathe. That's all I see. That's all I see. That's all . . ."

My hands slapped over my mouth. I felt like vomiting. "Oh my God, I'm so sorry."

She blinked rapidly, her pupils minimizing, bringing her surroundings into focus.

I swore liberally behind my cupped hand. I hadn't meant to influence her. I hadn't meant to lose control.

She whimpered, her little body shaking. "I'm scared, Mommy."

I collapsed on the bed and pulled her into my arms, burying my face in her hair. I sobbed. "I'm sorry, Cassie. I didn't mean to frighten you. Never again. I promise. It'll never happen again."

But it might. The admission whispered in my head. Somehow, some way, assuming I made it past Friday, I had to finally learn how to control my abilities. Because when I was emotionally out of control, my abilities naturally followed suit.

She cried on my shoulder. "I'm sorry I don't know more, Mommy. I promise to save you. I promise."

"Sweetheart, please don't think it's all up to you. You already have enough to worry about. Mom will take care of herself." Besides, mothers were supposed to take care of their daughters, not the other way around.

Clutching her to me, I felt like the worst mother on planet Earth. I didn't want her to lose me.

"I don't want to lose you either," she whispered.

Chapter 13

Tuesday, predawn

I adjusted Cassie's bedding over us and held her until her limbs relaxed and she drifted to sleep. I remained awake, swimming in a stew of self-loathing. It wasn't Cassie's fault she hadn't dreamed about the premonition, nor was it Nana's. She'd only done what I'd asked—help Cassie. However, I hadn't anticipated the nightmares suddenly stopping, and my reaction drop-kicked me into the past, leaving my mind reeling and my self-assurance that I could keep my abilities in check in shambles.

I had been nine when I first lost control. It was also the year I found my first piece of sea glass. Owen and I had been playing at the beach on Sunday afternoon. While he'd skipped stones into the surf and searched the tide pools for little crabs, I'd combed the sand hunting for shells and sand dollars.

Owen was telling me about where he'd spent his Saturday. He and his dad had gone to Laguna Seca to watch the car races. I half listened, and was scooping sand aside to get to the finer, wetter granules underneath when something flashed in the sunlight. A piece of glass. It wasn't ordinary. The texture was rough and pitted, as though it had been worn down and shaped by sandpaper, like the kind Mr. Torres used with his woodwork in the garage. He was always working on his house.

I held the glass against the sky, squinting at the sun. A green emerald, much more fascinating and pretty than the dull-gray shells lining my pockets.

Tucking the glass away, I searched for more. Fog rolled in, blanketing the bay, and the temperature dropped. I barely noticed. Owen tapped me on the shoulder and asked what I was doing.

"Looking for glass." I showed him the bits in my hand. Greens, browns, and blues glittered in the dimming sunlight.

"Those are cool." He pushed them round my palm, then looked at the sky. "We should go, it's getting late."

By the time we left, my pockets were full of sea glass. The shells I'd collected had been left behind in the sand for the next beachcomber.

The glass fascinated me, and I brought them to school the next day. I couldn't stop looking at them, and I wanted to show Phoebe what I'd found.

We sat across from each other on a picnic table at recess. I'd aligned the glass from smallest to largest on a white paper napkin.

Phoebe studied a blue, oval-shaped shard. "My mom collects these. We have a big vase in our living room full of glass." She returned the piece to my collection. "What does your mom collect?"

"She doesn't collect anything." She didn't get out of the house much unless she was grocery shopping, working, or taking me to school. I pushed the glass around the napkin, shaping them into a heart. It made me think of Owen.

Phoebe straightened her back, glancing over my shoulder. She scowled. "Don't look, but here comes Tyler."

I couldn't help it—I glanced over my shoulder. My stomach plunged like a stone in water. Tyler's quick stride ate up the hopscotch-marked pavement. He was short and scrawny, and his hair was always falling over his eyes. He snapped his head, whipping back his bangs, and stopped behind me. His friends Reese and Clayton bookended Tyler, towering over him by a head.

Tyler had completely ignored me last year, my first year in Pacific Grove. But this year, with Owen in middle school and no longer by my side, Tyler wouldn't leave me alone.

"Whatcha got, Ragdolly?"

"Her name is Molly, you jerk," Phoebe defended.

Tyler snorted, reaching over my shoulder. He snagged a piece of glass. I quickly hid the rest under my palms.

"Looks like junk to me." Clayton peered over my shoulder.

Tyler held up the glass in the sunlight. "I think you're right, dude." He chucked it over his shoulder.

"Hey!" Phoebe said.

I stood up. Reese shoved me back on the bench.

"Move it." I pushed him aside and went to retrieve my glass. I scanned the pavement for a moment before finding it winking at me against a white hopscotch line.

"It's trash, Ragdolly," Tyler said when I picked it up. I tucked the shard into my pocket.

He snagged the napkin of sea glass and wadded it into a ball. Phoebe reached across the table, grabbing for his hand. "Give that back."

He held the wadded napkin out of reach. "We aren't supposed to leave trash on the table." He walked away.

"What are you doing?" I asked in a high-pitched voice.

He stopped at the garbage can. "Doing you a favor. I'm tossing out the trash."

"No! Don't!" I'd spent hours looking for those pieces. I loved that glass, and so did Owen. He thought they were pretty. Little pieces of treasure.

"But, Molly," he said with mock sincerity, "it's just trash." His fingers uncurled, and the wadded-up sea glass dropped into the can.

I ran over. "It's not trash." I reached into the can. Tyler smacked my hand away. "Stop it!"

I tried again, and he shoved me back. He waggled a finger at me. "Now, now. You know it's against school rules to dig inside the garbage can. Unless"—he reached inside and pulled out a half-eaten sandwich— "you are garbage." He threw the sandwich at me. It smacked me in the chest, landing at my feet.

My hands fisted. A crowd had gathered, but I didn't care. "I'm not garbage," I screamed at him. "You are! You're garbage. Get in. *You* belong there." I pointed at the can, and he laughed at me, head tossed back. He laughed and laughed.

Heat radiated up my spine, and electricity popped and crackled in my mouth. *"GET IN!"*

Tyler pivoted to face the can. He popped the lid, dropped it on the pavement, and climbed inside. Kids started laughing and pointing fingers at him.

"Dude! What are you doing?" Clayton asked.

Tyler sat down so only his head was visible above the can's lip.

Reese ran over. He tugged Tyler's shirt collar. "Dude, get out before the yard lady sees you." He looked around, his gaze jumping madly over the yard.

Tyler's expression morphed from dull indifference to shock as the compulsion wore off. He shot to his feet. "Get me out of here." His hands flapped like a bird.

Mrs. Giles, the yard-duty lady, pushed through the crowd, blowing her whistle. "Tyler Eggleton," she yelled, the whistle popping from her mouth. "Get out of there this instant."

Tyler's wild gaze moved over the crowd until it landed on me. He pointed. "She made me do it!"

Phoebe whipped her head around and gawked at me. "Did you really?" she loudly whispered.

I cringed, fighting hard to keep the tears at bay. Now Phoebe would shun me, too.

"Did you?" she asked again.

I shrugged. "What would you do if I said yes?"

Her eyes dimmed with a cloud of fear, but she blinked and the light returned, full wattage. She laughed, a deep belly laugh. "I'd say that's the coolest thing ever." She grinned deviously. "Hey, Tyler! Dickwad!"

Tyler whisked his head around, searching for the person who had called out to him.

"You can't prove anything, you jerk!" Phoebe shot back, coming to stand beside me.

"Get out of the trash," Mrs. Giles yelled again.

"Molly made me!" He popped over the can lip as though jumping on a pogo stick. His sneakers landed with a thump on the pavement. His gaze zigzagged from one kid to the next. "You heard her."

They had heard. All eyes turned to me. I took an involuntary step back. Expressions turned leery. Whispers floated around me.

Phoebe scooted back with me, shifting her body to block me from their view. I'd never been so thankful to have her as a friend as I was in that moment.

The recess bell rang.

"Not so fast." Mrs. Giles's hand shot out. She snagged Tyler's upper arm. "It's the principal's office for you, young man," she said, hauling Tyler behind her.

"It's not my fault," he whined. "Molly made me do it. It's her fault."

Phoebe nudged me. "Come on. Let's get to class."

Inside our classroom, the phone rang about twenty-five minutes into math period. Mrs. Davenport looked over at me while she spoke to whomever it was on the other end of the line. I sank in my seat.

"Uh-oh. This can't be good," Phoebe mumbled beside me.

Mrs. Davenport hung up the phone. "Molly Brennan, pack up your things and report to the school office."

I slammed closed my math book.

"I'll call you this afternoon," Phoebe whispered as I gathered my belongings.

I murmured a good-bye and left. The heat of twenty-two pairs of eyes seared into my back as I walked out the door. The whispering started, and before the door had firmly shut, I heard Mrs. Davenport rap a book on her desk, calling for order.

Dad was waiting for me when I walked into the office. My step faltered when I saw him rising to his feet. Nausea coiled in my belly, like sand crabs wiggling and twisting along the shore to hide from the surf.

I stopped before him, my eyes glued to my Converse sneakers. He wore the leather loafers he used only for work, when he had work. The heels were scuffed to the point that brown polish no longer hid the marks.

His hand appeared in my line of vision. "Let's go, Molly. I've already signed you out."

My head snapped up. "I'm leaving?"

He grabbed my hand and pulled me out of the office and into the bright sunshine. I squinted against the glare, my eyes adjusting. It was early fall, summertime along the Monterey Peninsula. The sun was warm, and flowers perfumed the air.

"What did I do?" I asked, jogging to keep up with his purposeful stride. Tyler couldn't prove I made him get into the trash, so why would the school have called Dad?

Dad tugged me through the parking lot. He stopped at the car. "How about ice cream? Would you like a scoop?"

I blinked. "But I have school."

"I've decided you're taking the day off." He opened the rear passenger door. "Get in."

I crawled into the backseat and buckled my seat belt. My fingers kneaded my shirt hem, missing the special glass Tyler had tossed. The pitted texture soothed. Glancing at the back of Dad's head, I wondered when I could look for more. Hopefully he wouldn't ground me this weekend. I hadn't meant to make Tyler sit in the trash.

A giggle bubbled up in my throat. He'd looked funny, and I bet he smelled now, too.

"Anything you want to share?" Dad asked from the front seat.

I shook my head and stared out the window.

At Fester's Creamery, Dad ordered a single scoop of mint chocolate chip on a sugar cone for me, and French vanilla on a plain cone for himself. We took our ice cream to the beach, walking along the footpath that traced the shoreline. Oil painters standing at their easels captured the scene stretched before us: high, wispy clouds, yellow-blue sun, and an ocean of teals and deep blues.

Dad stopped at a park bench and sat down, patting the space beside him. I sat, swinging my legs. We licked our scoops, Dad finishing his with three large bites of his cone. He popped the last bite into his mouth, chewed, and crumpled the cone wrapper. He used it to dab the corners of his mouth, then folded his hands together, letting them hang between his legs.

He cleared his throat. "I understand there was an incident at school today," he said, watching a seagull land a few yards from us. A breeze moved past, lifting the thinning hair he combed over his scalp. "Do you want to tell me about it?"

I shook my head, wiping a dribble of melted ice cream from my chin with the back of my hand.

"You're not in trouble with the school. The office called to let me know a boy was harassing you. I felt it best to pull you from class today so we could talk." The seagull flew off. He watched it swoop down the rocky outcropping before turning to me. "Did you make that little boy sit in a garbage can?"

The ice cream curdled in my stomach. "He was calling me names and he threw away my sea glass."

"That's not the question I asked, Molly. Did you make that little boy sit in the garbage?"

"No one can prove I did it," I sassed.

"True. But I know how you did it, and you know. That's all that matters."

My shoulders bowed. I stopped swinging my legs.

"How did the other kids act when it happened?"

"They laughed at Tyler, and then . . ." I plucked at my cone's wrapper.

"Then what?" Dad coaxed.

I scratched my leg, wiped my bottom lip. "They laughed at Tyler until he pointed at me."

Dad pressed his lips into a ruler-thin line. "Did they look at you like you were an odd bird?"

Ice cream dribbled over my hand. "Yes, sir." I took a slow lick around the scoop.

Dad sighed. "There's something you must understand, Molly. When you do unexplained things, those kids go home and tell their parents. Those parents start talking to one another about you and about me. They'll think all of us are different.

"I work with some of those parents. When they start looking at me like I'm the odd bird, well, hell. That makes me upset. Do you know what happens when I get upset?"

I shook my head, chin bent toward my lap.

"I can't focus on my job. That's what happens, and that's not good, because then I lose my job. And when that happens, it won't be my fault. Whose fault will it be?" His gaze penetrated into mine.

My mouth worked. Cool ice cream trailed down my wrist to my forearm. I shivered.

"I'm waiting for an answer, Molly."

"Um, m-mine?" I said, even though I didn't believe it was. If I got a bad grade on a test, it was because I didn't study. If Dad didn't do well at work, it was because he wasn't doing his job the right way, not because of me.

But I took the blame. He'd be more upset than he already was if I answered his question any other way.

He remained calm, chillingly so. No wonder Mom acted so timid around him. My heart pounded in my chest as I wondered what he'd do next.

"Throw away your ice cream, Molly."

"Wh-what?" I sure hadn't expected that.

"I said throw it away."

"But I'm not done."

"Are you arguing with me?"

"No." I pouted.

"Then throw it away."

I looked around us. "There's no garbage can."

Dad's face hardened. "That's a good thing, or else I might make you sit in it so you'd know how that other boy felt." He ripped my cone from my hand and tossed it into the ocean.

I sat frozen, mouth hanging open, my hand cupping air.

Dad turned to me on the bench. "Did you see how I threw away the cone? You need to do that to your mind tricks. Lock them up tight in your head and toss the key. That's exactly what I tell your mom, every day. It's time you start learning, too."

"I don't know how."

"You'll just have to figure it out, then." He stood, holding out his hand. "Time to go home."

I reluctantly placed my sticky hand in his.

At the house, I followed him into the kitchen. He went straight to the fridge and pulled out a beer, popping the cap. I washed the ice cream stickiness from my hands at the kitchen sink.

Dad drew several long swallows, then set the bottle on the counter. "Follow me."

I doggedly tailed him into the hallway, my sneakers squeaking on the floor. He stopped in front of the hall closet and opened the door. "Inside you go."

My pulse jumped. "What? Why?"

"You need to learn a lesson. Now don't make me force you. Get inside, please."

The closet was overstuffed with coats. The vacuum took up half the floor space.

His grip tightened on the knob. "Molly." He put his hand on my back and guided me into the closet.

I swung around. "Dad?" Panic clawed up my throat. Sweat bloomed along my hairline, causing a prickling sensation on my scalp.

"You need to find that closet in your head and lock away your mind tricks. I won't ever have you embarrass this family again. I will not be looked at like a freak." He shut the door, snuffing the light, and flipped the bolt.

"Dad!" I yelled in the pitch dark, shocked to realize the closet had a lock. When had he installed it? "Dad, open up!" I banged my fists on the door.

"You yell again, Molly Poppy Brennan, and I'll have to punish your mother, too. She's the reason you have that mind ability."

"But, Dad," I sobbed. "I'm scared."

"Then find that closet in your head as fast as you can. The sooner you find it, the sooner I'll let you out."

"Is Molly home? I thought I heard her."

Mom. Her muffled voice came through the door. It sounded far away, as though she were at the top of the stairs.

"Molly and I were just having a discussion, Sheila." Dad tromped up the steps. I glanced up when his feet were above me. "I'll tell you about it." The ceiling creaked as they walked to their room, and a door slammed.

I squeezed my eyes shut, because the darkness I could control was safer and less scary than the one I couldn't. I waited, sobbing quietly for them to come downstairs and let me out. When I didn't hear anything, I slid to the floor. Over and over I tried to find that closet in my head because I realized *I* was the reason Dad had added the lock to the door. Until I figured how to lock up my abilities, I'd remain locked inside, which only made me cry harder.

I must have fallen asleep, because the next thing I heard was the front door slamming shut. Nana Mary's voice moved down the hallway. She was home from work, which meant it was after five o'clock.

"Put the bag on the counter, Owen. I have another bag of groceries in the car. Do you mind getting it?"

"Sure thing, ma'am." Footsteps walked past the closet and back again. The front door opened and closed. I held my breath, my heart in my throat.

A few moments later the front door opened and closed again. "Is Molly home, Mrs. Dwyer?" Owen asked as he walked by the closet.

Don't open the door. Please don't open the door.

I shifted where I sat, my bent legs burning, cramped from being stuck in one position.

I heard murmurs in the kitchen. Tears dampened my cheeks. More footsteps outside the door as someone approached.

Please don't open the door.

Shoes scraped the floor on the other side. A shadow moved in the sliver of light that peeked through the crack.

The lock flipped and the doorknob turned. The door creaked open, bright light flooding the tiny closet. I blinked rapidly and looked up.

Owen stood there holding out his hand. He didn't ask any questions; he just waited.

I reached for him, and he pulled me up. My legs wobbled, screaming as taut muscles extended.

"Your dad?" he whispered.

I nodded. "He's upstairs, I think."

He glanced at the ceiling. "You can come to my house if you want."

I shook my head. "He'll be mad." I sank back onto the floor. "Close the door, Owen."

He looked perplexed. "Why? Don't you want to come out?"

"He has to open it," I explained. "He'll get mad at me, and Mom, too, if I leave the closet."

Owen stood there, unmoving.

"Please, Owen. Close the door."

"Then I'm staying with you."

"In here?" I looked behind me. "There's no room."

"Then I'll stay right here." He slid to the floor outside the closet, legs bent, back to the wall.

"Close the door," I whispered.

He did, slowly, until the latch clicked. He kept it unlocked.

"Are you still there?" I whispered after a moment.

"Yes," he whispered back.

A scratching noise sounded, and Owen's fingertips peeked under the door. They wiggled.

I touched my fingertips to his. We sat there, barely touching, until Nana Mary's heels clicked across the wood floor a few moments later.

"Owen, what are you doing?"

His fingers disappeared. "Sitting with Molly."

The door flew open. Nana Mary looked down at me, her face riddled with shock until she noticed the shiny new bolt. She gasped, then her expression twisted into anger and her face turned red. She stomped to the base of the staircase. "Sheila!"

Owen poked his head in. "I think you can come out now."

I did crawl out, then I spent the evening at Owen's house. His mom fed us, and afterward we spent the evening stargazing. I didn't want to go home, and I didn't want to go inside. I needed wide-open spaces after spending six hours in a tiny closet.

Later, though, as he walked me home, I asked how he'd known I was in the closet. I hadn't made a sound.

He shrugged a shoulder. "I don't know. Just a feeling, I guess. Inside my gut." He patted his stomach.

Good thing he had opened the door when he had. Nana found my father passed-out drunk in his bed. He'd forgotten about me. I'd been too scared to make any noise, and I wasn't sure Mom even knew where I was. I'd been too afraid to reach out to her with my mind else Dad found out. I would have spent the entire night in the coat closet.

Chapter 14

Tuesday, morning

The next morning I woke at 9:40. I never slept that late. I didn't want to get up either, but I had to check on Cassie for both our peace of minds. She had every right to be upset with me. The way I'd influenced her had caught me by surprise. Then again, my compulsions always did. I once knew how to issue them on command, back when we'd first moved here. Mom had started to train me, but then Dad had found out and had convinced her to stop. Lack of training meant lack of use, which eventually led to a lack of control. My compulsions happened more infrequently over the years, but when they did, it usually was when I was overly emotional. I felt too much, whether anger, hatred, frustration, or fear. Last night I had been emotional. And I hadn't been that scared in a long time. We'd both been scared.

I burrowed farther under the covers. *God, I'm a horrible mother.*

Until last night, I'd never used my abilities on Cassie. I didn't even know the color of her aura. If I looked and then spoke with her in that special way I used to speak with my mom and Nana Mary, she'd start asking questions. She'd ask about me and what I could do. Then she'd want to know how I'd used them before. At her age, I'd asked my mother the same questions.

I'd remained with Cassie a couple of hours last night. I'd told her over and over how much I loved her. She eventually fell back to sleep, and I'd continued to murmur my love. I wanted to tell her I loved her again.

I also had to text Phoebe to see whether we could meet later than we'd planned.

Tossing aside the covers, I slipped on my robe and went downstairs. Nana's cooking pulled me into the kitchen. Lamb stock, thyme, onion. My stomach gurgled. Cassie stood on a footstool beside Nana. She held a measuring cup as Nana poured flour. They both looked up when I entered the room.

"Look who finally woke up." Nana sealed the flour bag and set it aside.

"Good morning." I gave Cassie a hard squeeze, plastering her back to my chest, and whispered in her ear. "Sorry about last night. Are you okay this morning?"

She nodded.

"Good." I planted noisy kisses on her neck.

She squealed and wiggled from my arms. "We're baking soda bread."

I sniffed the air and poured a cup of coffee. "Smells delicious. Lamb, too?"

"Braised lamb shoulder with root vegetables. Pour only half the flour," Nana instructed Cassie. She turned on the mixer.

I sipped coffee. Nana's lamb was a favorite, and she cooked it when company was expected. "What's the occasion?" I asked when the mixer shut off.

"Poker night. It's my turn to host. Pour the rest now, dear."

I groaned into the mug. *That's riiiight.* "Do you want me to pick up your dry cleaning?" I had to try to see Mr. Spencer Martin, Esq. again, anyhow.

"No, dear, I'll take care of that. Don't forget to call Ophelia," she reminded me.

Nana waited for Cassie to tip the remaining flour into the bowl before turning on the mixer. They watched the beaters twirl until Nana turned off the appliance to test the dough.

"Ruby is looking forward to seeing you."

I snorted. "Mrs. Felton? She cheats, you know."

Nana laughed. "We all do."

"Uh-oh."

"Care to share?"

"No," I mumbled under my breath.

She watched me, patient, as she shaped the dough into a loaf.

"Fine." I set down the mug. "At the last poker game I saw her—jeez, when was that? Thirteen, fourteen years ago?" I rubbed my face to clear my foggy brain. I was still drowsy. "Anyway, I chucked her purse on the porch and locked her out when she went to get it."

"I know." Nana giggled. "Thanks to you I won the game."

"How?"

"I peeked at her cards."

"Nana!" I held out a hand, palm up. Poor Mrs. Felton. Banging the side window and jiggling the doorknob. "It does explain things, though. Mrs. Paxton paid me to do it." I moved to the sink and rinsed the mug. "I'll make sure Cassie and I are out of the house tonight. We'll go see a movie or something."

"Nonsense." Nana waved aside my suggestion. "This is your home."

It would be my home if what Owen said were true. *Or it could be Cassie's,* I thought grimly. I watched Nana closely. She seemed to be fine this morning, no sign of a headache.

Cassie wiped her hands, dusting off flour.

"I have to stay here, Mommy. I'm going to be Nana's hostess. Right now I'm her Susie chef."

Nana giggled. "Sous chef," she corrected, moving to stand beside me. She dropped a handful of wooden spoons in the sink and flipped on the faucet.

"We need to talk."

Nana drew in a breath. Her hands paused in their washing. "I fell asleep last night, didn't I?" She hummed. "I was tired, and my head was bothersome. Migraines."

"About that—"

"Nothing for you to worry about, Molly, dear." She patted my shoulder. "I have to finish prepping for tonight. We'll have plenty of time to chat later."

That was the point. I might not have time. And neither did she, if Owen's suspicions were accurate.

The doorbell rang. "Will you get that?" Nana asked. "My hands are wet."

I gave Nana a penetrating look, one that told her she wasn't going to put me off much longer, and went to open the door.

Owen flashed a smile. "Nice pj's."

I tightened my robe belt. Underneath I still wore his shirt. It was comfortable and smelled like him—ocean spray and pine. "I'll return it to you later today after I do the wash."

He shook his head. "Keep it." Then he looked beyond my shoulder into the house. "Mary called me. May I come in?"

I moved aside, opening the door wider.

Owen stopped just inside the entryway. He glanced down the hall-way and waved. "I'm here to pick up Cassie."

I angled my head. "Excuse me?"

Owen looked at me, surprised. "You didn't know?"

I shook my head. "Know what?"

"I'll be right there, Mr. Torres." Cassie ran toward us, then up the stairs.

"Where are you taking her?" I asked, growing concerned.

"Mary said Cassie had an errand to run. She's coming with while I run mine."

I crossed my arms, not entirely comfortable that this arrangement had been planned without me.

Nana approached.

"Morning, Mary." Owen gave her a hard hug and kissed her cheek.

"Och, Owen! Behave." Nana blushed and swatted Owen with a dish towel. "Doesn't Owen look dashing this morning?"

He did fill out his fisherman-style sweater nicely, and the man definitely knew how to wear a faded pair of jeans.

He turned and looked at me. I felt my face burn and ducked my head, coughed into my hand. "Don't you work?"

"I'm in between jobs. New project starts next week."

"What time will you have Cassie back?" Nana asked. "I need her help in the kitchen this afternoon. She's my hostess tonight. She'll need time to bathe and dress beforehand."

Owen peeked at his watch. "It's ten now. How about one? I'll buy her lunch on our way back."

"Wonderful."

He gave me a questioning look. "Only if it's okay with you. Mary said Cassie had something to buy and that you and she were too busy to take her. I didn't realize you didn't know Mary called me."

Cassie bounded downstairs carrying Bunny and a purse. She held out her palm.

Nana glanced down. "Yes, I have it right here." She slipped three one-dollar bills from her apron pocket and handed them over.

Cassie counted the money before tucking the bills into her purse. She looked up at Owen. "Is three dollars an hour fair?"

"To help me shop? I don't know, Cass." He crossed his arms, tipped his chin, as though contemplating her request. "Three bucks is pretty steep."

"I won't take anything less than two."

Owen gave her an arch look. Cassie crossed her arms and dipped her chin. She looked up at him as though peering over eyeglasses.

"All right," he conceded. "Two it is." He extended his arm.

Cassie shook his hand. "Deal."

I eyed them both. "What's going on?"

"It's my new business. Here, look. I have a card for you." Cassie dug in her purse and gave me a paper scrap. "Just in case you need my services."

I looked at the paper, cut the size of a business card. Cassie had written neatly in felt tip pen: *Cassidy the Handy Girl. Sweeping, mopping, car washing, errand assistant, Susie chef (with adult supervision), and weeding.* Below that was Nana's house phone number. On the backside, Cassie had drawn Nana's purple house. Beside the house was a stick figure of a blonde girl holding a stuffed rabbit.

"I'm a handy girl, you know, like a handyman." Cassie beamed.

"I see." I pressed my lips flat. I trusted Owen with her, but I didn't want Cassie to tell him about the premonition. If he knew, he wouldn't leave me alone or let me out of his sight.

Cassie's smile faltered. "Don't be mad, Mommy. I'm keeping busy."

"Cassie, your mom has to agree with your coming along with me," Owen said.

Cassie clasped her hands against her chest. "Please may I go with Mr. Torres?"

I regarded Cassie with a serious look. She was right. She needed to keep her mind off me. And with her occupied, I could run my own errands. "All right, Cassie. Behave yourself and listen to Mr. Torres. Stick close to him while you're shopping."

"Aye-aye, Captain." Cassie saluted and clicked her heels.

I flicked Owen's arm with the card. "Don't let her out of your sight."

"Absolutely. And don't worry, I have experience with kids."

"That's surprising," I remarked, recalling his abrupt reaction to my comment about children the night before. Then again, I had no idea what he'd been up to or where he'd been over the years.

The corner of his mouth lifted. "I'm full of surprises."

"I bet you are," I drawled, sarcastic, and that old familiar flutter shifted in my belly again.

"Ready, Cassie?" Owen asked.

"Come here, honey. Give me a kiss."

She kissed my cheek, and I zipped her jacket, following her and Owen to the front porch.

"Bye, Mommy!" She waved back at me as they walked to his car. "I love you!"

I stood on the porch with Nana and watched them drive away. She glanced at the partly cloudy sky. "Storm's coming."

I looked toward the coast. "Another one?"

"Been coming for a long time." She removed her apron. "Soda bread is in the oven. Will you watch it for me while I shower?"

She handed me the apron and turned to the door.

I followed her inside. "I have to run an errand, so let's talk about Cassie before I go."

She gripped the stair banister and rubbed her temple. "Later, dear. My head is bothering me."

"Then tell me about the tea you gave Cassie. What was in it?"

"Valerian, and a few other things."

"She didn't dream about me drowning last night."

"Of course not. That's what the tea's meant to do. Closes the mind and allows it to rest." She looked at me curiously. "Isn't that why you came? To get help for Cassidy? She told me you wanted the nightmares to stop."

"Yes, but—" I stammered and blew out an exasperated breath. "That was before her vision about me."

"What difference does it make?"

"What difference does it make?" My voice shot to the ceiling. "The nightmares get more detailed each night. They show Cassie what's going to happen, sometimes the how and where, too. Without that information I don't know what to do! How am I supposed to survive if I don't know how to prevent it?"

"Hmm, well then"—she dipped her chin toward the floor, her gaze turning inward—"we'll have to figure another way for Cassie to see."

"You're going to help her, then?"

She moved up the stairs. "Of course, Molly, dear. Now, I have a lot of preparation to do and"—she glanced over her shoulder at me—"I believe you do, too."

Chapter 15

Tuesday, morning

While the soda bread baked in the oven, I read the text messages Phoebe had sent me earlier this morning. The first two asked when I expected to get there, as it was already past nine. The third asked that I call her, so I did.

"Hey, you," she answered. "What happened to you this morning? Did you forget about coffee?"

"No, I didn't. I'm sorry, I overslept. Can we meet later? I want to talk with you about a few things."

"Everything okay?"

"Um, yeah," I lied, pacing the kitchen. "I'll tell you when we meet up."

"I'm on my way to a doctor's appointment for Kurt, and then I meet with my attorney afterward." At the mention of his name, I heard a shout in the background. Phoebe ordered him to quiet down, then apologized to me.

"What's up with the attorney appointment?" I asked, my stomach fluttering as I recalled that I needed to do the same.

"King Asshole suddenly realized he no longer has the time to take the kids on his days. Then my afternoon and evening are crazy with afterschool activities and homework. I want to focus on our chit-chat when I see you, not herding four kids. Can we try again tomorrow morning, say nine o'clock?"

"All right. See you tomorrow."

After we said good-bye, I dialed Spencer Martin's number from the photo I'd snapped yesterday. His receptionist answered on the second ring. I explained that I needed a will, and she informed me that Mr. Martin's schedule was booked this week. Would I be available to come in next Tuesday?

There was the possibility I wouldn't be alive next Tuesday, and that thought sent my pulse skyrocketing.

"It's sort of urgent. You see, I'm leaving the country on a business trip," I told her. The little white lie was less outrageous than the truth. "I want a will finalized before I leave. I have a daughter, she's only eight, and I'd feel better traveling overseas if I knew her welfare has been considered."

A pencil tapped through the phone. "You said you're Mary Dwyer's granddaughter?"

"Yes."

"All right. Let me talk with Mr. Martin when he returns from court. I'll ask if he can fit you in before Friday. I'll call you back later this afternoon."

"Thank you," I said, ending the call.

With my calls out of the way, I paced the long, narrow hallway from the kitchen to the front door. It was already after eleven, and Cassie wouldn't return with Owen for another couple of hours. That was two hours when Nana wasn't training Cassie how to prevent her visions. And it was two hours when Nana wasn't doing whatever it was she intended to do to extract more details for me from Cassie's vision.

It was also two hours closer to my drowning, which made me think of all the things in Cassie's life I might miss, such as the report cards she would never show me. If something happened to me, I wouldn't be the one to buy her first bra, or teach her to shave her legs, or explain that warm water and soap worked better than shaving cream. I wouldn't be able to drive her to school, because I'd be dead.

"I'm *not* going to die," I said through gritted teeth.

Standing at the large window in the rear of the house, I looked in the direction of the ocean. Assuming Cassie's premonition followed the same pattern as the previous ones, I only had a few days left.

If I couldn't learn how and where I would drown from Cassie's nightmares, and if Nana wasn't able to get that information from her some other way, we needed to leave, and soon. Avoidance was still an option.

Although, I thought, tapping my chin, *there's still tonight.* As soon as Nana came back downstairs, I'd tell her not to give Cassie the tea. I needed that nightmare.

The oven dinged. I slipped on mitts and set the bread aside to cool. Then I went upstairs to shower. By the time I returned downstairs Nana had left the house. Running errands, according to the note pinned to the fridge with a magnet from Monterey Bay Aquarium.

I crumpled the paper.

Why wasn't she making the effort to talk with me? She should be showing me what she was working on with Cassie. Could she be avoiding me intentionally?

I think Mary might be dying. Owen's words came back to me.

My chest caved. Nana didn't want me to know.

She didn't have a cell phone, so I couldn't call her to come home. Until she got back, I needed to keep myself occupied, or I'd go nuts. I felt like a call that had been put on hold.

Going upstairs, I finished grading reports and uploaded the marks to the school's system. Then I fiddled with my tools, working on a pendant to show Ophelia tomorrow. An hour passed, and I checked my phone. Still no call from Spencer Martin's office. I tossed the phone aside in frustration, and when I couldn't get the wire to bend around the pendant the way I wanted it, I tossed my tools aside, too. Instead,

Kerry Lonsdale

I pulled out a sketchpad and a handful of colored pencils. My hand guided the pencils through contoured lines and sharp angels, and soon the form of a blonde mermaid with blue eyes took shape.

A short time later, voices rose from the entryway. Small feet bounded upstairs.

"Hi, Mommy!" Cassie burst into the room. She peeked over my shoulder at my doodling. "Pretty."

I flipped the pad closed. "All done with your errands?"

"Yep." She skipped to the doorway.

I frowned. "Hey, Cassie, how are you doing?"

"I'm fine."

I pivoted in my seat to face her. "How are you doing considering, you know, what you saw about me yesterday?"

She looked at her toes, shuffled her feet. "I'm doing okay."

My heart ached for what she must be going through. I wanted to whisk her away, pretend she hadn't foreseen anything. "I'm going to do everything in my power to avoid the water. You know that, right? I'll make sure I stay safe."

"Me, too, Mommy."

Nana called her from downstairs.

"When did she get back?" I asked.

Cassie glanced over her shoulder. "Just now. Gotta go! Nana's waiting." She blew me a kiss and ran off.

The front door slammed, and I started straightening up my sketches and packing supplies.

"Molly?" My name drifted up the stairs.

My skin tightened at the sound of Owen's voice. "Up here," I yelled, kneeling beside one of the bins. I stacked the sea glass trays back inside.

Owen stopped just inside the threshold to my room. "Hey there," he said in greeting.

"Hi." I popped on the lid and scooted on my knees to the next bin. "How was Cassie?"

130

"She was a great errand helper. You have a special girl on your hands."

My breath caught in my throat, wondering at his word. *Special.* What had Cassie told him?

He tucked his fingers into his front pockets and leaned against the doorframe. "She's smart, witty, and beautiful. She reminds me of you."

My breath eased out of my lungs. A smile tugged the corners of my mouth. "Thank you."

"Although she's not as shy as I remember you being at that age."

"Really?"

"She has no problem telling me what's on her mind."

Whereas I did. At Cassie's age, we'd just moved here and were living under Dad's no-mind-tricks rule. I had to keep my emotions in check to keep my abilities in check, which made me very quiet, and an easy let's-pick-on-the-weird-girl target.

"I hope she wasn't rude," I said.

"No, just outspoken. Which is a good thing. She'll make a great politician someday."

"Wonderful," I drawled. Now, that was a future I didn't see, but it was entertaining to think about.

"Mary sent me up here to get you." He came into the room and scoped the open box of pliers and cutting tools. "Are you working up here?" he asked in reference to my makeshift workshop on the floor.

"Only space available. The dining table is already set for poker night."

He made a noise in the back of his throat. "Thanks for the reminder to keep out of sight tonight."

His expression almost made me laugh. "What's so scary about old ladies playing poker?"

"Last time Mary hosted I was finishing work upstairs here. They roped me into a game. Those ladies are brutal. Took all my cards without the blink of an eye, and after Mrs. Felton left, they drank me under the table. They cheat, too."

"Did your ego take a bruising?"

"And my wallet. They beat both to a pulp. Anyhow, Mary thought you might be working with your sea glass. She's busy with Cassie right now and asked that I show you the changes in the backyard. Do you mind?"

"All right." I pushed to my feet and followed Owen.

He led us downstairs and into the backyard, where Mary's garden shed had been renovated to look like an in-law unit. He slipped a key from under a flowerpot and unlocked the door, pushing it open. He stepped aside.

"What's in there?" I arched my neck to look inside.

"Your new studio."

"My new what?"

He chuckled at my surprise and flipped on the light. *Wow!* I entered the shed, taking in the small space, from the design bench to the polishing work area and computer station, which was located across from a bench grinder. Right here, tucked in the corner of Nana's backyard, was the jewelry art studio I'd never imagined owning.

And I might never have the chance to use it.

My world tilted as the last thirty hours rushed over me. I gripped the corner of the desk beside me for balance.

Owen glanced around the room. "What do you think?"

I fumbled for something appropriate to say. Nana didn't expect me to leave, not with a studio like this built in the backyard. I thought of the stubborn sterling wire back in my room and the beginnings of Cassie's Sweet Sixteen mermaid pendant I'd been sketching in my pad. With these tools, I could tame the wire. My legacy to Cassie crafted into something magical.

But I wasn't sure I'd be here beyond the weekend.

A sick feeling advanced inside me like the evening tide, swift and powerful. Unstoppable. I burst into tears.

Owen looked horrified. "Not the reaction I expected."

To my dismay, the tears didn't stop. He swore and gathered me in his arms. After a few moments, he clasped my hand. "Let's walk."

⁓ꢃ

We entered Owen's house, where he offered me a jacket. He gathered the dogs' leashes hanging on the coatrack by the door. Hearing the jingle of their leashes and voices in the hall, Mudd and Dirt came running. Toenails skidded on hardwood. They planted their rumps on the floor and thumped their tails. Dirt let out a sharp bark, and I jumped. "I haven't walked a dog since that old Chesapeake retriever you had."

Owen clipped the leashes to collars and handed Mudd's to me. "Carmel was the best dog. Much more obedient than these knuckleheads," he said, opening the front door.

Mudd burst past him, tugging hard on my arm. "Oh!" I jogged to keep up. "He's strong."

"Give the leash a sharp tug and command him to heel. He'll fall back."

I complied and so did Mudd. We walked toward Ocean View Boulevard, and every so often I felt the gentle press of Owen's hand on the small of my back. He watched me closely when we crossed the street as though trying to measure my mood.

We reached the other side, and he allowed Dirt to tug him down the cement steps toward the beach. The dog pranced with nervous excitement. Mudd barked, and Owen looked at us over his shoulder. I remained frozen on the sidewalk. Wind stole through the unzipped jacket, twisting around my neck to lift my hair. Another gust, ripe with seaweed and salt and full of sand, collided with my torso. I locked my knees to keep from pitching forward. Mudd pawed the ground, tugging his leash. My arm burned. He let out another yelp.

Owen returned to the sidewalk, dragging Dirt behind him. "What's wrong?"

"I can't." I stared at the water. Sand rode the wind, punished the skin on my face, my bare hands. My cheeks stung.

He glanced over his shoulder, then back at me. "Can't what?"

I tore my gaze from the surf and looked at him where he stood, two cement steps down from me. Our eyes were level. "I promised Cassie."

He frowned. "Promised her what? What's wrong?" He moved closer. "What happened back at the studio? Why did you cry?"

I inhaled and took a leap. Just because I told Owen about my daughter didn't mean I had to explain why I'd left him all those years ago.

"Remember you asked if Cassie is like me?"

He slowly nodded.

"She is. But different. She sees the future and she saw me drown." My voice sounded like a car rolling over gravel. "Owen, I can't go near the water."

He stared at me. A typhoon of confusion and disbelief swirled in his eyes. His jaw hardened, and after an endless moment he redirected his gaze toward the ocean, where the horizon was as black as the storm in his expression. He wouldn't question my sanity, and he wouldn't judge. He would accept what I said about Cassie, and when he looked at me again, there was a glint of that acceptance in his expression.

"No wonder Cassie went ballistic yesterday," he said.

"She was pretty upset."

"How do her premonitions work? Is the outcome final or can it be changed?"

Mudd whined, and I rubbed his head. "Cassie was able to change one outcome by telling the girl what she saw. She told her friend Grace she was going to get hit by a car while riding her bike and that she'd wind up in the hospital with a severe head injury. The girl fared better than the premonition, because her parents bought her a new helmet after hearing what Cassie said."

"There's hope then. How much time do you have? When's this all supposed to happen?"

"Assuming this premonition follows the same pattern as the others"—I lifted a shoulder—"Friday." I eyed the violent shoreline. *It could happen within a few hours if I don't start walking in the other direction,* I thought morbidly.

Owen swore liberally. Dirt growled, and Owen tugged the dog's leash to get him to quiet. He then took Mudd's leash from me.

I rubbed sticky sand from my face. "The thought of never setting foot on a beach again. Or taking a bath . . ."

He shortened the leashes so the dogs pressed against our legs. "I can give you a sponge bath."

Our eyes met. The corner of his mouth twitched.

"Oh my God, Owen," I cried, shoving him. He stumbled down a step before regaining his perch. "This is serious."

"Exactly. I'll make sure to soap every inch of you. Linger over the softer parts."

I growled my frustration.

Holding both leashes in one hand, Owen rubbed my arm. "Relax, Molly. I'm not taking this news lightly."

I bundled his jacket around me, hugging my arms. "I feel like I'm being pulled in different directions. On one hand I want to leave town and put as much distance as I can between me and that." I motioned at the beach. "On the other hand, I want to stay because of Cassie. Nana's training her how to stop her visions. They're traumatizing."

Hair lashed the bridge of my nose, whipped my jaw. I wrapped the strands around my hand and held my fist against my shoulder. "On top of all this, I don't have a will, Owen. If Nana is dying like you think she is, who's going to raise Cassie if I can't? Never, ever did it occur to me I'd die when she was this young.

"And it's the little things that kill me. She's afraid of the dark and crawls into my bed all the time. I won't be there when she's scared. Who's going to hold her after I'm gone? I can't imagine who that person is, and it makes me sad it won't be me. That she'll have no one to love her. She'll be all alone."

A hoarse cry ripped from my lungs, tore up my throat. "It's like I have a disease and am dying. I just don't know when, and there's nothing I can do about it except hope I can hang on for as long as possible."

"Stop." Owen cradled my head. "Please stop." He pressed his lips to my forehead and held me to him.

My resistance crumbled, and I stopped fighting the feelings seeing him again had reawakened. Just for this one moment I melted against him.

Owen dragged his lips to my temple. "Stop tormenting yourself. I don't like this any more than you do, Molly, not one bit."

He stilled, keeping his face pressed to mine. The storm whipped around us, but he held us firm against the wind. He was my anchor, like he used to be. I gripped his forearms, my fingers digging into his jacket. He brought his lips to my ear. "I'll do everything possible to make sure you stay alive. Do you understand?"

I nodded.

"First things first, though. Let's give you some peace of mind."

He handed over the dog leashes and pulled out his phone, tapping the screen.

"What are you doing?"

He held up a finger, motioning for me to wait.

"Hey, Dave, it's Owen." He paused. "Yeah, I'm good. Listen, I'm calling in my favor." He paused again, his eyes meeting mine. I didn't know whom he was talking to or what he was asking, but I didn't care. I felt such relief having his help, I didn't feel so alone anymore.

"A friend of mine needs to see you," he explained. "Today." Pause. "Great. Thanks, man."

"Who's Dave?" I asked, somewhat anxious.

He tucked his phone away. "My attorney. You have an appointment with him in thirty minutes."

Chapter 16

Tuesday, afternoon

I made a quick detour to Nana's house to get my purse and my own jacket. I found Nana and Cassie in the sitting area by the kitchen. The fire crackled, and something delicious bubbled on the stove. Onions and herbs.

Nana knitted in her chair while Cassie sat cross-legged at her feet with Frankie curled in her lap. Eyes closed and delicate brows furrowed, she absently stroked the cat.

Nana looked up when I entered the room. She pressed a finger against her lips, her eyes darting to Cassie. Nana was training her, and by the intense look on Cassie's face, they were in the middle of an exercise.

My feet shifted toward the front door and back. I wanted to stay and watch, but I also had to think of Cassie's future, one that might not have me in it.

"I have to run to Monterey for an errand," I whispered. "Back in two hours," I estimated, holding up my index and middle fingers.

Nana nodded, waving me toward the front door. With one last glance at Cassie, I pushed aside that torn-up feeling inside me at having to spend time away from her, even if only for a couple of hours, and left the house.

Owen was waiting in his Camaro at the end of Nana's walkway, motor rumbling. He leaned across the seat and popped open the door as I neared the car.

"Ready?" he asked, and I nodded, strapping on the seat belt. He shifted into gear and pulled away from the curb. The car lurched forward, and I gripped the door handle. The engine gave a rough-and-tumble growl that vibrated through me.

"So," I began, dragging out the one-syllable word. "The car parts I saw last night on your coffee table?"

His grin spread like a leaf unfolding to catch the sunlight. "They don't belong to this car."

"That's a relief." I loosened my grip and coaxed myself into relaxing, even if only for a bit. For over thirty hours, I'd been wound up tighter than the reels on the fishing poles Owen had used when we were kids. I was making progress. There would be a clear plan outlined for Cassie if I couldn't avoid or outwit her premonition, and Nana was working with her at this very moment to hone and, hopefully, to put a stop to her visions.

"Do you remember Paul Conroy?" Owen was asking. "Big guy, wide shoulders. He played on the football team."

I shook my head.

"Only dude in high school with flaming-red hair."

My eyes lit up. "Oh yeah," I said, picturing a tall redhead in the hallway at school. He had the fairest skin that reacted to everything. Whether embarrassed, angry, or winded from PE class, Paul's face flushed to match his hair. Beefsteak-tomato red. He also had a TR7 that he drove everywhere. The car was as distinct as his hair.

"Anyhow," Owen continued, "he still has that old Triumph. It finally died, so we've been rebuilding the engine over the weekends."

"What's he doing now?"

"He's a marine biologist. Works out at the aquarium."

"Married? Kids?"

Owen shook his head and shifted into third. The road passed under us, and fir trees sped by outside the rain-drenched windows. Folding my hands in my lap, I admired Owen's hand resting lightly on the gearshift. He pushed it into fourth, his forearm muscles flexing. My stomach knotted, and I released a long, steady breath. I'd neglected to realize that driving with Owen in his car meant being cocooned with him in a tight and intimate space, inhaling the same air.

In an attempt to settle my fluttering nerves, I took a deep breath. Raw lumber and car seat leather filled my senses, along with the subtle scent of pine and ocean spray that I knew was a part of him.

He glanced at me. "What about you? Mary mentioned you teach art history at Cuesta College."

"I do and I love it. It's not the best-paying job, but it's rewarding. It gives me the flexibility to be off school when Cassie is. And, of course, there's my sea glass. I still design jewelry."

The Camaro coasted up Highway 1 toward Monterey. Owen scratched his jaw. I admired his profile. The hard lines and angles. His throat rippled, and he glanced at me quickly. "If you don't mind me asking, what did you tell the school to get the time off?"

"Family emergency," I said simply. The rain hadn't let up, and the wipers played a mad game of chase across the windshield.

"What do you plan to tell Dave Pearson, the attorney? It's probably best that I know, too, in case he asks."

"Same thing I told the receptionist at Nana's attorney's firm. She was supposed to call me back this afternoon." I glanced at my phone's screen. No missed-call notifications.

"Anyhow." I waved my hand, dismissing Spencer Martin Esq. as an option. "My story is that I have to go overseas on business, maybe a lecture or something I was invited to at the last minute, since I'm a teacher. I want to have a will drafted and notarized before I go in the event something happens to me while I'm there."

"That's good." Owen fell silent.

I didn't like the quiet. It made me all too aware of him. "Thank you for going out of your way to drive me."

"Of course," he said, sounding surprised. "I want to help. I've always wanted to help you." He grinned. "Maybe I'll force you to walk around in a life jacket."

I snorted a laugh, although it came out sounding sadder than anything.

"I'm having a hard time with what you told me," he emphatically admitted. "I can't imagine how difficult this must be for you."

I looked out the window, the corners of my eyes burning. It was tremendously hard. Parents weren't supposed to leave young children behind.

In my peripheral vision, I saw Owen shovel his hand through his hair. He gripped the gearshift and slipped it into third, merging onto the off-ramp.

"Even when we were apart," he said, "it was always in the back of my mind that you were somewhere, living and enjoying your life. Just thinking you could die on—" He didn't finish his sentence.

Reaching across the seat, he clasped my hand. I gripped his tightly, cursing the tears that quickly flooded my eyes.

"Tell me about your attorney," I said, needing to change the subject before I lost it again in front of him. "What favor did you call in?"

He cleared the emotion from his throat. "I repaired Dave's roof after a major rainstorm on short notice. Like really short notice. He bought an old fixer-upper and it had a lot more leaks, and a bucket of other issues, that didn't show on the inspection report. I showed up that day after canceling one project and postponing another so I could get it done. That was last November, and he told me if I ever had a legal emergency, he'd clear his calendar."

And he'd turned in his free pass on my behalf. Owen had always been the thoughtful one.

A short time later, we arrived at Dave Pearson's law office. Dave had the lean build of an ultra-marathoner and a high, shiny forehead. He was short, barely reaching my nose, and I was five foot seven. Owen towered over him, but Dave had a booming voice and a handshake with an exceedingly firm grip. He and Owen kept up a good banter for a few moments after Owen introduced us. When Dave turned to me and asked whether I was ready to get started, Owen excused himself, saying he planned to run an errand and would pick me up in a couple of hours. He met my gaze, and I sensed there was something more he wanted to say. Instead, he squeezed my hand and left the office.

For the next hour, Dave explained everything from a *power of attorney* and an *executor of an estate* to all the various components of a will, including the distribution of assets and guardianships. Once I couldn't think of any further questions, he gave me a worksheet to complete. In the interest of time, he suggested I fill out the form in their conference room. His clerical assistant could type up the document tomorrow morning. She'd then securely e-mail a copy, and if it was to my liking, I could return Friday morning to sign and have it notarized before I left on my trip. He then asked me about life insurance.

I stared guiltily at him. "I'm afraid I've been remiss in that area, too."

"Hmm." He pressed his lips flat and dug into the center drawer of his desk.

I stared at my hands folded in my lap, disappointed that I hadn't bothered to do any of this until now, what was possibly the eleventh hour of my life. I was the single parent of an eight-year-old. These were projects that should have been done the moment after her birth.

But I had been young, and struggling through my last year of college. I'd had student loans to pay off.

Dave slid a business card across his desk. "Give my insurance agent a call. Gayle won't be able to have a policy issued before your trip. Life insurance policies require blood work. But she can get started on quoting a term policy for you." He then showed me to the conference room where I could complete his worksheet. He had a few calls to make in the meantime.

For the most part, the worksheet was straightforward. I easily listed my assets, financials, and personal property, which wasn't much. I indicated that I wanted to be cremated and buried near my mother. As I wrote the name of the cemetery on the line provided, I refused to allow myself time to consider that I could be laid there to rest next week.

I quickly moved on to the guardian section and stopped. My pen hovered above the line as I wavered between Nana Mary and Phoebe. Nana Mary might be dying, and I didn't know whether Phoebe could emotionally or financially handle another child. Without a life insurance policy, I had minimal funds to offer. The only hope I had was that Cassie inherited Nana's house, which Phoebe could sell.

I glanced at my phone. Owen would be back in a few minutes. *What about Owen?*

He once held such an important place in my life that I knew I could trust him with my life, and with Cassie's. But asking him to take on the responsibility of my child was a huge request. I couldn't consider such a thing only twenty-four hours after seeing him for the first time in twelve years.

In the end, I put down Nana Mary as my primary for power of attorney and guardian, with Phoebe as my secondary in the event Nana couldn't perform her duties. I did ask Dave's assistant to hold off typing the will until I followed up tomorrow. I had to verify that Phoebe agreed with this arrangement. I also wanted to ask Nana about her health.

I might need to remove her from my will altogether. As to whom I replaced her with, I had no clue and had maybe less than seventy-two hours to figure out.

Owen was waiting for me by his car. The rain had let up, but clouds still hung thick and dark overhead.

"All done?" he asked as I approached.

"Pretty much." I stopped in front of him and met his eyes. "Thank you."

He smiled, and my traitorous heart took a tumble, splitting open on the sidewalk. Leaving him again was not going to be easy for either of us. I knew he hoped I'd stay, probably as much as Nana did. They'd put so much love and care into remodeling a house I'd run away from as soon as I graduated from high school.

I thought of the little studio in the backyard, and of how Owen, not Nana, had always been fascinated with my passion for sea glass. He was the one who had cased the shores he'd fished with his father, looking for glass to gift me while his dad iced their fish and packed their rods. I recalled his expression when he'd first opened the studio door, inviting me to take a look inside. Expectant and hopeful.

"The sea glass studio, that was your idea."

Owen took a step back, brows raised in surprise. "Uh . . . why do you ask?"

There was no way Nana had purchased the equipment, not after all she'd spent on the remodel. It was too expensive. "You bought the supplies to build the studio shed and purchased everything inside, too."

He watched me for a moment, then nodded.

"Why?"

"Because"—he shrugged a shoulder—"it's what you love to do."

He'd been keeping tabs on me all these years. God, he didn't hate me for breaking up with him. He still loved me. And he wanted me to stay. The proof was in the beautiful studio in Nana's backyard.

My heart thudded in my chest, and I took sudden interest in the traffic moving at a steady pace behind him. Grief and guilt, that nasty little pair of emotions, wreaked havoc inside me.

"Owen." I sighed. "I can't—"

He held up flat hands. "Hey, don't worry about it. Just enjoy it. Come on, let's get back."

∽

We drove to Pacific Grove in relative silence. Owen's admission only added fuel to my desire to get out of town as soon as possible. Before I fell for him all over again, and definitely before I broke down and confessed. Leaving him had had nothing to do with us as a couple and everything to do with me. My father had been right. My mind tricks should be locked tight in my head. And for the past twelve years, I'd kept them securely sealed.

Until last night.

I'd panicked. Been scared and angry. So much so that the door in my head had flown open. I'd influenced my daughter, and I'd manipulated her actions. I'd forced her to do something against her will. I could have put her in danger.

It had happened before and could happen again. It could happen with Owen.

But not if I could help it.

He dropped me off at the curb, mentioning a new project he had to quote. The rain had started again. Large drops fell at an angle, pushed inland by strong offshore winds. I ran up to the porch and into the house with my head ducked. Warm, spicy scents greeted me. Melted butter, heavy cream, and whiskey. I moaned. Nana's bread pudding.

Movement where the parlor adjoined the dining room caught my attention. Cassie stood beside a felt-covered, green table, counting plastic chips. Behind her, the dining table had been set with Nana's china and crystal. It wasn't lost on me that while Nana and her friends played poker like scoundrels and swore like sailors, they dined like ladies.

I went to Cassie, and she glanced up. "Hi, Mommy. Nana asked me to set up the poker table."

"I hope she didn't ask you to play."

She pushed out her lower lip. "She said I'm too young." She counted six green chips. "Nana and her friends play Texas Hug'em."

My cheek twitched. "You mean Texas Hold'em?"

She laughed. "Yeah, that's what I meant." Her brow scrunched as she counted red chips, then moved to stand behind the next seat. "Each player gets one white chip, three blue, six green, and ten red. That makes"—she counted her fingers—"twenty." She grinned. "I'm helping Nana cook, too."

I picked up the cards on the table and shuffled the deck. "You like helping people, don't you?"

Cassie counted more chips. "Some people don't think they need help. Ethan didn't."

The little boy who'd broken his leg. He'd ridiculed Cassie about her vision, mocked her in front of her classmates. I straightened the cards and returned the deck to the table. "Sometimes people don't want help."

She closed the poker chip case. "They're the ones who need it most. All done!" She skipped from the room before I could ask about her training this afternoon with Nana. Instead, she left me wondering about what she'd said.

The people who didn't want help needed it the most.

She knew I didn't want her help, not the kind that could jeopardize her own life. But I hadn't told her that exactly that way last night.

Had she sensed the reason why I didn't want her help?

She must have seen my aura, discolored with fear, I reasoned.

Then I remembered what she'd said to me last night. As I'd hugged her, I'd been thinking about her growing up without a mother. I hadn't wanted her to lose me. I'd thought that in my head, yet she'd replied out loud that she didn't want to lose me either.

My gaze tracked to Cassie. Had she learned to read thoughts? She must have heard mine about why I didn't want her help. She'd endanger her own life.

How had she broken through my barriers without my knowing? She couldn't be that strong at her age.

Although I had been emotional. I'd sent her a compulsion. Maybe my barriers had been weaker.

I trailed her into the kitchen. She'd donned an apron and stood on a stool beside Nana. The lilting notes of Celtic fiddles from the stereo competed with the buzz of the electric mixer. I said hello to Nana and spied the opened whiskey bottle on the counter. It was half-empty. I snatched the bottle and screwed on the cap. "Starting early, Nana?"

"Och! It's for the pudding."

I raised a brow at the dark amber liquid in the lowball. Nana's rosy cheeks matched the pink lipstick kissing the rim.

She wagged a wooden spoon at me. "Unless you plan to help cook, out of my kitchen."

"Nana says I make a great Susie chef." Cassie smacked her forehead. "I mean sous chef!"

"Yes, you do. Now pour this in, dear." Nana gave Cassie a bowl of egg yolks.

"You shouldn't drink." I returned the bottle to the pantry.

"It won't make a difference at my age."

"It's not about that. I don't like people drinking in front of Cassie. Dad always—"

Nana paled, and her face took a greenish hue. The knife she gripped hovered above chopped onions. She squeezed her eyes shut and swayed. My heart lurched. I caught her upper arm and steadied her. "Nana?"

"It's done!" Cassie peered into the mixing bowl.

"I'm fine," Nana said.

"You sure?" I asked.

"Yes, I'm sure. Look!" Cassie pointed at the bowl.

Nana nodded, and I rubbed her arm before stepping back. She resumed chopping, carefully pressing the blade through the onion's flesh until it connected with the wood chopping block. The putrid color clung to her complexion like tree sap on carpet.

"Nana—" Cassie pointed at the rotating beaters.

"Just a sec, Cass." I leaned closer to Nana. "You're doing too much." Hosting relatives, cooking, entertaining guests, and training Cassie. I was sure she was worried about me, too. And all of this was weighing her down. Making her ill.

She released a long, steady breath and pasted on a smile. "I'm fine, dear. I can handle it."

"No, you can't," I disagreed, and her face tightened as though in pain. "You're sick, aren't you?"

Nana's eyes snapped to mine. Fear and apprehension swirled in the depths of her faded blues. What was she hiding from me?

"Nana, please, you can tell me. Let me help you."

Nana only stared at me. Didn't she hear me?

I took the knife she white-knuckled, and set it on the counter. "Nana?"

She worked her mouth. Her eyes watered.

Sweat bloomed across my back as I watched her. Was she having some sort of attack?

Cassie raised the beaters out of the bowl as they whirled at high speed. Batter slapped against the ceiling, lobbed across the counter. She squealed. Nana gasped.

A chunk slapped me on the cheek. "Oh!"

Nana scooted around the island and yanked the plug.

Horrified, Cassie wiped batter off her face. It oozed from her fingers to the countertop and dripped from the ceiling. Nana glanced up. She laughed and an unladylike snort escaped. She covered her nose, smearing batter on her face. "Oh my."

A smile blossomed over the stern reprimand I had been preparing for Cassie. Another glob landed on Nana's head, and laughter burst from deep inside me.

Nana wiped tears from her eyes with the back of her hands. "That was fun. We need to do this more often."

"Do what? Make a mess?"

"No, laugh. This house needs more laughter. Don't you think so, Cassie?"

Her lower lip quivered. "Am I fired?"

Nana's cheeks pillowed with her smile. "No, no dear." She removed Cassie's apron. "Run along upstairs and change, put on your pretty dress. Your mommy and I will clean up."

Nana moved to the sink and started washing dishes. I picked up the dish towel and wiped down the countertop beside her.

"You're doing too much. Promise no more parties and entertaining?"

"Of course, dear," she agreed too readily.

I bit the inside of my cheek. Nana had no intention of slowing down, and that worried me. Because I couldn't force her to do what she didn't want to do.

My hand stilled. *I could.* If I focused hard, I probably could force her to slow down. Ease up on her activities. Rest.

Nausea rolled around my stomach like a boat on waves.

Why was I even thinking this?

I scrubbed the counter harder, and changed subjects. "How did it go with Cassie this afternoon?"

She put a wet dish in the dishwasher. "She asked about you."

I stilled. "Me?"

"She's curious about you and what you can do. You know"—she rinsed another dish—"Cassie might not feel so alone if she saw she was more like her mother than she thinks she is."

Nana had mentioned that yesterday. I set aside the dish towel, shaking my head. "I haven't used my abilities in years." Except last night, and I wasn't sure she knew about that. "She doesn't need to see what I can do. I don't want her to."

Nana turned off the water and faced me. "Why not, Molly? Your gifts are incredible. Why did you stop using them?" She covered my hand where it rested on the countertop.

"I don't want to talk about it." I slipped my hand from under hers.

"Can you at least speak to her in her mind? She'd feel more connected to you."

I shook my head harder. "No. I won't talk to her in that way. Just like you don't talk to me that way anymore."

She flinched, and I wanted to apologize for my defensive tone. But my emotions were riding the surface. Heat pulsed up my spine. My mouth sparked. I needed to get away from her before I did—or said—something I'd regret later.

"I should go help Cassie." I started to walk out of the kitchen. "Oh!" I stopped and turned around. "Please don't give Cassie the tea tonight." I left the room before she had the chance to object.

Chapter 17

Tuesday, late afternoon

A plastic shopping bag had been left on my bed with a Hello Kitty–shaped sticky note stuck to the side. *I love you, Mommy!* Cassie had drawn two stick figures, one taller than the other, with triangular skirts. They held hands. I peered inside the bag, the plastic crinkling, and my chest clenched. Water wings.

"Cassie," I softly moaned.

Sinking onto the bed, I pulled the bag onto my lap. She'd want me to wear them. She expected them to save me.

"Did you see my note?"

Cassie stood in the doorway. She wore a new dress, a navy-blue knit with matching tights. A present from Nana. The sea glass bracelet slipped from her sleeve, and the corner of my mouth tugged upward. She still wore it. The golden hair I'd blow-dried and brushed a few moments ago fell flat and straight over her back like an ironed sheet. She twisted her fingers and chewed her bottom lip.

"Come here." I opened my arms and she came to me, burying her face against my breast.

"Did you see the water wings I bought?" Her words were muffled by my sweater.

"Did you buy them while shopping with Mr. Torres?"

She nodded.

A ribbon of anxiety tightened around my chest. "Does he know why you bought them?"

She shook her head. "I didn't tell him anything. Only that I wanted to have them."

He probably thought they were for Cassie, I surmised, looking at the size on the plastic wrapping.

"Will you wear them? You won't drown if you wear them."

"Cassie, the floats won't work. They're too small for me."

"But I got the biggest ones. It says right here." She removed the floats from the bag and pointed to the size. "See? XL."

"For children." I tapped a fingernail under the word *child*.

Her shoulders and chin dropped. She let the water wings fall onto the mattress. "I guess I'll exchange them."

I lifted her chin. "I don't think they come in adult sizes."

"What can I buy you then? Something that helps you float."

"A life vest?" I suggested somewhat jokingly. "But those are really expensive," I quickly added before the idea formed in her head. She'd stress with the worry from trying to earn enough money in time. Hopefully, though, we'd be back home by Friday, and it wouldn't matter.

Cassie stared at her feet and worried her fingers, tugging the digits. Silence fell between us. Outside, rain pelted the window, pinged the metal gutters. The dreary weather had been almost constant since we'd left San Luis Obispo, and I wanted it to stop. I wanted to see the sun, to turn my face heavenward and absorb its warmth. And I wanted Cassie to do the things kids do. Run outside. Construct obstacle courses out of stones and sticks on the sidewalk for her scooter. Draw pictures to decorate Nana's refrigerator. I didn't want her worrying about how to save me.

But she liked helping people.

Here I was, acting exactly like her friends. Discounting her premonition and disregarding her efforts to assist. Not listening as a mother should. I shook my head, disappointed in myself.

"Maybe you can borrow a life vest. I bet Mr. Torres has one. He likes to fish and probably has one in his garage. If he does, I'll wear it."

Relief flooded Cassie's eyes. "Really?"

I nodded, unable to stop the tear that sneaked down my face.

Her gaze buzzed around my head. She was looking at my aura. "You're afraid," she murmured. Swirls of gray would be distorting the orange glow surrounding me.

"I am."

"Me, too. Nana tells me to be brave."

I kissed her forehead. "Nana is right. I think you are one brave girl."

Cassie hugged me. "I love you."

"I love you, too, Mermaid."

Nana called Cassie from downstairs. She squeezed me as though afraid to let me go.

"You're late for work," I teased. "We'll talk later about what Nana's teaching you."

After Cassie left, I showered, rinsing dried batter from my hair, and then headed downstairs. The doorbell rang when I reached the bottom step. "I got it!" I called out and opened the door.

An elderly woman, about six inches shorter than me, lips pursed, stood on the porch. She held a baking dish covered in tinfoil, and she was dressed like she'd stepped from a Talbot's catalog. Names churned in my head. Sweet Sadie Paxton or cantankerous Ruby Felton.

Faded brown eyes widened like an opening window, and a smile expanded across her face, pillowing wrinkled cheeks rouged with bright-peach powder. "Are you going to let me in, Molly, or leave me shivering in this dreadful weather? Now, I know you did that to Ruby, but the shriveled prune deserved it."

"Mrs. Paxton." I gave her a bright smile and opened the door wider.

"I haven't seen you in years." Sadie came into the house. "You look wonderful." She juggled her purse with the foil-covered dish as she fumbled with the coat buttons.

"Here, let me help." I took the dish as Cassie skipped down the hallway.

"I always knew you'd grow into a beautiful woman." Sadie unbuttoned her coat. "You have the look of your mother. Now, there was a woman who was more precocious as a child than anyone else I knew. Speaking of children, who is this pretty little thing?"

Cassie dipped in a dramatic curtsey. "How do you do? I'm Cassidy Brennan."

"Nice to meet you, Miss Cassidy."

"Cassie, this is Mrs. Paxton."

Cassie held out her hands. "May I take your coat and purse?"

"Thank you, dear." Sadie handed Cassie her purse and turned around. Cassie helped the older woman slip free of the garment.

"Your things will be in the hall closet." Cassie skipped away.

My gaze tagged along, watching as she opened the closet door. A slight uneasiness flipped inside my stomach.

Sadie grasped my forearm, pulling my attention back to her. My eyes trailed from her veined fingers to her eyes. They shined brightly. "I'm glad you moved back. Mary needs you."

The corners of my mouth lifted in apology. "We're only visiting."

"But Mary fixed up the house for you, said you needed a place to live."

I frowned, glancing quickly in the direction of the kitchen where Nana prepped the meal. "I'm sorry." I switched the dish to one arm and ran fingers through my hair. "You must have misunderstood. We live in San Luis Obispo. That's where Cassie goes to school and I work."

"No, no." Sadie shook her head. She looked at the floor and tapped a finger on her lips. "No, Mary clearly stated you were moving home to be with her."

What had Nana been telling her friends?

The doorbell rang. Sadie looked at the door. Her brows arched high, folding the skin on her forehead. "Is that Ruby? Quick, lock the door."

My jaw dropped. Sadie was the one who'd gotten me into trouble with Mrs. Felton last time.

Sadie peeked through the narrow window alongside the door. She scowled. "Drat. It's only Francine."

"Guess we'd better let her in." I twisted the knob, and both Sadie and I peered around the door.

"Molly!" Francine gasped. "You're here!"

The tall, rail-thin woman, dressed as fashionably as her poker partner, from the wool sweater and silk blouse ensemble to her pointed red heels, gave me a broad smile. Her teeth were too straight and white to be her own. She held a foil-covered dish.

"Mrs. Smythe, come in," I greeted, pulling the door and Sadie out of the way. "I'll take that." I reached for the dish as Francine walked inside. It was still warm. I smelled potatoes, rosemary, and butter. My stomach rumbled. "Smells delicious."

Over Francine's shoulder, I saw Ruby Felton approach.

"Here she comes," Sadie barked, ripping the knob from my fingers. She slammed the front door. The side windows rattled.

Sadie flipped the lock and leaned back against the door. Her shoulders shook in merriment when Ruby rang the doorbell. Sadie pulled aside the curtain and finger-waved. I caught a glimpse of the other woman's rigid face. She was not thrilled.

"Be nice, Sadie," Francine scolded. She nudged the tittering woman aside and opened the front door.

"Hello, Mrs. Felton." I peeked over Francine's shoulder and smiled.

Ruby Felton glowered at me. "Up to your old tricks, no doubt."

I kept smiling, moving aside when she pushed past Francine.

"Can you believe how beautiful Molly is?" Sadie said to Ruby. She took Ruby's plastic-wrapped tray of goodies as the other woman struggled from her coat and stacked the dish on top of the others I carried. I did a quick balancing act, shifting the bakeware. "Mary shows us pictures of her visits with you and your daughter," Sadie continued. "Of course, it's hard to see what people really look like on those tiny screens." She held her index and thumb an inch apart and whistled at me. "You're the spitting image of your mother."

Sadness poured through me like the rain outside. The hole in my chest that had appeared when Mom passed ached. "Thank you," I said, and kicked the door shut behind me.

"Have you settled in nicely?" Francine asked me.

I shot her a puzzled look. "No, we're not—"

"Mary's been planning your move home for months. Isn't the house beautiful?"

My head spun. "We aren't moving back," I explained again.

"That's a pity." Francine clutched her purse at her waist.

"She and Cassidy have a place in San Luis Obispo. They're just visiting," Sadie explained on my behalf. She sounded perturbed.

Ruby handed off her coat to Cassie, who had returned to help the newly arrived guests. Ruby looked down her nose. "I understand your house is a rental."

"What Ruby means to say," Francine interjected, moving between Ruby and me, "is that Mary misses you. She's alone in this big house. We worry about her. She hasn't been herself lately. She needs the company."

"Are we moving here?" Cassie asked hopefully.

"No, we're not."

"It's safer for you if we stay, Mommy."

Blood roared swiftly through my head, whistled in my ear. My gaze narrowed on Cassie. Did she know something I didn't?

"Will you take my purse, too, dear?" Francine asked Cassie.

"Sure." Cassie took the bag and skipped downed the hallway to the closet. I watched her drop the purse inside, thankful she had no idea about, and would never experience, the hours I'd spent locked in that confining space.

I shifted the dishes in my arm. "Let's take these to the kitchen."

The ladies followed me through the house. Rich and savory scents filled the kitchen. We found Nana slicing braised lamb. She aligned several cut portions on a platter already laden with an assortment of food, then covered the platter with tinfoil. I maneuvered the dishes I carried onto the countertop.

"Will you join us tonight for a round of poker?" Sadie asked me.

"No thank you." I waved my hands in front of me, remembering Owen's tale. "Count me out." A quiet evening hanging with Cassie sounded way more appealing. Maybe we'd watch a movie.

"What about you, Cassie?" Sadie asked.

"She'll be upstairs with me." I didn't want Cassie downstairs when they started drinking. And I especially didn't want to risk her having a vision about one of them.

Nana lightly touched my hand. Her fingertips singed my skin like a shock of static electricity. "Francine doesn't drink anymore, so we don't drink around her." She spoke quietly, for my ears only, as though she'd read my thoughts.

I sucked air through my teeth and pulled my hand from under hers. "Nana—?" I started to ask, but held my tongue. I hadn't felt her probe my head. But I hadn't felt Cassie probe my head either, and I swore she'd read my thoughts last night.

"Will you sneak around the poker table and steal our snacks?" Sadie was asking Cassie. "That's what your mother did."

"She did?" Cassie gave me a skeptical look. I saw mischief brew in her eyes.

"And she locks elderly ladies out of the house," Ruby griped.

"Mommy!"

My neck flushed to my face. "Well . . . I—"

"Sadie, check Ruby's sleeves," Nana suggested. "Make sure she hasn't stashed any cards there before we play."

Ruby stuck out her tongue.

"Molly." Nana shoved the platter she'd fixed into my arms. "Take this to Owen."

"Wh-what?" I stammered. "Now?"

"Yes, now. It's his dinner."

"Can't the man feed himself?"

Nana pushed me toward the hallway.

"Fine, fine. I'll be right back," I said to Cassie. "We'll watch a movie tonight."

She frowned. "But Mr. Torres expects—"

"Sh-shh." Nana waved at her while looking at me. "I need Cassie's assistance tonight." She shooed me away. "Go, go. Food is getting cold."

Chapter 18

Tuesday, dusk

Keeping my head ducked against the rain, I jogged to Owen's house. He answered the door after the first knock. Light spilled onto the porch like honey from a jar, all golden. Raindrops glittered in their downward descent. Dressed in faded jeans and a fitted long-sleeved shirt, Owen braced a hand on the upper edge of the door. He smiled, ivory teeth bright against the shadows playing on his jaw. A shiver wound up my torso that had nothing to do with the wind chill.

"Hey." His voice was calm and low.

"Hi," I managed. My forearms quivered under the food platter. "Nana made you dinner."

"You mean us."

I did an awkward shuffle with my feet. Owen chuckled. "Mary made us dinner. She thought you might want to eat here while Cassie helps her with her friends. That's what she told me," he added when I gave him a skeptical look. "Don't worry; I'll have you home by curfew."

"Ha, ha." But I glanced toward Nana's house. The party would keep Cassie busy for a few hours, and if I remained there I'd stay holed up in my room. In that house.

Noticing my hesitation, Owen opened the door wider. "Come in. It's cold out."

My fingers clamped tightly to the platter. I peered inside the house, on guard for a furry onslaught. Nothing charged at me. It was unusually quiet. "Where're the dogs?"

"Garage. They're filthy and on restriction. They escaped from the backyard again."

"Gotta fix that fence, Owen." I crossed the threshold. Candlelight flickered from the dining room on my right, the table set with fine china. I stopped in the middle of the entryway, hesitating.

Owen glanced at the dining room. "Too much?" A stilted laugh rumbled from his chest.

"Uh, sort of. Yeah."

"I thought so." His eyes dimmed slightly. "Follow me."

He led us through the dining room, snatching the wineglasses as we passed the table.

"Wine?" he offered.

"A small glass."

I set the platter on the counter, and he selected a pinot from the wine rack.

Restless, I wandered into the family room and studied the framed photos on the bookshelf. There was a photo of Owen, a school picture when he was ten and wearing his favorite red-and-white-striped T-shirt. I'd once had the same picture tucked in my wallet for years. It had been the first picture of him that he'd given me, right after I'd moved to Pacific Grove. Beside Owen's photo was a picture of his parents, faces sunbrowned, as they posed in tropical-print shirts before a turquoise-blue backdrop that stretched far to the horizon.

"How are your parents?" I asked, making small talk to fill the silence.

"Good." A cork popped. "Spoke with Mom this morning. They're flying out next month to see what I've done with this house."

"They haven't seen the improvements?" I returned the photo to the shelf, maneuvering the frame into its dustless spot, and peeked inside a small reed basket. It was filled with old fishing lures. I remembered these. Souvenirs from the surfperch he'd caught fishing with his father off the piers that fringe Monterey Bay. For a long moment I stood there, inspecting the lures, thinking of those days. Owen waiting for me while I hunted glass by Cannery Row, then me standing beside him on the wharf while he fished. A perfect Saturday, the memories as fresh as though they had happened yesterday, not twenty years ago.

"I've sent them pictures," Owen was explaining. "I only finished the house last month."

"You were working on yours and Nana's at the same time?"

"Wasn't too difficult. My crew worked on both while they were here." He crossed the room, carrying with him the scent of warm wood and rich spice, along with the heavy fruit of wine. He handed me a glass. Our fingers brushed, and gooseflesh rose along my forearms.

Another snapshot caught my attention. A young boy I didn't recognize. I pointed at the picture. "Who's this?"

Owen looked at the photo like he'd forgotten it was on the shelf. His smile disappeared. He rubbed the back of his neck and circled away.

"Owen?" I gently prodded.

"His name was Enrique."

Was.

The boy with café mocha skin and espresso hair stared back at me with a jack-o'-lantern smile. He had four missing teeth. Bright eyes crinkled at the corners. The basketball he held was three times bigger than his hands.

"I knew him in Tijuana." He paused a beat. "He lived in a children's shelter."

"What happened to him?"

"He drowned."

My hand trembled. I set the wineglass on a shelf. "How?"

His gaze shifted between me and the picture, finally settling on the glass in his hand. He fisted his other hand and pressed it against his lips, the way he did when he felt unsettled or wasn't quite sure how to express himself. "I messed up."

I sucked in a short breath. Had he been responsible for Enrique's death?

"I haven't talked about him in a long time," he said after a moment.

But I was positive he thought about him every day.

Owen lowered to the coffee table and sat on the edge. "The crew I worked with was assigned to construct a new building at an orphanage. During the weekends and evenings, some of the guys and I volunteered with the kids. We played hoops at the park, did workshop projects. Those kinds of things. Some days we went to the beach." He paused, drawing a long drink of wine.

Then he bent his head and seemed to steel himself.

I moved to sit beside him, leaving a few inches between us to give him the space I sensed he needed. He propped his elbows on his knees and let his hands hang loose. He angled his head and looked at me. I almost cried out at the self-loathing that masked his expression. It was like looking in a mirror. My heart cracked.

"I don't know Enrique's entire history, but his biological father messed him up pretty bad. Took him a long time to warm up to me."

"You grew attached to him."

He nodded. "Loved him like a son. I wanted to adopt him."

I felt the urge to comfort him and rested my hand on his thigh. We stared with him into the fire. Snapping flames bathed our skin in an orange glow, warming the jeans covering my shins.

His leg tensed under my fingers. "There was a new guy on my crew. Dex. Cocky sonuvabitch. Always had to one-up me."

"And you rose to the challenge."

He nodded. "We'd finished the project and it was our last day at the beach with the kids. Dex started a game of Ultimate Frisbee. We split the kids into teams. Enrique was on mine and we were winning. Then out of the blue this woman charges into the water screaming, 'He's drowning, he's drowning! Get help, he's drowning!'

"Dex and I counted the kids and"—he swallowed—"and that's when we noticed Enrique was missing. He'd just been standing right beside me seconds before." He indicated the space beside him as though reliving the moment. "I didn't even see him leave my side, let alone go into the water."

Owen pinched the bridge of his nose and took a moment. "Drowning doesn't look like what we see on TV. There's no splashing. No yelling. It's a quiet death. Do you know it's impossible to scream for help while you're drowning?"

I slowly shook my head, my eyes wide.

"It's called the instinctive drowning response, what you do to avoid suffocating. You can't yell. You can't do anything but breathe when you come up for air.

"The tide had pulled him from the shore. We swam to him as fast as we could, but by the time we reached him, he wasn't breathing and we couldn't revive him."

Owen stopped. His throat rippled. He rubbed his face.

"After the ambulance took away Enrique's body, I asked the woman how she knew he was drowning. She was a college student on spring break who happened to be a lifeguard. She told me Enrique's head never fell below the surface before he submerged, but his mouth did. It kept bobbing up and down, up and down." He raised and lowered his flattened hand to demonstrate. "He only had time to exhale and quickly inhale before his mouth went under again. No chance to call for help. He never called for help."

"Owen." My eyes burned for him. As a mother, I felt every ounce of his burden, a burden he shouldn't have to carry. "What happened isn't your fault. You can't blame yourself."

He gulped his wine. "Can't I? I should have had my eyes on him the entire time."

"Kids disappear from sight like that." I snapped my fingers. "Trust me, I know. It happened with Cassie. We were at Avila Beach last summer with Phoebe and her kids. Cassie was sitting beside me on the blanket. I turned around to get a bottled water from the cooler and when I turned back she was gone. I sat there, looking every which way, trying to pick out her pink ruffled suit among all the other little-kid bathing suits in the crowd. It's shocking how many kids her size wear pink.

"When I finally found her, she was in the water. Had there been a riptide or a large wave that knocked her under, she would have been gone in an instant. All that happened within seconds, from the moment she left the blanket to my finding her in the water." But it had seemed like a lifetime and wasn't something I wanted to experience again.

"You must have been scared to death," Owen said.

"It was only a couple seconds, but during that time, your heart races and you're trying not to panic, and then when you find them you just want to yell and scream. Then you feel sick because you start thinking *what if.*"

Owen held the rim of his wineglass between his knees, watching as he swirled the wine. "Unfortunately, my *what if* is a *what did happen*, and it's something I have to live with every day."

An ache lodged in my throat. "I understand how you feel," I said in a strained whisper, averting my gaze toward the fire.

"Do you?" There was a note of surprise in his voice.

My eyelids drifted closed and I swallowed, unable to dislodge the lump. I felt his gaze on me.

"Well," he sighed deeply after a moment, "I didn't expect our conversation to go in this direction. You're the first person I've told since I got back from Mexico." He lifted his face toward the ceiling and blinked rapidly as though his eyes stung. "That's about . . . oh, nine or ten years now. My parents don't even know what happened."

"Thank you for sharing with me," I said, truthfully.

"You're the only one I ever opened up with. I guess it's still that way." His mouth pulled up at one corner. "What did you mean, though, that you understand how I feel?"

An anxious flutter shifted in my stomach. I buried my nose in my glass. "It was nothing. I was only commiserating." I took a large swallow of wine.

I felt him stare at me for a few long moments before I met his gaze. He frowned. "What are you not telling me?"

"Nothing."

I pushed to my feet, going into the kitchen, where I set my empty glass on the counter. Nana's food waited. My stomach gurgled. I returned to the family room. Owen still sat where I'd left him. "Let's eat," I suggested. "I want to get back to Nana's." I wanted to tuck Cassie into bed.

"I've been thinking about what you said yesterday." Owen slowly stood, turning his back to the fireplace, facing me. "How you did something vile. And last night. You said you didn't think I was safe around you." His gaze met mine across the room. "Then just now, after I confessed something I've never told anyone, that I felt responsible for a little boy's death, you told me you understood how I felt. There is no way in hell"—his hand slashed in front of him—"you understand how I feel unless you've been in a similar situation."

I was shaking my head as he spoke. I held up both hands, palms forward. "I don't want to talk about it."

"Why, Molly? Please, I'm just trying to understand what happened between us." He approached me.

"Please. Stop."

He lifted a shaking hand as if to cup my cheek. I turned my face away.

He let his arm fall. "Molly."

My name sounded like it had been torn from his throat. It struck me right in the chest. Like a dam broken during a heavy rainstorm, tears flowed unhindered down my cheeks.

"Molly, honey, why isn't it safe for me to be around you? What did you do that you think is so vile?"

I shook my head. He took a step toward me, and I moved back.

"Molly." One more step.

I shook my head, retreating. My shoulder blades connected with the wall.

Our gazes locked, frozen in a battle of wills. Pain and rejection swirled in the depths of his eyes, mixing with a strong desire to help me battle my own pain. A pain I'd kept locked away and buried for twelve years, and tossed aside the key.

Good old Owen, with his bucketloads of compassion for and trust in me, had just found the key. He'd shared his deepest, darkest secret with me. And that was my undoing. He'd unlocked the door, and the thing I was most ashamed—and guilty—about wanted out.

I blinked rapidly, glancing away quickly before I sucked in a harsh breath, shoulders rising.

"I killed my father."

Chapter 19

Twelve years ago

Mom died in late afternoon on a Monday, two weeks before my high school graduation. I spent the previous day at Owen's, studying in his bed, the same bed where we'd spent our Saturday evening. His parents had gone out for dinner and a movie. The moment they left, Owen had grabbed my hand. "Change of plans." Our own date out had suddenly become a date in.

It wasn't often we had the house to ourselves. We dashed to his room and kissed and loved until breathless. Then we talked about our plans for after graduation. He would finish his second year at community college this month and then leave for Mexico at the end of summer.

"Two years, Owen. That's a long time."

He dropped a kiss on my bare shoulder. "You'll be so busy with school you won't notice I'm gone." He trailed kisses up my neck and nipped my chin. While he spent those two years building homes with a charity organization through his church, I would be at the Jewelry Arts & Design College in Los Angeles.

"When I'm done, I'll move to L.A. with you." He kissed my lips. "Time will fly. You'll see." We'd finish our last two years of college at the same time, with him studying construction management at Long Beach and me earning a bachelor's degree in jewelry arts.

"Two years can't come soon enough," I murmured, angling my neck as he traveled back down. Excitement skipped through me, leaving a heated path to my center.

He lifted his head and locked his eyes on mine. Desire and adoration swirled in their depths.

"What?" I asked, my gaze buzzing over him.

He moistened his lips. "I plan to marry you, Molly."

My heartbeat quickened. I clasped his face. "Really?" I asked, breathless.

"Really." He grinned. "You're my girl. I love you."

And I loved him. He was the boy I'd grown up with and the man I adored. Eighteen hours later, propped against his pillows in my sweats, I still basked in the afterglow of his declaration. It was nearly impossible to concentrate on chemistry. The chemistry between Owen and me was much more fascinating than the periodic table staring up at me from the open book resting on my lap.

Carmel, Owen's Chesapeake retriever, blanketed my feet at the end of the bed, and the house was quiet. Owen was working at the lumber-yard, and his parents were running errands. I kept myself holed up in Owen's room, not necessarily because I liked being there with his scent on the sheets, but because my father was home. He was watching a baseball game and probably moving on to his second six-pack.

Nana worked Sundays at the hospital's ER registration desk, and she had been requesting longer shifts in the recent weeks. My father had lost another job, and Mom's part-time position at a dental office brought in barely enough money to keep decent clothes on my back. She didn't want me working while in school. Rather, my time should be spent studying. She wanted me to go to college, and she wanted the school far enough away that I didn't live at home. She knew I avoided being at the house whenever possible. But I also believed that without me there, Mom didn't have to block her thoughts from me. She tried shielding me, embarrassed about how she let Dad treat her. It didn't always work. I heard it every day, the blaming, demeaning comments and the judging.

The sun dipped lower, elongating the room's shadows. I glanced at the clock. Five forty-five. Mom would be cooking dinner.

I flipped my book closed, intent on going home to see whether she needed help. Carmel grumbled, lifting her head as I extracted my legs. Ripping a piece of ruled paper from my notebook, I scratched a quick note to Owen.

O. Hope you had a good afternoon at work. Loved last night. Love you. Will see you in the morning. I'll meet you at your car. 7:30. Love, M. xo (your girl)

I folded the paper and left it propped like a tent on his pillow.

"See you tomorrow, you big bear." I scratched Carmel behind her ear and kissed her head.

Back at my house, Dad was parked in the parlor watching the game. Several empty beer bottles and a fifth of JD littered the coffee table. Great. He'd moved on to the hard stuff.

I quietly shut the door, determined to get to the kitchen unnoticed. I smelled dinner. Baked meatloaf and roasted mushrooms and onions permeated the stale air. My father preferred watching TV with the windows closed and drapes drawn.

Five paces in and my heel caught the edge of that dratted creaky board. I cringed.

"Molly," Dad said, his eyes glued to the TV, "tell your mother to hurry up with dinner."

You tell her, drunken asshole.

"Yeah, sure," I mumbled.

He leaned forward, elbow perched on his knee and tapped the coffee table. He threw me a look over his shoulder. "Tell her to bring it here. Game's not over yet." He drained a finger of bourbon, then refilled his glass with three more fingers.

"Yeah, okay." *Whatever.*

I had no intention of telling Mom. I'd make his plate for him. She already did enough around the house, trying to appease him.

Scooting into the kitchen, I came to a screeching halt, almost running over my mother. Crouched on the floor, she picked up tiny slivers of glass. Malted barley and hops assaulted my nose.

"What happened?" I asked, my mind immediately jumping to Dad.

Mom glanced up. The lines etched below her eyes deepened, her mouth curving into a tired smile. "Hello, honey. How's studying going?"

"It's fine. What happened here?" The pungent odor of beer filled the room. Liquid amber soaked into Mom's shins where she worked on the floor.

"The shelf your father's beer was on was too full. The entire six-pack fell and shattered when he opened the fridge."

Of course he didn't clean up his own mess, I thought. This explained why he'd switched to liquor. The shattered bottles must have been the last of his beer.

"I'll get a broom and help clean."

"It's too wet to sweep." Mom scraped glass bits from her palm into the trash.

"Then let's soak up the beer first. I'll get some rags."

"The glass will get stuck in the towels," Mom replied, stopping me on my way to the laundry room. "It'll ruin the clothes washer."

I watched her methodically pick up the glass. Her reasoning made no sense. The broom could be rinsed and the glass shaken from the towels before washing.

My stomach clenched as I realized my father must have ordered her to clean up this way. It was tedious and would take longer. Proper punishment for wasting his beer.

"Sheila," Dad yelled from the other room. "Where's my dinner?"

Mom dropped a large piece of glass in the trash can beside her. Glass rattled inside. She swiped her forehead with the back of her wrist. "Just a minute, Brad. I'm almost done."

No, she wasn't. Glass sparkled everywhere on the tiled floor, from every corner of the kitchen. It looked as though the bottles had exploded on impact.

Dinner cooled on the stove. I cautiously tiptoed around the mess and retrieved a plate from the cabinet. "I'll get his dinner."

"No!" Mom straightened on her knees. She inhaled, her eyes momentarily closing. "No, Molly, please. Don't trouble yourself. I'll take care of it."

Because she had to be the one to serve him. My grip tightened on the plate. "Then let me help you clean." I set the plate aside on the counter and sank to my knees.

"Molly, please get up."

"Sheila," Dad snapped. Footsteps clunked on hardwood, and my heart picked up speed.

I quickly scooped up glass and beer, not caring that shards clung to my palm like splinters. I shook my hand over the trash, wanting the kitchen cleaned so Mom could fix his plate and Dad would shut up and go back to watching his game.

"Sheila, I'm tired of asking."

"Molly, get up," Mom pleaded.

"No," I said firmly. This had to stop. Dad's disrespect for Mom and Mom's disregard for her own worth sickened me.

"Dammit, Sheila"—Dad rounded into the kitchen—"it's time for . . . Molly, get off the floor."

Mom lifted her head, giving me an I-warned-you glare.

"No," I argued. "Mom needs my help." I scooped more of the shattered stew of beer and glass.

"Get up. Your mother packed the fridge wrong. This is her mess to clean."

"No."

"I said. Get. Up." He gripped my upper arm, his fingers digging into my armpits, and yanked me upward.

My knees lifted off the floor. "Don't touch me." I rotated my arm, twisting from his grip.

"I'll touch you if I want to."

He grabbed at me again, and I shoved him. "Leave me alone."

Dad stumbled back against the fridge. His eyes widened in shock, then his face hardened, his intoxicated blush deepening to purple. He raised his fists. "Damn you, girl." He lunged at me.

I gasped, scooting from his reach. Heat zipped along my spine. Words arced in my mouth. "Get out! *LEAVE!*"

And he did. He turned on his heel, marched down the hallway, and out the front door. I crawled across the kitchen floor, glancing down the hallway to make sure he was gone. He'd left the front door wide open.

I crawled back to Mom. "Let's hurry." Without a mess on the floor, he wouldn't harass us about it.

"He'll be back," Mom said matter-of-factly.

"I know." Standing, I snagged the paper towel roll off the counter and tore off several pieces, wadding them in a ball.

"He'll be stinking mad when he gets back," Mom pointed out. She continued picking the glass among the beer puddles with her bare fingers.

I knew that, too, but still, I was relieved to have him out of the house. Dad had never touched me before in anger, and it had rattled me. I'd panicked when he'd lunged, and the compulsion shot out.

Mom and I worked in silence. I quickly made my way through the paper towel roll and was soaking up the beer that had flowed under the fridge when Dad returned.

Heavy footsteps resounded in the hallway. My heart leaped into my throat, pounding hard. Rising to my knees, I quickly gathered up the towels and turned to dump them in the trash.

A hand grabbed my ponytail and yanked. My head snapped back, and I landed smack on my rear.

"Ow!" I gasped. My scalp seared and tailbone throbbed.

Dad tugged me to my feet with the ponytail. "I told you to get up."

"Dad!" I screamed in pain. "What the hell?" My hands flew to my head, gripping the hair band. I held on, counteracting the burning pull as Dad dragged me from the kitchen.

"Brad, let her go," Mom pleaded, following us.

"She's interfering with your work. And she used her mind tricks. She needs to be taught a lesson." He yanked open the closet door, and with the jerk of his wrist I stumbled inside, landing face-first into the coats. I scrambled to turn around, panting.

Dad shook his finger at me. "Don't you ever, *ever* use your mind tricks on me."

I swallowed, tasting fear, thick in my mouth. The walls were closing in, and he hadn't yet shut the door. My entire body broke out in a sweat. "I'm sorry. I didn't mean to make you leave. Don't close the door. Please." I gasped, sucking in a harsh breath, and shook my head. "Don't close the door." He hadn't locked me inside since I was thirteen, which seemed like yesterday.

Bile thickened in my mouth. Air blasted from my lungs.

Dad tsked. "Once again, you need to find that closet in your head. This time make sure you throw the key away." He started to close the door.

I swung up my hands, stopping it.

Mom came up behind my father. "Brad, darling," she said, using her sweet voice, placating. That tender tone was the only way she knew how to defuse my father's anger. "Send her to her room. She's too big for the closet." She curved her hands on his forearm, rested her cheek against his shoulder, looking up at him. "Please, Brad. This isn't her fault. It's mine."

Dad patted her hands. "You're right. She wouldn't be able to do those mind tricks if it weren't for you." He lifted Mom's hands off him, then, with the flat of his palm pressed to her shoulder, maneuvered her out of the way.

He started to close the door again. I stuck out my foot. "Why are you doing this? Do you hate me that much?"

Dad cocked his head. He studied me, and for a moment his eyes cleared. "I don't hate you. I could never hate you. I just don't like those parts of you that embarrass me. You need to fix those parts. And if you can't fix them, they need to stay hidden."

He kicked my foot into the closet. It threw me off balance. I sank against the hanging coats and sweaters, my arms flying out to press against the side walls so I wouldn't drop on my rear.

"Let me tell you a little story," Dad said, leaning against the door frame. "I had a lisp as a kid. Damn embarrassing. I talked funny and the other kids made fun of me. They ridiculed me." He scrunched his lips and inhaled sharply through his nose. "You can't hide a lisp, Molly, so I fixed it. I practiced and practiced the exercises the therapists gave me. That lisp went away and the kids stopped talking about me. The teasing and ridicule stopped. I was finally normal, like them. There was nothing about me that drew their attention.

"But your mother's fortune telling and the things you can make other people do? Well"—he scratched the back of his neck—"that draws attention back to me. My coworkers and peers, they look at me oddly when they hear about you two. I really, really, really don't like that kind of attention. It's upsetting."

"Then leave us if we embarrass you so much."

Dad shook his head, a slow back-and-forth motion. "I can't. I love you both too much." He closed the door, and my cramped little space turned pitch black. The lock flipped. "Be quiet as a mouse, find that closet in your head, and I'll let you out after dinner."

"Open the door, Dad. Please."

He didn't answer.

"Dad. Dad, I love you, too. Did you hear me? Please open the door. Please let me out." My fingernails scratched at the wood and jiggled the knob, my heart racing and my breath coming in short bursts. I felt light-headed and closed my eyes.

The sound of dishes and utensils came from the kitchen. They ate dinner and then the floor creaked outside the door, and a moment later, above my head. They'd gone to bed.

I sank to the floor, whimpering. My mind drifted to Owen. Thinking about him kept my mind centered and me calm. Soon I drifted to sleep, knees pressed to my chest.

The closet door swung open, and the bright hallway light spilled inside. I blinked, rubbing my eyes, and looked up. Nana stood in the doorway, holding the sweater she wore when she worked the night shift at the hospital.

Her lips scrunched, and her face hardened. A blush bloomed on her cheeks. "I've had it with him. This needs to stop now. Come on, Molly, it's late. Go to bed."

It was after two in the morning when I crawled under my sheets. I dreamed of moving away, and I dreamed of Owen cradling me in his arms. Being with him and away from home was where I felt loved and safe.

In the morning, I left the house before anyone else stirred and met Owen by his car. He drove me to school in the mornings, dropping me off before he headed to his own classes.

He kissed me good morning, then pulled away, his expression concerned. "You look exhausted. Did you get any sleep?"

My gaze lowered to the binder I hugged to my chest.

He lifted my chin. "Staying up late studying?"

I shook my head.

His jaw clenched. "Your father?"

"He was drunk again last night." Lifting to my toes, I kissed him, cupping the nape of his neck. Out here in the sunshine and fresh air, he made me forget about where I'd spent most of the night.

I dropped back to my heels. "Let's get going. I have an exam this morning."

Owen's forehead creased. "Promise me you'll study at my house this afternoon. I have to work again today. I don't want you at your house when your dad's there, especially if he's drunk again, at least not until I get home. That way you can call me if you need me. Has he found a new job yet?"

I shook my head. "I think he has a couple interviews this afternoon."

"Either way, hang out with Carmel." He grinned. "My dog loves you."

By the time school was done for the day, Nana's car was parked out front, but my father's wasn't. Still, I took Owen up on his offer to study in his room, letting myself in with the key he'd given me. Both his parents worked, so it was just me and Carmel.

For an hour I attempted to study. Carmel stretched out on her back, plastered to the side of my leg as she snoozed. My mind kept drifting away from English and toward Owen. He wouldn't be home for another half hour or so. I wanted to kiss him and tell him that I loved him. I wanted to go for a drive and park. Gaze across the ocean as his hands and lips did all those delicious things to me that made me wild and crazy for him. I wanted to discuss our future again, one where we lived far from Pacific Grove.

I shifted on the bed, feeling overheated from my thoughts and the living furnace glued to my side.

Realizing I was procrastinating, I shifted my focus back to my studies, only to have a heavy weight of dread cinch my chest. I gasped as

Mom's tired face appeared in my mind. A ghostly touch along the back of my neck lifted the fine hairs there. The faint whisper of a kiss brushed my cheek. Then it disappeared, the dread and ghostly touches, leaving an emptiness behind that I didn't understand.

"Mom."

An all-consuming urgency to see her struck me. I ran from Owen's house to mine, flying up the front porch. "Mom," I shouted, throwing open the door. It bounced against the wall.

Nana stood at the base of the stairs, her expression stricken.

"Where's Mom?"

Her mouth worked. Her hand flew to cover her mouth. "Molly." My name was a muffled cry torn from her throat.

"Mom!"

I bounded up the stairs, taking two at a time, coming to a dead stop in my parents' bedroom doorway. There she was, sprawled across my father's lap. Her eyes open and empty. Deep red and blue ovals marred her neck. Behind them on the bed was an opened suitcase half-full of Mom's clothes. Garments spilled from the dresser, drawers still open as though Mom had packed in a rush.

"What have you done?" My voice came out high and thin.

Dad's head jerked up. "Molly?"

I stepped into the room. "What did you do?"

His mouth opened and closed several times. "It—it was an accident," he sputtered. "You have to believe me."

A deep, wrenching sadness moved swiftly through me, almost buckling my knees. Gasping, I pressed my hands flat against my sternum, directly over the hole where my heart had been. My father had just ripped it from my chest. "You killed her."

"I didn't mean to. She had a vision about me. She told me about it and she wouldn't stop talking. She kept talking, and talking, and talking." He briefly gazed down at the woman he claimed to love. "She wouldn't shut up. I only wanted her to shut up." He caressed her cheek.

"Don't you touch her!" I shrieked.

His face snapped back to mine, and he narrowed his eyes. "It was you who did this. You made me do this." He stood quickly. Mom's lifeless body crumpled to the floor at his feet. He stepped over her, pointing a finger at me. "This is your fault. You did this to her. You made me kill your mother with your mind tricks."

Rocks tumbled in my stomach. Sweat dampened my palms. "I did not. I wasn't even here."

He crossed the room, shaking his finger. "It's your fault; don't deny it. Your fault!" He raised a fist, pulled back his arm.

My eyes bugged out, and I shrank back. Heat shot up my spine. Electricity arced wildly in my mouth. "*GET OUT OF HERE! GET OUT OF THIS HOUSE. LEAVE US ALONE. GO! JUST GO AWAY!*"

He did. His arm fell to his side, and he walked past me like a puppet on strings, leaving the room. I followed him to the top of the stairs, watching. He moved down the stairs like an apparition floating across the room and out the front door I'd left open. He walked, and he kept on walking.

This time he didn't return.

Chapter 20

Tuesday, night

Owen leaned forward, elbows on thighs, hands cupping his nose and mouth, eyes open wide in shock. We'd moved to the couch. He'd poured us two fingers of bourbon at some point during my confession. Aside from a couple of sips, the crystal lowballs sat untouched on the coffee table.

When it was apparent I'd finished my story, he frowned and slowly shook his head. "I don't buy it."

"You don't believe me?" My voice came out rough and scratchy, like sandpaper on wood.

"No, not that." He laid a hand on my shoulder, then touched my cheek. "I mean I don't believe you killed him."

"He was under my influence, Owen."

"How long is the effect? A few minutes, seconds?"

I nodded slowly, not quite sure. "Something like that."

"Where was your dad killed?"

"Corner of Third and Central, why?"

"That's at least a fifteen-minute walk from here. Your influence would have worn off by then." He flicked his hand to emphasize his point. "He was most likely drunk, and he'd just murdered your mother. I think he was on the run."

My chin quivered. I pressed a hand to my stomach and shook my head, still in denial, as much as I wanted to see his point of view. God, I wanted to believe his reasoning.

"I know, Molly. It hurts. But let's think this through."

"He wouldn't have been there, crossing that street, if I hadn't sent him a compulsion to leave us in the first place," I objected.

"You don't know that. There's a good chance he walked in front of that car on purpose."

"You think he committed suicide?"

He shrugged a shoulder. "I don't think you should rule that out. I also don't think you should blame yourself for his death. There are too many outside factors at play. Just like—" He stopped and a corner of his mouth lifted. He tapped his chest. "Just like I probably shouldn't blame myself for Enrique's death. He wanted to go into the water, and no matter how hard I kept an eye on him, he would have found a way in."

"It still hurts, though."

"Yes, it does."

"You'll make a great father someday," I told him honestly.

His brows lifted. "You think so?"

"I do. My father . . . he was a horrible man, but he didn't deserve to die that way."

"He'd just killed your mother."

"I know, and he should have gone to prison for that."

Owen lifted my hand and pressed his lips to my knuckles. "Mary doesn't know about this, does she?"

"I don't think so. It's why I've kept my mind closed to her all these years."

"Thank you for helping me understand what was going on with you back then," he said sincerely.

I slipped my hand from his. "It still doesn't change anything between us."

"Then do you mind explaining why you think I'm not safe around you?"

I stood, wiping damp palms on the back of my jeans. I felt raw, my emotions too close to the surface. "Look, Owen, can we eat? I'm hungry and I've got a lot to do tomorrow."

He scratched his jaw and rose to his feet. "All right. You still owe me an explanation, though."

I was sure Owen would do what he could to entice it out of me, which was another reason Cassie and I needed to leave. Because as I looked up at him, standing before me, I acknowledged that I'd never fallen out of love with him. It had been simmering on the back burner for twelve years.

And that scared me. Because when I left, I doubted I could lock away the hurt and pain and guilt like I'd done before.

Owen tossed more logs onto the fire. I fixed our plates, and we ate on the floor, the fancy dining room forgotten. He kept our talk light, sharing stories about everything, from how difficult it had been finding the parts Paul needed for his Triumph TR7 to his dogs' antics.

When we'd cleared our plates, I took them to the kitchen. Owen followed, carrying our water glasses. The oven clock glowed eight forty-five.

"I should go," I told Owen. Cassie would be getting ready for bed shortly.

Owen poured out the remainder of our water and set the glasses aside. He leaned back against the counter edge, arms folded, and studied me. "How are you feeling about what you told me?"

I searched inward, finding the usual shame and sadness. But I also felt something new. Relief. A slight lessening of the burden I'd carried for so long. Owen's questions had made me look at the tragedy from a different perspective. Maybe my father had been running away. Maybe he'd been too drunk to stop and look for oncoming cars. Or maybe, as Owen surmised, he intentionally walked in front of the car, grief-stricken over what he'd done to my mother.

My mouth curved slightly. "I feel okay. Honestly," I added when he quirked a brow. "You?"

He crossed his ankles. "Surprisingly all right."

I reached out and tugged his shirtsleeve cuff before letting my arm fall against my side. "Me, too."

He pushed from the counter and tucked my hair behind my ear. My skin warmed where his fingers traced my lobe.

"Let's go," he said. "I'll walk you home."

Outside, the rain had stopped, and the winds calmed, leaving the night air crisp and salty. Above us, a fitted sheet of stars glittered behind clouds outlined in moonlight.

"Think we'll get a break from the rain?" I asked, looking up.

"Maybe for a bit tomorrow, but another front is due Thursday."

We climbed the steps to Nana's purple Victorian and into the dim glow of the porch lamp. A soft glow peeked through the curtains from inside.

"Speaking of Thursday," he began. He leaned against the door-jamb while I unlocked the door. "I have a full-day builders' conference in San Jose. My crew and I go out to dinner afterward and I won't be home until late. Usually, the dogs are fine on their own for the day, but since Cassie seems to like them and is interested in earning money, would she want to play with them and feed them dinner?"

I pulled the key from the lock and kept my eyes fixed on the handle. "Those dogs are a bit much for an eight-year-old."

He flashed a smile. "I guess I'm asking if you can check on them while I'm gone. I'm going to keep them inside, because I won't have the chance to repair the gate until this weekend. They'll need to be let out at least once or twice."

"All right. Cassie and I will come by in the morning. You can show us what to do."

"Thanks," Owen said. He scooped the hair that cloaked my face behind my shoulder, coaxing me to peer up at him. He cradled my jaw, his thumb brushing over my cheek, skimming my lips.

My mouth parted. "Owen."

"I've missed you, Molly."

His face drew closer, lashes fluttering closed, and curse me and my damned heart, I didn't lean away or stop him. I sighed as his lips touched mine.

It wasn't a long kiss, and it wasn't deep. But it touched my soul. *I miss you, too!* The words floated through my head.

He ended the kiss before it barely started. I followed him up, rising to my toes, our lips breaking apart when he'd fully straightened. I dropped back to my heels.

"Good night. See you in the morning."

I watched him leave, speechless, still reeling from his kiss and the stories we'd shared. When he disappeared around the hedge between his and Nana's yards, I went into the house.

Inside, I found Sadie and Francine cleaning the kitchen. "Where's Mary?" I asked, slightly alarmed.

"Hello, Molly," Sadie greeted over her shoulder. She waved a wet rubber-gloved hand. "Mary went to bed. She wasn't feeling well."

"Really?" I angled toward the stairs, my forehead creasing with worry. Nana had left her own party. "Is Mrs. Felton up there with her?"

Francine shook her head. "She left a few minutes ago." She swiped a damp towel across the countertop, moving aside a teacup that was in her path.

My breath lodged in my throat. Heart racing, I snatched up the cup and sniffed the damp tea leaves. Dirty socks.

"That's Cassie's." Francine nodded at the cup in my hand. "She said Mary makes it for her, that it helps her sleep. I hope you don't mind I made some."

I set down the cup with a loud click. "Where's Cassie?"

"Upstairs, getting ready for bed," Sadie replied. "She was a wonderful helper tonight."

I didn't acknowledge Sadie. I ran upstairs, taking two steps at a time. "Cassie!" I followed the light to the hallway bathroom.

She stood at the sink in her jammies, brushing her teeth. Toothpaste frothed from her mouth. "Hello, Mommy," she said in the back of her throat, trying to keep the paste in her mouth.

"Hi, Cass," I leaned against the doorjamb. "Did you have fun tonight?"

"Uh-huh." She spit the paste into the sink and rinsed her mouth, cupping her hand under the running water. "Nana wasn't feeling well so she went to bed early."

"I heard. And you? How are you feeling?"

"Nana's tea is really gross. It makes my stomach feel funny. I had to ask Mrs. Smythe to make me some because Nana forgot." She tapped her toothbrush on the towel to dry it, then tucked it away in her toiletries case.

"Actually, I'd asked Nana not to give it to you. I was hoping . . ." Her dreams would show her more about the premonition. But I stopped at the surprised look on her face.

"Nana said it was dangerous for me *not* to drink it."

I blinked. That was concerning. "Did she say why?"

She slowly shook her head. "Will you read me a story?"

"Sure, sweetheart." I kissed her forehead, anxious to talk about this in the morning with Nana. "Go pick out a book. I want to check on Nana."

Nana's door was opened a crack. I eased it open and slipped into the room, careful to not make noise. Under the glow of the hallway light, Nana slept on her back, a pillow hugging her neck and head. Soft snores vibrated the room's air. I stood above her, brushing aside the thin wisps of hair covering her forehead. As she slept, her eyes darted under thin lids. Lips quivered in reflex.

Why did you shut me out, Nana, all those years ago? I found myself wondering. *What are you hiding from me?*

A depth of worry for Nana I'd never felt before had me looking at her more fully, using senses inherent to the women of my family. Bright yellow unraveled from her body like rays of sunshine. I exhaled in a rush, air thick like steam in the back of my throat. I'd forgotten how beautiful her colors were. Seeing them again was like setting my eyes upon her the first time I remembered meeting her, when we drank hot cocoa at the kitchen table.

I lifted my gaze to her sleeping face, her eyelids thinner, more purple than the skin on her hand. The barriers she kept erected had weakened with her exhaustion. Her colors flickered, dulled. Yellow morphed, mutating with brown, creating mustard. It gave her aura a smokelike appearance that meant one thing. Sickness.

Nana. I petted her hand as the reality of my situation settled over me, sinking into my stomach. I couldn't stay in Pacific Grove. Without Cassie's dreams, avoidance was my only weapon against Cassie's premonition. She and I would both feel better when I was far from the shoreline.

But I couldn't leave Nana either, not when she was as sick as I was beginning to suspect she was.

What to do? What to do?

The question swirled around my mind like a whirlpool threatening to suck me under.

One more night, I reasoned. That was all I needed. One more night where Cassie could dream. One more night to see whether asking Nana to move in with us was even an option. She might be too sick already.

In the quiet darkness of Nana's room, I sent out a silent prayer, hoping I'd get this all worked out by Friday.

Chapter 21

Wednesday, morning

Early the next morning, after Cassie and I met with Owen about his dogs, I sat at the kitchen table sipping coffee. Nana shuffled around the kitchen, complaining about the attic. It was a mess, unorganized. She wanted to toss old clothing and furniture. Dust collectors, she called them. Things that had no beneficial use for any of us.

As I listened to her muddle on, I contemplated the discoloration of her aura I'd seen last night and her overall weariness. "Shouldn't you rest today?"

"I'm fine," she insisted, carrying a dirty pan across the kitchen. Her wrist wobbled, and the iron skillet clanged into the sink.

I rushed to her side. "Let me help."

She didn't say a word but stepped aside, hovering nearby as I scrubbed the pan. She hadn't changed from her sleeping gown, which was unusual for her.

"Promise me you'll rest?" I asked.

She fiddled with her robe's quilted sleeve. "That might be a good idea, now that you mention it. Perhaps later. Are you meeting with Ophelia?"

I nodded. "I'm heading over after I visit with Phoebe."

"Ocean's Artistry was your mother's favorite jewelry store. She'd spend hours looking at the trinkets in the window. I hope Ophelia puts you on commission. That little bit of extra income would be nice for you."

It would, but I had other plans to discuss with Ophelia.

"When you get back, I want to talk about Cassie."

Finally. "How's the training going?"

"It's fine. I gave her some exercises, little tricks to help her focus. They worked on your mother and seem to be working with her." Nana tugged her sleeve.

I stopped scrubbing. "How's her progress?"

"Coming along. When you get back this afternoon, I want to show you what I taught her."

I resumed scrubbing, working a stubborn spot along the edge. "That sounds good. I should be back around two or so," I said, thinking I might need to swing by the attorney's office. I still had to give his assistant the go-ahead to draft the will.

Nana patted my shoulder, telling me she wanted to shower and get started with her day. The attic was a big project.

She shuffled from the room.

"Nana, Cassie said something odd last night about the tea you made her."

She stopped. "Is her stomach bothering her? It can be a little harsh at times."

"Yes, but that's not my question. Cassie said you told her it was dangerous if she did not drink it."

"Oh, that." Nana bit the corner of her lip, then swirled a hand by her head. "She needs her mind well rested while doing the exercises I teach. She can't focus if she's up all night from dreaming. Besides, telling her that gets her to drink the tea. It's nasty-tasting."

Nana was telling little white lies. Although I'd been guilty once or twice myself to coax Cassie into eating something she considered gross. Like broccoli and Brussels sprouts.

"You're sure that's all?"

"Of course." She flashed a smile, then shuffled from the room.

I finished washing the dishes and then dressed for my meeting with Ophelia. I'd cleaned and ironed as best I could the blouse and skirt I'd worn the day we arrived. I hadn't packed anything else as nice.

I collected my portfolio and every finished project I'd brought with me, kissed Cassie good-bye, and drove to Phoebe's for coffee.

Ride-on toys, wet from days of rain, dotted the small lawn in front of her house. Shoes and umbrellas were piled by the front door. Overwatered plants in desperate need of TLC and sunshine withered in their pots. There were two chairs on the porch. Toys cluttered one, and on the other rested a calico cat. His head popped up when he heard me approach, my heels loud on Phoebe's cement steps. I scratched the feline's chin. "You're missing the catnip bonanza several blocks over."

The cat stretched his front legs and flexed its paws, claws elongating. He kneaded the air. I patted his head, then rang the doorbell.

Kurt answered wearing a spoiled shirt and pull-ups. Purple jam framed his mouth like clown makeup, dotted his shirt like misshaped buttons. He smiled around the thumb stuffed between his lips. "'Ello."

"Hey, Kurt, where's your mommy?"

"Right here!" Phoebe, flapping both hands, briskly walked toward the door. She tugged it farther open. "I'm right here."

Kurt scattered out of the way. Phoebe pulled me in for a hug. I grunted. "Morning."

She smelled like coffee grounds and boysenberry jam. "Good morning!" she sang, and moved aside for me to come in.

A messy bun flopped on her head. Her terry robe, threadbare and stained at the bottom hem, billowed around a stretched-out Laguna Seca T-shirt and flannel pj bottoms. My brows lifted. "You look—"

"Ravishing, I know." She popped a hip and patted her hair. "I dressed up for you."

A morning news show blared from the parlor. "Turn that down, Kurt!" She rolled her eyes for my benefit. "Kid can't figure the difference between the volume and channel buttons." She raised her index finger. "Excuse me a sec."

Phoebe stomped into the parlor. "Give me that." She reached for the remote.

Kurt ran around the coffee table and held the remote away from his mother. Phoebe reached over his head and snagged the device. Kurt shrieked. My ears rang. He picked up a magazine and threw it at Phoebe. It bounced off her thigh. She swore under her breath. Kurt's eyes bugged like a Whac-A-Mole popping through a hole. He shrieked and ran from the room.

"Kurt!"

She started to go after him, but stopped and tossed up her arms. "See what I put up with?" She turned off the TV. "Child abuse, my ass. This is parent abuse."

My chest caved a bit. Phoebe had her hands full, even with Jeff and Dale in school most of the day.

"Anything I can do to help?" I offered.

"Your being here is good enough. But smack me if I start talking baby, 'kay?"

"Deal."

She tossed the remote on the table and gave me a tight smile. "Lattes?"

"Yeah, sounds great."

Phoebe led us into the kitchen, which looked like a cereal factory had exploded. Cheerios and wheat flakes crunched under our feet.

Kitchen table chairs were pushed out. Dirty plates littered the counter-top, filled the sink. Danica, who was screaming, red-faced, in her high chair, immediately shut up when she saw me. I was someone new and different in her kitchen. She watched me curiously from her perch.

"Sorry about the mess." Phoebe moved aside cracker boxes and a pretzel bag to get to the espresso machine.

Danica cooed when I waggled my fingers at her. Except for a Christmas-card picture, I hadn't seen her since last summer, when she was barely three months old. "Look at you, Danica! So big." She thrust pudgy fists at me and kicked her legs. I dragged a chair beside her and sat down.

"Whole milk, right?" Phoebe asked and I nodded, digging out a handful of Cheerios for Danica. "Good. 'Cuz I don't do that skinny soy stuff." She smacked her belly.

I arranged the cereal bits into a little-girl stick figure. Danica squealed and scattered the design. I moved the O's into a smiley face.

The espresso machine bubbled and hissed. "Would you believe me if I told you the kitchen was spotless when I went to bed last night?"

"I think you have gremlin problems." I tickled Danica's cheek. She giggled and messed up the smiley face.

"Freaking infestation. Can't get rid of them." Phoebe swept crumbs into the sink and finished the lattes. She hissed. "Shit."

"Sheet!" Kurt repeated. He marched into the kitchen.

I raised my face from the tower of O's stacked on the high chair tray. "You okay?"

"Yeah." She sucked her knuckles. "Watch out. Coffee's hot."

"Sheet, sheet, sheet." Kurt marched around the kitchen island, his voice rising. "SHEET!"

"Watch your mouth, Kurtis Riley!" Phoebe warned as she brought mugs to the table.

Danica kicked and squealed, smiling up at her mother. Phoebe planted a kiss on her cheek, noisy and slobbery. Danica stuffed a wet cheerio in Phoebe's mouth.

"Mmm. Thank you, sweet pea."

"SHEET!" Kurt screamed one last time before running from the kitchen.

I watched him go, thankful Cassie had never been that unruly at his age. I did wonder whether adding one more kid to the mix would tip Phoebe's sanity scale and drain her wallet.

Phoebe groaned and dropped her forehead in her hand.

"When does he start preschool?"

"August. And I'm red-X-ing the days off my calendar." She nodded toward the calendar pinned to the fridge with a race car magnet. "Can't wait."

I drank the latte. "You make good coffee."

"At least I did something right today. So, how long are you staying in town?"

"Another day or so, I think."

Phoebe quirked her brow. "You think?"

"Nana's not feeling well."

Phoebe pressed her lips together, her mouth curving into an upside-down smile. She patted my hand where it rested on the table. "I'm sorry. It's not easy when family grows old."

"No, it's not."

"Is that why you came to visit with her?"

"Ah, not initially," I hedged. I skimmed a finger around the mug rim. "Cassie's on suspension. She has the week off."

Phoebe grimaced, exposing the bottom row of teeth. "That's not good."

"No, it's not." Phoebe didn't know the half of it, and I wasn't ready to tell her about Cassie's abilities. "She's been bullying other kids."

Phoebe gasped. Her hand flew to her chest. "My sweet little Cassie?"

I gave her a weak smile. Sweet little Cassie had quite the temper when people didn't listen to her.

"Speaking of Cassie, I know you're stretched thin on time and money since the divorce, but you are Cassie's godmother. Would you be all right if I made it official and put you down as her guardian? I'm having my will drawn up."

Phoebe thrust out her chest, sitting straighter. "Your will? Is there something I need to know? Are you dying?" She leaned forward. "Don't you dare die on me."

I inhaled sharply and dipped my chin, turning my attention back to Danica's Cheerios. Phoebe's tone was teasing, but the remarks hit too close to home. "No, I'm not dying." I sipped the latte. A creamy nut flavor filled my mouth. "This is something I should have done a long time ago."

Phoebe visibly sighed, sagging in her chair. "Good, you had me scared there for an instant." She covered my hand with hers, her expression turning serious. "My attorney drafted my will when I divorced Vince. But yes, yes, put me down as Cassie's guardian."

I exhaled. "Thank you. I have you as the secondary guardian. Nana is primary, but I'm not sure what's going on with her yet. I may have to change that. I only wanted you to know because"—I looked around the room, took in the results of the morning's pandemonium, and tried not to imagine my daughter getting lost among the cereal crumbs and upturned furniture—"you already have four mouths to feed, and adding Cassie might be too much for you."

"Puh-leeeze, Molly. I'll manage. My life is the spittin' image of chaos, but should something happen to you, and don't you dare let it"—she wiggled a finger at me—"I'll make sure Cassie is taken care of. Do whatever it is you have to do."

My eyes misted. I couldn't promise her I wouldn't die, but at least I knew Cassie would be in loving hands if I did.

When I was young, and before Dad's emotional abuse had started taking its toll on Mom, she and I had spent many hours strolling Ocean Avenue and the narrow streets of Carmel-by-the-Sea, peeking inside windows and browsing shops with cottage roofs, gingerbread eaves, and Dutch doors. She never purchased anything except saltwater taffy, her favorite. We would eat as we walked so there wasn't any left to bring home, or else Dad would know where we'd been.

He hated the quaint seaside village's rustic affluence as much as Mom loved it. It represented everything he wasn't. Wealthy, worldly, and handsome. Instead, he became a victim of his own abuse and neglect. An unemployed alcoholic. He spent days wasting away in his La-Z-Boy and nights tormenting Mom. He blamed her for his failures. Her foresight of his drunkenness had produced a drunk. The knowledge of his fate had acted like poison in his mind, shredding his confidence and ambition. But he had refused to let Mom leave, and his daily threats had kept her by his side.

I stood outside Ocean's Artistry's front window, looking through my reflection at the display. Delicate works of freshwater pearls encased in gold filigree decorated the window ledge. I had always wanted to see my jewelry here, in this window.

"One day," Mom had said during one of our many afternoon walks, "your glass will be here on Ocean Avenue with all the premier local artists."

"Do you think I'll be that good?" At fourteen I had just begun wrapping glass in silver wire.

Her ocean-blue eyes shimmered, the creases at the corners deepening. The white candy bag crinkled, and she gave me a peppermint taffy, pink-and-white-striped, wrapped in wax paper. "I've seen your sea glass in these windows." She nodded at the boutique we passed.

I lifted my chin to the wood sign with the gold lettering we walked under. **OCEAN'S ARTISTRY.**

I stood under that sign now, smoothing my skirt before I went inside. A bell above my head announced my arrival.

The lady behind the countertop looked up. She wore a light-blue chambray shirt under a wool knit sweater vest with a Western-style print. Silver chains draped her neck, hung from her wrists. Hammered silver earrings dangled from her lobes, and rings adorned each finger. She smiled, weathered cheeks fanned upward, creased like worn leather, giving her face a rustic appearance that blended well with the artistic community of the Monterey Peninsula.

"Can I help you?"

"I'm Molly Brennan." I approached her. "I have an appointment with Ophelia Lorimer."

"Molly!" she exclaimed. She stood and extended her arm over the display counter. "Mary had so many good things to say about you. I'm Ophelia." Her voice was smooth and welcoming.

"Hi." I clasped her hand, her skin leathery and warm. An artist's hand, a kindred soul. "I brought the items I told you about."

"Wonderful." She nodded, her earrings swaying like little children on swings. "Let's sit at the table and talk." She came around the counter and led me to a glass table in the corner. "Tea, coffee? Some water?"

"No, thank you." I opened my jewelry case, unrolled a square of black velvet, and arranged a few of my favorite and more intricate pieces.

She slipped on her glasses and leaned over the table. "These are amazing. Better than the photos you e-mailed." She sank into the chair across from me and reached for an earring. She hesitated, fingertips hovering above the kelly-green-hued sea glass. Her eyes lifted to mine. "May I?"

"Please," I encouraged, drawing my hand over the display, inviting her to touch and inspect.

She studied the jewelry, complimenting each design. The quality of the silver, the details of the craftsmanship, the striking colors of glass. I wanted to show her everything I had.

We spent the next twenty minutes looking through my portfolio, at photos of bracelets, charms, rings, and pendants I'd sold in the past. I showed her sketches from my summer and fall lines as she asked questions about my experience, where I had studied, and the processes I used to shape the metal. Our conversation veered into pricing and commissions, and eventually into life on the Monterey Peninsula, Carmel Valley, and growing up on the coast.

When there was a break in our conversation, she splayed her hands on the table. "My counter display has limited space, and I only feature local artists, but I must make an exception. Your work is spectacular. Here's what I propose.

"I'll give you twelve inches in my display case until June. It's not much but it's a start. Assuming those pieces sell, we'll do a big announcement and promo this summer. I'll host an open house." She clapped her hands. "This will be fun. What do you think?"

"I think it's a wonderful offer and I can't thank you enough for such a generous opportunity. But . . ." I paused, glancing at the sea glass shining bright against the black felt. Those pieces reflected hours spent first combing beaches along the Pacific Coast, then wrapping the glass in sterling silver wire. I spent even more hours imagining not only the finished product but also the person who might treasure it. A surge of melancholy flowed over me, flooding my senses, bathing me in sadness. Would I ever again be safe enough to hunt my glass?

"But," I began again, "I'd like to propose another arrangement. A situation has arisen that prevents me from hunting for sea glass. I'm afraid it may be a long time"—*if ever*, I thought to myself—"before I can spend time designing and crafting jewelry."

Ophelia's face fell in disappointment. Then she gasped and her brows lifted high. "It's Mary, isn't it? I was telling myself she didn't look well when I saw her. Is she all right?"

"I'm not sure, but yes, Mary is part of the reason."

Ophelia moistened her lips. "What are you proposing?"

I breathed deeply. "I'd like to sell you all the stock I have with me."

She blinked. "Everything?"

"It's not much, but it'll only sit around and collect dust otherwise. I'd be much happier knowing my pieces were being appreciated by someone."

Ophelia leaned back in her chair, lips pressed as she contemplated my counteroffer. "All right," she said after a moment. "Let me look at what you have, but only on one condition. When you start designing again, you come see me first."

I nudged the chain of a necklace into place and sighed with relief. "Thank you."

Over the next half hour, after I brought in the bin from the car, Ophelia combed through my selection. She took everything I brought, concluding our deal with the reminder that I come back to her first should I design anything new.

When we finished, I left, going outside into the sunshine. I turned my face skyward, absorbing the first rays of sunlight I'd felt all week, and sighed. I slipped a folded check for an amount much greater than I'd expected into my purse. Something extra to leave for Cassie. Just in case.

Chapter 22

Wednesday, noon

"How'd it go?"

I turned around. Owen lounged against the stucco wall between Ocean's Artistry and the window of the clothing boutique next door. Mudd and Dirt obediently sat at his feet. I shielded my eyes against the sun, ultrabright after days of overcast skies, and peered at him. He smiled, and I felt a responding pull inside me. "Hey, there! What're you doing here?" I asked. I'd mentioned my appointment this morning to him while he showed Cassie and me where he kept the dog food.

He pushed away from the wall, the dogs following on their leashes, and ambled over. "Thought I'd convince you to have lunch with me."

"What time is it?"

He glanced at his phone screen. "Noon. What time do you have to be back?"

"I told Nana around two. Sure, why not," I agreed, making a mental note to call the law office on the way back. They were awaiting my go-ahead to type the will.

Owen gave me an amazing smile and folded his hand around mine. "There's a great Italian place around the corner. It's a hole-in-the-wall but the food's good."

We walked along Ocean Avenue. Mudd and Dirt sauntered ahead on the lead Owen gave them. The sidewalk bustled with shoppers. The entire town seemed to be out and about, dogs included, enjoying the sunshine before the rain returned.

"Tell me about your interview," he prompted.

"It wasn't an interview, per se."

"No?"

I shook my head. "She wanted to put me on commission but I proposed another arrangement."

Owen glanced at me curiously, the dogs tugging at his arm.

"I sold her the stock I'd brought with the promise to let her know if I start designing again."

Owen stopped. He yanked the leashes. Mudd whined. "Why in the world would you do that? And what do you mean by 'start designing again'? Why would you stop?" He gave me an incredulous look. "You love sea glass."

"I do, a lot," I said, brokenhearted. I started walking again, feeling anxious, like my clock was ticking. I needed to move. "I can't make any product if I can't comb beaches for sea glass. Besides, I needed some money to leave behind for Cassie." My voice broke when I spoke my daughter's name. I cleared my throat, pressed the back of my hand against my mouth.

Owen stopped again. This time he grasped my upper arm, angling my torso to face him.

I gasped at his grip. "Owen."

His jaw hardened, and his gaze bore into me. "You're giving up."

"No, I—"

"You expect to die."

My mouth worked, demanding I passionately object, but I couldn't. My shoulders bowed. "I honestly don't know what to expect. I'm just trying to be prepared, like with the attorney and the will."

Owen's grip loosened, and he rubbed my arm. "Being prepared is good. But don't you dare give up. The Molly I knew was a fighter."

No, she wasn't.

I angled my face down and away. Mudd and Dirt, rumps to the ground, pranced, their front paws itching to move. They wanted to run, which was what I always did. I wasn't a fighter. I was a runner. And I planned to run again come Friday.

"The only way I know how to outwit Cassie's premonition is avoidance. I can't drown if I don't go in the water." A soggy chuckle bubbled up my throat. "As we saw the other day, I clearly can't avoid the beach. The ocean is too much a part of me and what I love to do. It's also why Cassie and I must leave. The ocean's too close here and too much of a temptation."

"You're leaving," he said, simply. A pained expression crossed his face. Then he frowned. "Back to San Luis Obispo? Which is also near the beach?"

"A fifteen-minute drive," I argued. "Not quite the same as seeing it outside the front door." I motioned toward the beach at the end of Ocean Avenue.

Owen shook his head. "You aren't thinking straight. Avoiding the ocean doesn't mean you have to give up your sea glass. You can buy it online."

I balked. "You mean machine-tumbled beach glass? The fake stuff?"

"I bet you can find real sea glass," he challenged. "What's that website all you crafty people use?"

"Etsy?"

"Yeah, that." He grinned, putting an arm across my shoulders. We started walking again. "You're resourceful. I'm sure you can find some without ever going to the beach again."

Mudd nudged the hands passersby allowed him to sniff. Dirt kept his nose to the ground. Both tails waved like flags.

"You can still design, too." He dipped his head toward me. "Then sell those designs, like fashion designers. Did you think of that?"

"No," I admitted glumly.

He gave my shoulders an encouraging squeeze. "There are always options, Molly."

I prayed he was right, not solely about my sea glass passion, but about my life. My death couldn't be the only outcome of Cassie's premonition.

On the drive back to Pacific Grove after lunch, I called the attorney's office and spoke with Loretta, Dave's assistant. She'd type up the will this afternoon, leaving Nana as Cassie's primary guardian and Phoebe as secondary. I still had time to make changes, she told me. She'd do a quick edit and reprint tomorrow. Before concluding the call, we scheduled a time tomorrow afternoon for me to come in and sign the document. They had a notary on staff, so everything would be completed onsite and I could go home with my copy.

My next call was to Gayle Piedmont, the life insurance agent. After a quick round of questions asking about my age and health, how much I drank and whether or not I smoked, she anticipated having quotes for me by early next week. Fingers crossed I was still around to consider them.

Feeling a little better about Cassie's future, I returned to Pacific Grove and parked in front of the purple Victorian behind a Hyundai Sonata with a plastic license plate frame from a dealership in San Luis Obispo. Who could be here?

I hurried into the house. Voices drifted from the parlor as I hung my sweater on the coatrack. I walked to the room and stopped abruptly in the doorway. Jane Harrison sat on the couch, head inclined. Cassie knelt on the floor, eyes squeezed shut. She clutched Jane's hand in her two small ones.

Jane leaned forward and quietly asked, "What do you see?"

The portfolio slipped from my fingers. It landed on the floor with a loud thud. Jane and Cassie jolted. They gave me startled looks.

"What's going on?'

Jane slowly stood. "Hello, Molly."

I stumbled back a step.

Cassie popped to her feet. "Mom! Principal Harrison is going to have a baby. Well, she's not having one yet, but she will soon."

My eyes narrowed on Jane. A smile flashed on her face. "Cassie told me the news."

"It's going to be a girl."

Jane's hand fluttered to her chest. "A girl?"

Cassie nodded. She curved a hand along her mouth. "You'll name her Hannah," she whisper-yelled.

"My mother's name." Jane sounded amazed. "Thank you, Cassie. Thank you so much. Mr. Harrison and I have waited so long for a child." She clasped Cassie's hand.

I moved swiftly into the room and maneuvered my daughter behind me. Jane gasped and retreated a step.

"I should have called," Jane said to me.

"You should be fired."

She watched me for a beat. "Please let me explain—"

"You came here to have your fortune told," I accused. "You took advantage of my child."

We stared at each other. Jane's lashes fluttered. "Yes, well . . ." She looked left then right, and then picked up her purse on the couch behind her. "I should go."

"Yes, you should."

Cassie tugged my sweater. I turned to her. "Go to your room."

Her jaw dropped. "B-but . . . what did I do?"

"Tea's ready." Nana shuffled through the adjoining door between the kitchen and dining room and into the parlor. Porcelain pots and cups and silver spoons rattled on the tray she carried. Mint and lemon filled the room. They were having a tea party.

"Principal Harrison was just leaving," I said in a flat tone.

"Oh? So soon?" Nana said.

"It was wrong of me to come. I'm sorry to have bothered you, Mrs. Dwyer."

"It was no bother at all."

I gaped at Nana.

Jane started walking toward the door.

As she moved into the entryway, I backed up and opened the front door. She paused at the threshold. "You have a special daughter."

"Then don't treat her like a freak," I blurted, not thinking how my words might affect Cassie.

Jane's eyes widened for a split second before her face fell. "You're right. I apologize for my intrusion." She stepped onto the porch and turned around to face me. I slammed the door.

Nana gasped. "Molly Brennan!"

"Don't you start with me." I thrust a finger at her. "You had no right to let that woman in here. How did she find us?"

Nana shrugged. I turned to Cassie. She shook her head. I pursed my lips and blew air out my nose like a bull ready to charge. "What did she want? Her palm read? For Cassie to predict her future?"

Nana's gaze darted to Cassie.

"That's it, isn't it?" I sneered. My mind cranked to make sense of what I'd heard. It was like guessing song titles without a CD cover. Then it hit me. "Let me guess . . . she's had trouble getting pregnant and wants to know if she'll ever have a child."

Nana's shoulders dropped. I swore. My fingers dug into my scalp, scooping hair. I tugged hard at the strands. "Did Jane call?" She must have finally found the note I'd left with the front receptionist. Then I remembered: Nana's address was on Cassie's emergency contact form. "Did you invite her here so Cassie can test her abilities?"

Nana straightened. "I had no idea she was coming. She found a lump in her breast three days ago and is scared it's cancerous. She and her husband have been trying to have children for years. She's afraid she'll never be a mother."

Through the window, my gaze followed Jane to her car, my heart reaching out to her.

No! I wouldn't feel sorry for her. My daughter was my priority.

I whirled on Cassie. My mother had honed her abilities enough to see fairly far into the future. How had Cassie learned to do that in such a short amount of time? Was she that much more powerful than Mom? Was that why her premonitions were so intense? "What the hell has Nana been teaching you?"

"What your mother and I should have taught you years ago," Nana answered for Cassie. "How to harness your abilities so you embrace them. Cassie shouldn't be afraid of using her gifts, and neither should you be."

"I—I had a good vision, Mom." Cassie's lips quivered. She twisted her fingers.

"I don't care what you saw. Your visions have to stop. Don't ever do that again! Not with anyone!"

She flinched like I'd slapped her. "I only want to help . . ."

"Your visions don't help people. They scare the shit out of them." My own fear echoed in my tone.

"Molly!" Nana yelled.

All those times Dad had told me my abilities made me a freak. That they were wrong. Abnormal. His words reared their ugly heads and howled. Making me sound just like him.

Tears poured down Cassie's face. Deep, ragged sobs tore up her throat. Her shoulders shook. My chest deflated. She was too young to understand. "Cass—"

"I hate you." She sucked in a gulp of air and exploded. "I don't care if you die! I hate you! HATE YOU! HATE YOU!" She ran from the room and up the steps.

"Cassidy!"

A door slammed upstairs. I kept myself from chasing after her. Inside my stomach, a roiling heat expanded outward to my limbs like a firestorm, moving swiftly, uncontrollable. I whirled on Nana. "You're supposed to be teaching her how to suppress the visions, not induce them!"

Nana shook her head, disappointed. "Calm down, right this instant, Molly. I'm not going to discuss this while you're in such a foul mood." She walked away.

"Why? Is it because I'm yelling?"

"No," she snapped over her shoulder.

I dogged her down the hallway. "It's because *he* always yelled, isn't it? You hated when he berated Mom, screaming and yelling. And you never did a damn thing about it. I'm trying to get help for Cassie, something you never did for your own daughter!"

Nana stiffened. Her pace slowed.

"Why did you block me out, Nana? Why did you stop opening your mind to me? It's because you think I'm just like him, isn't it?"

She stopped abruptly, teacups knocking, and turned. "No, but you do."

I gasped.

"You scorn your abilities like him. You control them, Molly. They don't have to control you. And they don't make you a terrible person. That's what I'm teaching Cassie, and it's what we never took the time to teach you. You weren't . . ." Her brows bunched. She breathed unsteadily. "You weren't the only one afraid of your father—"

The tea tray crashed to the floor. Cups and pots shattered. Hot tea splattered on my shoes and bare shins. I jumped backward, inhaling sharply through my teeth. Nana swayed. She folded against the wall.

"Nana!"

Chapter 23

Wednesday, afternoon

I leaped to Nana's side and grasped her elbows. "What's wrong?"

She shook her head in a slow, constant sway. Her eyes were glassy, her face pasty. Arms quivered and hands trembled.

"Let's sit down." I tried to coax her from the wall. She moaned, a wounded sound in the back of her throat. "On second thought, we'll stay right here." I rooted around the purse still hanging from my shoulder and searched for my phone. "I'll call an ambulance."

"No." She pressed herself into the wall. "No, Molly, dear. I'm all right."

"No, you're not. You're pale and shaking."

She moistened her lips. Her eyelids lowered like blinds drawn over a window. "I'm tired. Help me upstairs."

I glanced up the steep staircase. "I really think I should call an ambulance."

"No." Impatience edged her tone. "Please. I'll be fine." Her gaze drifted to the floor.

"Don't worry about the mess. I'll clean up."

She hesitated a beat before nodding. "Help me to my room, then."

"Fine." I relented against my better judgment and walked slowly with her to the base of the staircase. We both looked up the steps expanding heavenward. "I'm going to call 9-1-1 if you get worse. Or drag you to the hospital myself," I said when she positioned a wobbly foot on the first step.

"That's fine, dear." She gripped my forearm.

I wrapped my arm around her shoulders and tucked her into my side. She was frailer, her shoulder blade hard and angular under my hand. We climbed the stairs, each step a mountain. Every few steps we stopped for Nana to catch her breath. She held her head steady, the muscles in her neck rigid, as though moving hurt.

"I think you overdid it in the attic this morning," I told her as we maneuvered around the attic ladder at the top of the landing. She'd been overdoing it for the past couple of days.

Nana shook her head. "That's not it."

"Then what's wrong?" I pleaded, my voice heavy with concern.

"Shh." She cringed. "Lower your voice, please."

I sighed heavily, looking inward, and latched on to my last ounce of patience. Not that there was much there to begin with. "Sorry." The week was taking its toll on all of us.

We shuffled into her bedroom, and I barely had a moment to acknowledge that I hadn't spent much time in this room all week. It had been my parents' room.

After pulling back the covers, I eased Nana into bed and removed her shoes.

She settled against the white-sheeted pillows and patted my hand. A tiny smile curved her lips. "I'm fine." She stayed my hands to stop my fidgeting with the blankets and closed her eyes.

"You're not fine." I stood by the bed and watched her rest, a medi-tating rise and fall to her chest. Slowly, tension eased from her face like ice melting on hot cement. The thin lines softened at her lips. I chewed mine. "I saw your colors." My voice was quiet, barely above a whisper.

Nana shifted under the covers. She sighed, but she didn't look at me. "I have cancer."

Air cycloned from my lungs. Quickly, our surroundings came into focus. The prescription medications and water pitcher on the bedside table. The sour odor that came with age and sickness. It clung like mildew to every item in the room. Sheets, clothing, drapes, and furniture.

I sank onto the bed with my face upturned, fingers pressed over my mouth. Gradually the news settled, and it brought a sense of understanding. Owen's suspicions about Nana's health. My own observations. She had been weary and slower. I'd been somewhat mentally prepared. I'd seen her colors. Now I knew. Owen had been right. Nana was dying.

I picked up a bottle of pills, the drug's name foreign to me. "What type of cancer do you have?"

"Brain tumor."

My fingers tightened around the plastic container. Pills rattled.

"It's inoperable," she added.

I covered my mouth, briefly closed my eyes, and breathed deeply through my nose, the sour odor stronger. How had I missed that smell before?

I hadn't, I admitted. It was there, on the first day, the tang hiding under Nana's perfume.

I lowered my hand. "Chemo?"

Nana rolled her head back and forth on the pillow. "Chose not to."

"Why?" I stared at her. She was only seventy-three. Plenty of years left. Where was her will to live?

Nana turned her face to the window. In her prone position, gravity pulled her skin toward the bed. Wrinkles smoothed over wan cheeks and bunched around her jaw and thinning hairline. Over time, her brilliant blue eyes had faded to a dull gray, and in them I saw the answer.

Without treatment, she'd go quickly. Her suffering wouldn't last long. She didn't want to be a burden.

"Nana," I whispered. Then I glanced at her, her aura emanating, unrestricted in her weakened state. "Does Cassie know?" She must have seen Nana's colors.

"She's asked." The corner of Nana's mouth twitched. "I told her I had a head cold." Truth enough so her aura didn't reveal the white lie.

The weight of the week's news and events fell hard on my shoulders. "I'm scared, Nana. I'm scared about what you're going through. I'm scared for Cassie. She'll have no family left if we both die."

"You're too stubborn to die."

"I don't want you to die either." I returned to the bed, resting my head on her chest. "I'm sorry I left. I should have visited more often."

"There, there." Nana patted my back. "We both could have done more."

I sighed. "I love you."

She rubbed my back, light, back-and-forth brushes of her hand. "I've always loved you, Molly, dear."

I listened to her heartbeat. Strong and steady, belying the malignant mass expanding in her brain, her beautiful mind.

For a length of time we lay that way, her rubbing my back, me listening to her breathe. When her hand stilled, I straightened, smoothed my hair, and rubbed my eyes.

She looked peaceful, her head framed by the pillow. I thought she'd fallen asleep until she turned and looked up at me. "What is it?" she asked as though she felt the weight of my stare.

"How much time do you have?"

She glanced at her body, a thin outline under the blanket. "I'm thirsty. Will you get me some water, honey?"

The near-empty pitcher towered over pill containers, cups, and books on the bedside table. "Yeah, sure." I collected the pitcher and left the room.

On my way to the kitchen, I folded the attic ladder, closing the hatch, and skirted the mess in the downstairs hallway. I filled the pitcher and returned upstairs to find Nana had fallen asleep. I poured a glass and left both glass and pitcher on the table. The sun had drifted lower, ducking behind a bank of clouds. Long, gray shadows stretched across the room. I drew the curtains, the room falling into darkness, and left, keeping the door cracked in case Nana needed me. Downstairs, I cleaned up the shattered porcelain. The pieces had been in Nana's family for generations. It broke my heart they couldn't be repaired or replaced.

The house was quiet when I'd finished, too quiet. I stared out the back window, unmoving. The wind from the past couple of days had died. A fog bank had moved in while I'd cleaned, obscuring the sun. It gave the outside world a flat, mattelike appearance. A thousand thoughts cluttered my head like a word cloud, the biggest and boldest being Cassie and her future now that I had my answer. Nana was dying.

Where was Cassie, anyhow? By now she should have been slamming her door over and over to get my attention.

She was still mad at me, I reasoned. Not ready to talk. Or she might have fallen asleep.

I went upstairs to check and found Bunny sprawled on the floor outside her door. The stuffed animal's ears had been knotted together, and the thread attaching the leg to its body was unraveling like the limb had been stretched and yanked. Poor Bunny.

I picked up the toy and lightly knocked on Cassie's door. It creaked open. "Cass?"

When there wasn't an answer, I peeked inside. Her bed was made. She wasn't asleep, nor was she in her room. I went to Nana's room and poked my head inside. "Cassidy?" I whispered.

No answer.

Where was she?

I called her name from the top of the stairs. The house moaned, boards settling, but no response from Cassie.

"She's really angry with me," I said out loud. "What do you think, Bunny?"

The toy's beady eye stared blankly at me.

After checking Cassie's closet and the cabinets in the bathroom and hallway, I went to my room. "I know you're angry, Cassie. Please come out so we can talk."

The room remained quiet. She wasn't here either, but there was a bright-orange life vest on my bed.

I only want to help.

Cassie's words shredded through me. My chest deflated, and I collapsed onto the bed.

I'm going to save you, Mommy.

"Cassie . . ." I wept.

My issues with our abilities weren't Cassie's issues. I was the one with the problem. It was me who was ashamed, who didn't want to be seen as a freak, who was afraid of what I could do to someone I loved. If only I had the courage to embrace my oddities as Cassie seemed to do today with Jane. As she'd been trying to do all along.

"God, Cassie. I'm so sorry." Recalling my promise to her yesterday, I slipped on the vest and clipped the front clasps. The vest was bulky, definitely an awkward fit. I tightened the straps and hugged my middle, rocking on the bed. "I'm sorry."

Nana had been teaching Cassie to harness her foresight so the premonitions weren't uninvited and tragic, those emotionally charged visions she didn't have the skill to block. She was helping Cassie develop control, to see what she wanted and when. To know who to help and why. Like Mom had done.

I shot to my feet. "Cassidy!" I ran from the room. I needed to apologize, tell her I'd been wrong to force my fears on her before allowing her the opportunity to try, to let her abilities grow and flourish along with her.

Jogging through the house, I hollered her name as I searched rooms and cabinets large enough to fit her petite frame. I checked the backyard and my studio, finally ending at the hallway closet. I stood in front of the door. Perspiration flared between my shoulder blades, trapped by the life vest.

Please don't be in here.

My fingers flexed on the doorknob. To think she willingly hid here made me sick. Then again, she didn't know about the hours I'd spent locked inside.

The ceiling pressed down, and the floor rose as I thought about the confining space. My breaths came in short bursts. *Do it, Molly.* I yanked open the door, somewhat surprised to find it unlocked, but even more shocked to discover it empty. I almost expected to find myself crouched on the floor with tear tracks on my cheeks, nails bloody from picking at the lock in the dark.

"Cassidy?" Her name was a whimper as I backed from the door. I rubbed my neck and circled around, my eyes darting over furniture to doors and rooms.

Where is she?

The beach.

I don't care if you die! I HATE YOU!

Dizziness swirled around me. I pressed my hand on the wall, took a deep breath, and exhaling, opened my mind. *Where are you?*

Emptiness greeted me.

Panic lodged in my throat. Was she blocking me? Or worse, had she left the house?

I imagined Cassie running to the beach, angry at the world, much like I'd done at her age. Then I saw her caught in the storm-crazed waves, her little body tossing and turning. I watched the current drag her away, then me swimming frantically after her.

"No!" This couldn't be the way it happened.

My heart pounding like a mallet on a kettledrum, I ran out the front door and flew off the porch, screaming for Cassie. But I didn't head toward the beach. I went to Owen's and pounded on the door. He'd told me, anytime, no matter what, to come to him should I need him. And I needed him.

Mudd and Dirt barked from inside. I heard Owen order them to sit. He opened the door and chuckled. "Nice look."

His gaze lifted from the vest and snared in mine. His smile faltered. He clutched my shoulders. "What is it?"

"Cassie's gone."

Chapter 24

Wednesday, late afternoon

"When did you last see her?" Owen yanked his jacket from the hanger in the hall closet.

"Over an hour ago. Cassie's principal was here when I got home," I explained, out of breath. "She'd come all this way—on a school day—to see Cassie."

"That's considerate of her." Owen knew Cassie was on suspension. He zipped his jacket, and we left his house.

I jogged to keep up with Owen's brisk pace. "She wasn't here to check on Cassie. She wanted Cassie to look at her future, like she was a fortune teller."

Owen jolted to a stop where his walkway met the sidewalk. He gaped at me. "You're kidding."

"I freaked. I kicked her out. Yelled at Cassie. Nana hollered at me. Cassie screamed she hated me and ran upstairs. Then Nana collapsed."

His head quickly drew back. "What?"

"Owen." My hands flew to my cheeks. "Nana has a brain tumor."

He stared hard at me for a moment, as though processing everything I'd dumped on him. He blinked, then swore. "Where is she?"

"Nana? In bed, resting. She's fine for the moment." I anxiously glanced over my shoulder toward the ocean. The sky had darkened, night coming quicker with the fog. "I think Cassie's at the beach."

Owen lifted his face and looked down the road. He frowned. "Has she gone there yet this week?"

I shook my head, bouncing on my toes. My heart raced.

"Then I don't think she's there."

"Are you sure? Because that's where I always went when I was mad, and we're so much alike, and I've never seen her so angry with me, I mean—God, Owen—she hates me. I totally screwed up."

"Hey, hey." Owen gripped my shoulders. "Calm down. Take a deep breath. We'll find her."

I inhaled long and deep, my lungs fighting for space in my chest.

"That's it," he said as I exhaled. "Now, let's think through this. I'm sure she didn't go far. Have you tried reaching out to her?"

I nodded rapidly. "I couldn't sense her; I don't know why." It was the first time in Cassie's life that I'd tried talking to her in that special way, and she hadn't answered.

He arched his brows. "Is she blocking you?"

"I hope so." Because I couldn't stomach the alternative.

"All right, let's go back to Mary's and look around."

"I already checked the house," I said.

"Then we should definitely check the beach."

We both glanced toward the water, and my stomach plummeted.

"Do you want—" He stopped as I rapidly shook my head. "Would you like me to run down there and check it out?"

I nodded. "Yes, please." The words burst from my mouth.

"Wait here." He took off at a sprint. He couldn't have been gone longer than three minutes, but those minutes were the longest stretch of time I'd experienced in my life.

Owen ran back up the street. I met him at the sidewalk in front of Nana's house.

"She's not there," he said, winded.

"Thank God."

He grabbed my hand. "Let's try the house once more to see if she's come back. Then we should call the police."

My face contorted. Tears burned. *God, don't let it come to that. Please be inside. Please be inside.*

I repeated the prayer in my head as the metallic taste of fear filled my mouth.

We stopped in the foyer and looked up the staircase. "You say she ran upstairs when you last saw her?"

I nodded.

"Did you hear her after that? Any running footsteps? Perhaps a door opening or closing?"

I shook my head.

"Let's start upstairs, then." He headed up the steps, taking two at a time. I jogged to keep up, the life vest bouncing on my shoulders.

"She wasn't in her room when I last looked," I mentioned as we stood outside Cassie's door. "Bunny was right here when I came up to check on her." I pointed at the floor. "She never goes anywhere without Bunny."

Owen watched me unknot the rabbit's ears. "Where were you before you came upstairs?"

I twisted Bunny's ear. "Downstairs. I . . . um . . . Nana dropped the tea tray, so I cleaned up the mess."

A pained expression passed over his face. "And before that?"

"I was with Nana. That's when she told me about . . . about the . . . you know . . ." I flapped my hand, at a loss for words. My throat hurt from yelling and sobbing. The life vest pressed into my ribs with each breath, tight and constricting. My skin was sweltering underneath. Perspiration beaded my hairline. I started sucking in short breaths.

Owen unsnapped the front latches. I sighed heavily.

"Better?" he asked in a low and calm voice.

"Much. Thanks."

"Tell me about Mary." He rubbed my upper arms. It kept me grounded and focused. My breathing evened and my head stopped spinning.

"I told her I knew she was sick. I'd seen her colors. That's when she told me about the tumor. When I asked how much time she had left, she asked for water."

"So you went downstairs?"

"Yes . . . *no!*" I looked left and then right and then up. I gasped.

Owen followed my gaze. "You think she's in the attic?"

"She must be! I put the ladder up when I got Nana's water," I explained. Owen was already pulling the hatch open. I smacked my forehead. "Stupid. I can't believe I didn't look there."

He unfolded the ladder. "Given what the last couple of hours have been like, I think your oversight is understandable. Let me take a look." He climbed up the ladder. "Hey, Cassie! You up here?"

A light shuffling sound floated down from the attic. Two hands grasped the ledge and Cassie poked her face over. Her beautiful, smiling face. Long golden tresses cascaded over her shoulders.

"Hi, Mr. Torres."

I practically melted into the floor. "What are you doing up there?"

"Looking at pictures. There's lots of your mom when you were little. She's pretty."

I dragged fingers through my hair. "Yes, she was pretty."

"Come look." She waved me up and disappeared from view. The ceiling moaned with her footsteps, the same sound I'd heard earlier when I was calling for her, I realized.

I climbed the first rung and looked at Owen.

"Go ahead." He nodded up at the attic. "I'll check on Mary."

"Thank you."

He kissed my forehead. I handed him Bunny and clomped up the ladder. The life vest snagged on the edge, so I angled my torso away from the ledge and climbed into the attic. Crouched like a hunchback so my head didn't hit a rafter, I skirted boxes and old furniture. The attic smelled of dust and mothballs and aged newspaper.

Cassie sat near the far wall at the back of the house, legs crossed. A photo album lay open across her knees. Above her head, a small window allowed enough of the fading daylight into the room for her to see the pictures.

I eased onto the floor beside her.

My fingers itched to touch her, so I scooped the hair draping her shoulders. I wanted to see her beautiful face.

"What are you looking at?" I asked.

"Pictures of you and your mom. I think you're at a park." She angled the album for me to see.

There I was, no older than five, chasing Mom through a field of wildflowers. I remembered that day. The flowers' perfume overpowered the hillside where Mom took her daily walks. The picture had been taken from behind us as we ran away from the photographer, my father. Long platinum hair flowed down our backs.

There was a close-up of Mom on the opposite page, me in her lap. We smiled at the camera. My eyes a shimmering green, hers a deep ocean blue. She looked so young.

"See how pretty your mom is?" Cassie asked.

"She's beautiful." I touched the photo's plastic cover.

"How did she die?"

My heart clenched. "In a tragic accident," I said, sparing her the ugly details. She was still too young.

"Do you miss her?"

"Very much."

Cassie put her hand on my knee. "I'm sorry you lost your mom."

"Me, too." I looked at Cassie. She floored me. Here she was, comforting me when it should have been the other way around.

We looked through the album together. Cassie asked questions, and I answered each one the best I could.

What was your mom like?

Wonderful. I loved her.

What did she like to do?

She liked walking the beach. She looked for shells.

Was she special, too?

Yes.

What could she do?

The same thing as you, I said. Then I told Cassie she reminded me of my mother every day. And that I loved her.

The photos were from a time when life had been good with my parents, before my father had lost his job. Before he had brought alcohol into our lives, and before he'd broken Mom with his words, blaming her for his failings. The album ended right before we moved to California.

Cassie closed the album and set it aside. The attic had grown too dark to look at more pictures, but I didn't want to disturb this moment with her. Which was why I didn't get up and flip on the light.

"Thank you for the life vest." I spoke in a low voice.

Cassie inspected the vest. She clipped the latches. Thick pressure clamped tightly to my rib cage. I took a meditative breath. Cassie's eyes flew to mine. "It's bulky."

"Just a bit," I said tightly. Suffocating, too, despite it being a size too big. "I'll keep it on if it makes you feel better."

She unclipped the vest and slipped it off me.

"What're you doing?"

"Giving it back to Mr. Torres. It doesn't fit right." She hugged the vest to her chest.

I scooped hair from her face and smoothed it down her back. "Sorry I yelled."

She pressed her lips flat and nodded. She didn't look at me, her gaze fixed at some point on the unfinished wood floorboards. "You embarrassed me. Principal Harrison was starting to like me again. She was sad and I wanted to help her."

While I didn't have much sympathy for Jane—and should we all get through this week, I planned to call the school district—I did feel like a heel for how I'd treated Cassie. "I'm sorry I didn't listen to you, and I didn't give you the chance to explain."

Her only response was the blink of her eyelids.

"I was angry and scared. Moms get scared, too. It hurts me when I see how others treat you because of your . . . special skills."

She scratched at a knothole in the floor with her fingernail. "But I can help people."

"I know you can, but"—I took a deep breath—"sometimes helping people hurts others."

She raised her head. "Is that why you don't read minds anymore?"

"It's part of the reason."

"Nana says you don't use your gifts because it scares you."

"You're fortunate to have Nana train you. I didn't learn to control my abilities."

"Nana or your mommy didn't train you?" Cassie looked at me, stunned.

I shook my head. "My daddy wouldn't allow it."

"Why not?"

I opened my mouth, searching for the words she'd best understand. "I think, like your friends, our abilities scared him." Tears burned my eyes, either from the dust or from long-ago regrets. Perhaps both.

Cassie rubbed my cheeks. "Don't cry, Mommy. Maybe I can teach you what Nana taught me."

A watery laugh bubbled from my throat. "You know what? I think I like that idea."

Tossing aside the vest, I pulled her onto my lap. Her clothes smelled dusty, tickling my nose. She'd been sitting up here for a while.

The ladder creaked. Owen's head and shoulders popped through the opening. "Mary's awake," he told me. "She's asking for you."

"All right. Be right down."

I lifted Cassie to her feet. "You okay?"

She nodded, and I kissed her cheek. "I love you, Mermaid."

She gave me a hug. "Love you right back."

"Hey, Cass," Owen said. "Come down and I'll fix you dinner."

Cassie started to walk away.

"Do you want to call Grace after dinner?" It had been a couple of days, and I thought Cassie would like to hear directly from her friend. Cassie had helped her.

She exuberantly nodded and hugged me again.

Owen took Cassie downstairs to scrounge up some food for dinner while I went to see Nana.

Color had returned to her cheeks, and she was sitting upright in bed. She'd changed into her nightgown. The covers had been tucked neatly around her slight form. She put aside the book she was reading when I entered the room.

A little smile touched her lips, smoothing the wrinkles around her mouth. "Finally found Cassie?"

"Yes, thank God." I dragged Nana's favorite rocking chair to her bedside. The seat creaked with age when I sat. It made me think of Mom.

We'd spent many late nights in this chair, rocking in Nana's old room. The chair's gentle sway and Mom's soft humming had lulled me to sleep.

There was a twinkle in Nana's eyes. Her shoulders vibrated. "She had you going there for a bit." She found Cassie's disappearing act amusing.

"The attic is the first place I should have looked," I said in retrospect.

"We had fun up there this morning. She loved looking at the pictures, especially the ones when you were her age."

"I don't have any albums at home."

"Then you'll have to bring these downstairs for her to enjoy. There's plenty of space on the shelves Owen built in the parlor."

She removed her reading glasses and rubbed the bridge of her nose with her index and thumb. A heavy sigh expanded and deflated her lungs.

Too many years had gone by since Nana and I had opened our minds to each other. Instinctively, I wanted to leave the room and pretend she was healthy, but time was of the essence, for both of us. "How are you . . . considering . . . you know?" The words came out strained, as if wrung from a twisted wet towel.

Her eyes briefly closed. "I'm tired." She folded her glasses and laid them on her book. "There's been a lot of excitement this week."

That was an understatement.

She shifted, scooting farther upright in bed. Her movements were slow as she adjusted her position.

"Let me help." I started to rise.

"Sit, sit." She gestured me away.

"Are you hungry? Can I get you something to eat?"

"Owen's bringing up dinner." She tugged the blanket, tucking it below her chest.

"How about water?" Her glass was half-empty. "I'll pour you another." I pushed up from the rocker.

"Molly. Sit."

I obediently plopped back into the chair.

She searched my face. "The only thing I want right now is your company."

"All right," I said, clasping my hands.

She watched me twist my fingers, a nervous habit Cassie had picked up from me. I'd picked it up from Mom. "Did your meeting with Ophelia go well?" Nana asked.

I nodded, refraining from telling her the details so she wouldn't worry about me. I absently rocked in the chair, the hardwood floor groaning under the chair's runners. A thousand questions tossed around my head like sea glass tumbling in the surf. How much time did Nana have left? How long had she been sick? Why hadn't she told me sooner? And why had she decided not to get treatment?

I should have come home sooner. I should have visited more often. I should never have left home.

"I'm sorry," I said simply.

"For what, Molly, dear?"

"Everything." My breath shook and my stomach gave a lurch. "For everything."

Nana looked at me for a long moment, her eyes sad and weary. "You don't owe me an apology."

I nodded vigorously. "I do." I turned to the window, where earlier Owen must have opened the drapes. I stared beyond the glass and into the evening sky. "Where do I begin?" I murmured.

Nana sighed. "How about the beginning?"

"The beginning," I repeated in a whisper. I ingested a sudden onslaught of emotion and took a deep breath. "That afternoon, when Dad killed Mom, I was studying at Owen's house. I suddenly thought of Mom. I felt a brush across my skin and a kiss. And then I felt nothing. Just a vast emptiness that terrified me, so I ran home. That's when I saw you at the bottom of the stairs. I ran to Mom's room, and there she was, lying in Dad's lap with purple fingerprint blotches around her neck. He'd just killed her, Nana. I'd just missed it. I have always thought if I hadn't been at Owen's, he never would have killed Mom. Or maybe I could have stopped him. Mom would still be with us."

"Molly, Molly, Molly." Nana rolled her head side to side on the pillow. "Sheila's death wasn't your fault. I was home, too, remember? He still murdered my daughter." Her voice broke.

"There's more, though." Before I lost the courage, I soldiered on. "I surprised Dad when I showed up. He dropped Mom. Literally. He let her fall on the ground like a discarded doll." I extended my arms toward the floor. "He stepped over her as though she meant nothing to him and came after me. He started making excuses how it was an accident, that he didn't mean to do it. Then he got this crazed look in his eyes. He was all sweaty, blaming me. He said Mom's death was my fault. That I'd compelled him to do it.

"I got so scared, Nana, that I did exactly that. I issued a compulsion before realizing what I was doing. I told him to leave us."

"That's why he left so suddenly." Nana whispered the realization.

I moved to the bed, sat down beside her. "Yes. And that's when he was hit by a car. That car hit him because of me. I killed my father."

Nana reached across the bedsheet, seeking my hand. I grasped hers tightly.

"Your compulsion would have worn off by that time, Molly. You didn't kill him."

"That's what Owen said, and I want to believe that. But he wouldn't have been there if I hadn't sent him away."

Nana cocked her head. "Owen knows about this?"

"I told him only last night. I've been so ashamed."

"You've kept this to yourself all this time. It's why you left, isn't it?"

I nodded. "That and the house bothered me. Every time I passed their bedroom, this room"—I glanced around—"I saw that image of Mom in Dad's lap. I'm sorry I left, and I'm sorry I closed my mind to you."

"You poor girl." She patted my hand. "I closed my mind to you first. Don't you remember?"

I slowly nodded. We'd closed our minds to each other. Guilt closed off mine, but I didn't understand Nana's reasons.

"Why *did* you shut me out?"

She slid her hand from mine and twisted the covers. "We all did things that night we regret."

A chill rippled through me. Something about her tone. "What did you do?"

Her throat convulsed. She shook her head.

"Dinner's served," Owen announced, entering the room. He carried a tray of food.

"Perfect timing. I'm famished." Nana smoothed the sheet she'd worried.

Owen adjusted the tray over Nana's lap, and she clapped her hands together. "I haven't had a handsome man bring me dinner in bed since . . . never," she teased, and winked at Owen.

He chuckled, and I caught a blush deepening the color over his cheekbones. "The good thing about Mary's cooking," he said to me over his shoulder, "is there are always leftovers in the fridge."

"Lamb is much better the second day. Don't you think so, Owen?"

"I sure do."

Nana picked up her utensils, but lacked the strength to slice into her meat. The knife sawed back and forth without progress. She raised the utensils from her plate and tightened her hands around them.

Owen gently rested his hands over hers. "Allow me."

"If the gentleman insists . . ."

"I do." He took the utensils and cut her food.

She was weak and helpless, a shell of the independent and vibrant woman she'd once been. I turned my gaze away. It was too hard to watch her. I already missed the woman I'd known as a child.

Another gust rattled the windows, and an odd feeling settled inside me. Nana's time was short. She didn't have months or weeks left. More like days.

Just like me.

My gaze circled the room, landing on the doorway as my thoughts went out to Cassie. It was likely she could lose us both within a very short time.

I couldn't let that happen.

Owen backed away from the bed and rested his hand on my shoulder, coaxing me to look up at him, his expression concerned. "You okay?"

I frowned. "I don't know."

"Go eat. There's a plate for you downstairs."

I nodded and rose from the chair. I didn't have the strength to object.

He gave me a quick hug and whispered in my ear. "I'll stay with Mary while she eats."

I nodded again and left the room.

Chapter 25

Wednesday, evening

Every muscle in my body ached as I went downstairs. The railing kept me upright, but when I reached the bottom, I sank onto the last step and dropped my forehead on my knees. Rain tapped the porch on the other side of the front door. The rhythmic patter soothed me, and my eyelids grew heavy, my weary mind drifting to Nana. I sensed her cancer was more advanced than she'd let on. She'd pushed herself these last days, entertaining friends and mentoring Cassie. She didn't want to look or act like a sick and dying woman.

The hallway floor creaked, and air stirred around me. I lifted my head. Cassie stood toe-to-toe with me. She clasped my cheeks, her hands warm on my face. "Why are your colors sad?"

I debated telling her about Nana, but she was already too afraid for me. She didn't need to know, not yet.

I twirled a finger in the hair falling over her chest. "I'm fine, honey. Just tired."

She patted my shoulders. "You need to eat dinner and go to bed."

A smile cracked my face. "Yes, ma'am." I stood slowly and noticed my shoulder bag on the floor by the coatrack. "Shall we call Grace now?"

"Yes!" She clapped her hands and bounced on her toes.

I grabbed my bag, dug out the phone, and sat back down. There were two missed calls and one voicemail from Jane. I ignored them and dialed information to get the number to Grace's hospital.

"Hello?" Alice Kaling answered after the hospital's operator transferred me to Grace's room.

"Alice, it's Molly. Cassie's mom."

Alice gave an uneasy laugh. "This is so weird. I had just picked up my cell to call you."

"Principal Harrison told me that you wanted to speak with me," I began. I scratched my temple with my index fingernail. "How's Grace?"

"Exceptionally well, given the circumstances. We didn't know"— she stopped and cleared her throat—"we didn't know about the helmet. Cassie scared her into wearing it. If she hadn't . . ." She pushed out a deep breath. The sound of air rattled through the phone. "I'm sorry."

"You don't have to apologize. I understand."

"Grace will be released tomorrow. Her head scans came back negative. She'll be back in school Monday with a few scrapes and bruises and a hot-pink cast." Alice gave a choked laugh.

"I'm happy to hear that." I parked an elbow on my knee and rested my forehead in my hand.

"Molly, I . . ."

Alice grew quiet, and I imagined her pausing in the middle of the hospital room where she paced, looking down at her daughter, awed she'd survived the accident.

"You don't need to tell me."

"No, I do. Your daughter . . . Cassie saved Grace. She saved her," she repeated in a low voice heavy with emotion. "I can't wrap my head around how Cassie knew about the accident, but I'm so thankful she did. You have a gifted daughter. She's welcome in our home anytime. Grace misses her, and I . . . I think I now understand why Cassie acted out. It's a hard age. You can't find the right words, or you don't know how to communicate them. People don't listen to you, or worse, they don't believe you. I swear, Molly, we'll listen if Cassie sees Grace's future again."

"Thank you," I said in a strained whisper as I swiped a finger under each eye. Cassie rubbed my shoulder. I clutched her hand and held on.

"Is Cassie with you?" Alice asked. "Grace wants to say hello."

"She's right here." I said good-bye to Alice and handed Cassie the phone.

She squealed and walked into the parlor. "Hi, Grace!" She paced around the couch as they talked about everything, from Owen's crazy, big dogs to her Susie chef skills and the icky homework they had to do next week, to designing new outfits for their dolls.

I didn't have the heart to tell her she might not be at her old school on Monday. Nana needed us.

The stairs creaked behind me. Owen sat beside me and set the tray on the floor at our feet.

"Nana asleep?" I asked.

"Yep."

"She doesn't have much time left."

"No, she doesn't." His tone was void of emotion. He'd known her since he was a boy. Her death would to be hard on him, too.

"I think she's going to go quick."

He put his arm around me. "I think you're right."

Cassie's high-pitched giggle drew our attention. A closed-lip smile curved my mouth. "She did it. She used her skills to save someone."

It occurred to me Nana had been right: instructing Cassie to harness her visions gave her the skills to focus on those premonitions that helped people.

She needed a good role model, someone who went out of his way to help people.

Owen rubbed my back. "Cassie's a good kid."

"I wish I'd had her confidence at her age."

He tilted his head and looked at me. "Funny, I was thinking the exact opposite. She reminds me a lot of you."

He picked up the tray and stood. "I'll heat up your plate. Come eat."

Owen went into the kitchen to prepare dinner. I returned my bag to its spot on the floor by the coatrack. My arm grazed Nana's coat.

I stared at the coat and clicked my tongue. Ten clicks before I snatched the lapels and held the coat at arm's length. Instinct told me to leave the coat there, to avoid the hall closet. Nana would put it away later.

Still, I pushed on, taking long strides down the hallway.

I'd peeked inside the closet earlier during my search for Cassie. No one had shoved me inside and locked the door. Thinking of Cassie, and of her bravery and determination this week, even when she was scared, I yanked open the door and hung the coat on a hanger, stuffing the sleeves between a rain slicker and a thick sweater. Then I stood there, facing down the small, cramped space. That was when I noticed the light fixture on the ceiling.

Skimming my hand along the wall and under a coat sleeve, I found the switch. LED light flooded the closet. It never had to be dark in here again.

My thumb absently rubbed the doorknob. I inspected the knob. There was no lock.

Stepping into the closet, I closed the door behind me. Sweat blossomed under my breasts, and a chill tiptoed across my skin. But the walls didn't close in. It wasn't pitch black. I didn't panic because I could get out when I wanted to leave.

My legs buckled. I slid to the floor and laughed.

"Molly?" I heard Owen call me, my name muffled through the door.

My laugh morphed into a cry. He must think me crazy.

Under my legs I felt the floor vibrate. Shoes shuffled outside. Knuckles lightly rapped the door.

"Molly? You in there?"

"Yes." I swiped away the dampness on my cheeks.

He opened the door. I looked up, and he looked down. I smiled awkwardly at him. His brows arched high. "What are you doing?" He lowered to his heels.

"You put a light in here."

He nodded.

"There's no lock on the door."

He shook his head.

I took a calming breath. "Thank you."

Something passed between us. A level of understanding. He inclined his head before looking at me again. "You're welcome."

"Both you and Nana have made this house feel like a home to me." The home it had been meant to be.

"Good. That's what Mary wanted." He flashed a smile. "So did I."

"Why are you in the closet?" Cassie asked, coming up to stand behind Owen. She propped fists on her hips and scowled. "Are you playing hide-and-seek without me?"

I snorted. Laughter burst from my chest.

Owen grabbed Cassie and dragged her across his lap. He tickled her.

Cassie squealed and kicked her legs. Her giggly, bubbly laughter filled my heart and warmed my soul as only a daughter could. As I watched them together, I thought how Owen would make a wonderful father someday.

My head eased back against the wall, my heart growing heavy with melancholy and regret. I wouldn't be the mother of his child.

Perhaps, though, he might consider becoming a father to mine.

Owen and I ate dinner while Cassie watched TV. Afterward, I helped her get ready for bed. Then Owen read a story to her and Bunny—Cassie's request. I watched them from the doorway and felt a tug. Something about how Cassie was drawn to Owen spoke to the maternal side of me. I'd never seen her warm to another adult as quickly.

The same with Owen. He seemed at ease around her. Interacting with children wasn't foreign to him, and I wondered about his time spent in Mexico at the orphanage. I thought of Enrique. How Owen had loved and then lost him.

The backs of my eyes burned, and my throat rippled with unshed emotion. Hopefully Owen would consider raising Cassie. Perhaps someday he'd love her as much as he'd loved Enrique.

Pulling myself away, I went to check on Nana. She slept under the glow of her mustard-yellow aura and the street lamps reflecting off the low clouds. I closed the drapes, smoothed her blankets, and held her hand. Her flesh was cool. Gentle snores rippled through the room. I kissed her forehead and left the room.

Downstairs, I lit the fire. Owen came into the room a short time later and collapsed in Nana's favorite chair. Frankie popped into his lap.

"Is Cassie asleep yet?" I asked, and poured him a glass of scotch.

"Not yet. I gave her a pocket flashlight. She's reading to Bunny under the covers." He stroked the cat, who kneaded his jeans.

"I'll go up in a moment and say good night." I capped the bottle. "What time do you leave in the morning?"

"Early." He yawned and rubbed his face. "I have to go home soon and prep. I'm a speaker at one of the sessions."

"Cassie and I'll let the dogs out in the morning." I gave Owen the scotch. My hand shook, shifting the ice.

He looked up. "What's this for?"

"You. It's been a long day."

"Where's yours?" He took the glass. "You need one more than me."

I shook my head. "I'm fine."

He sipped the scotch. I rubbed my hands. His right brow rose over the rim of his glass. "What?" he asked, and drank again.

I squeezed my hands tight together and took a deep breath. "I want you to adopt Cassie."

Chapter 26

Wednesday, night

Owen choked back his scotch. He coughed. Frankie leaped off his lap and ran from the room.

"What?" His voice was thin. He coughed again.

I should have waited until he'd swallowed.

"Will you adopt Cassie if I die?"

His face hardened. He held my gaze for several breaths. Flames popped in the fireplace. Firelight flickered in the grays of his eyes. "What happened to not giving up? Have you changed your mind?"

"No, of course not," I quickly replied. "But Nana is the primary guardian on the will Dave's drafting for me, and I need to change that. I don't have anyone else to consider."

Owen lifted his face to the ceiling. "God, Molly. I'm sorry." He dragged a hand through his hair. The ends stood up. "You scared me, that's all."

"I'm scared, too," I confessed. "But I have to be realistic about this. With Nana this sick, I can't leave her alone, and she's not going to leave the house." This was her home, and she'd want to stay here, not at an assisted living facility, and not at my rental. It was starting to dawn on me why she'd put so much money into the remodel. She knew she wouldn't be around much longer, but for the time she was, she wanted me comfortable while I stayed with her. And then she'd want me comfortable enough to live here permanently when I'd inherit it. She loved this house.

"I can't leave Pacific Grove by Friday like I'd planned. And Friday is—"

"—the last day in the cycle. Do you think Cassie's nightmares will stop and the premonition is done if you avoid getting near the water and you survive Friday?" As he spoke, he set the scotch on the side table. He stood.

"I sure hope so," I said, my gaze following him up. I was anxious to get past this week. Nana needed me. Cassie needed me.

I need Owen.

The thought hurtled through my weary mind. After years of doing everything on my own, and being alone, I longed for someone's support. *His support.*

"I also can't take any chances," I explained. "If, by some freak accident, I wind up at the beach and drown, Cassie needs someone to care for her. Phoebe is my secondary. I know she'd do everything within her means to give Cassie a happy and stable upbringing, but she's already stretched thin. Cassie likes you, and you seem to like her, and I like seeing the two of you together." So much so that I agonized that I wouldn't be around to watch them.

"I know what I'm asking for is a lot. Taking on a child is a huge responsibility, so think about it. I mean, don't take too long. I have to tell Dave by tomorrow afternoon, but will you at least consider my request? Cassie is a wonderful girl, and most of the time she's even-tempered. You'll have to help with homework once in a while, and attend her school activities.

"Besides," I paused, gathering courage for what I really wanted to tell him, "you'd make the perfect father for her."

"I would?" he asked with surprised wonderment.

"You're kind, and giving, and patient. Well, for the most part." A teasing smile touched the corner of my mouth. "And you have so much love to give," I added, thinking of Enrique, and wishing with all my heart he'd share some of that love with Cassie. Should something happen to me, I didn't want her to grow up wondering whether or not she'd been loved. My father hadn't been able to love me the way a father should. I didn't want Cassie to experience that.

I grasped both of his hands and held them against my chest, over my heart. "If my circumstances had been different," I continued with a passionate whisper, desperate for him to understand, "I'd have wanted you to be the father of my children."

"Molly." He rested his forehead against mine. "You're killing me."

"Please say yes." I released his hands, skimmed mine over his shoulders, cradled his neck. "Please."

Owen buried his fingers in my hair, keeping our foreheads pressed together. We stood that way for some time, not moving, simply sharing the air between us.

After a long moment, he swallowed. I felt the ripple under my fingertips, and then he whispered, "Yes."

"Yes?" I pulled back slightly. My eyes searched his. "You'll be her primary guardian?"

"There was a time once, I thought we'd get married. I told you that, remember?"

I nodded. "I remember."

"Cassie's *your* daughter, Molly. If only for that alone, I'll watch over her."

"Thank you." I clung to his wrists. "Thank you so much."

He enfolded me in his arms and dropped a kiss on my head. "I'll watch over Nana, too." He breathed into my hair.

God, he was amazing. I squeezed my eyes tight and hugged him just as tightly. Listening to the steady rhythm of his heartbeat, I wondered how I'd ever walked away from him, and how I'd ever told him I didn't love him.

Because I did love him. Very much so.

$$\sim\hspace{-0.3em}\textgreek{9}$$

Owen stepped from our embrace, and I immediately felt his withdrawal and his mood drop a few degrees. He rubbed his face and picked up his scotch.

"What's wrong?"

He shook his head, taking interest in the liquor he swirled. "Nothing. You mentioned you wanted to say good night to Cassie. I'll go clean the dinner dishes." He walked over to the sink and set the scotch glass aside. Facing the counter, he gripped the ledge and lowered his head. I fought the urge to go to him, because I couldn't tell him everything would be all right. I had no idea what would happen between now and the end of Friday. Turning away, I went upstairs.

Under Cassie's thick cover I found a brightly lit flashlight and a fast-asleep daughter. I turned off the light, setting it and her book aside on the table, and adjusted the covers under her chin. The glow of her night-light illuminated the soft lines of her face. Tracing those lines, the rise of her nose, the curve of her jaw, and the jut of her chin, I committed each dip and angle to memory. Then I sent out a silent prayer that I would be blessed enough to see this face grow into the beautiful woman I knew she'd become.

"Good night, Cassie." I bent over and kissed her cheek, then left the room.

Owen was waiting for me at the bottom of the stairs. My step faltered as I caught his sullen expression. He watched me descend.

I stopped two steps up from him, our gazes level. His eyes, red-rimmed, searched mine.

"Owen?" I asked, concerned. "What's bothering you?"

He gripped the banister by my hand, which brought him a couple of inches closer. "I don't want to lose you."

My mouth angled downward. "I know."

"I already lost you once, and I refuse to lose you again."

He moved up one step so I had to tilt my head to look up at him. A glint of determination brightened his gray eyes, highlighting the blue specks. Looking into them was like watching the blue sky peek through the clouds when a storm broke.

"I have a plan," he said.

"A plan?" I asked cautiously.

"The don't-let-Molly-out-of-your-sight plan."

"The what?"

He moved his hand over mine. "The way I figure it, if you can get through Friday, you're in the clear. We need to make sure between now and then you're always with someone. We'll help you stay away from the water. You'll also be less inclined, or tempted"—he gave me a look—"to go to the beach.

"Hang out with Phoebe tomorrow," he suggested. "Call Sadie to stay with Mary while you go to Dave's office, and have Phoebe go with you. Better yet, have her drive.

"And tonight"—he leaned in close—"I'll stay with you."

My chest rose sharply. "Owen." I started shaking my head.

"Invite me upstairs, Molly." His lips swept over mine. "Let me stay. Let *me* keep you safe."

He kissed me again, and this time I kissed him right back. My hand slid over his shoulder, and my fingers traced the edge of his collar.

"Molly." He breathed against my mouth. "Tell me yes."

He wanted to stay, and he wanted to keep me safe. He would protect my family should I not survive Friday. And he loved me.

But just as important, I loved him.

How could I say no?

"Yes." I kissed him as my mind cried out with relief. I wasn't in this fight for my life alone.

"Yes," I said again, deepening the kiss. I was so tired of being alone and on my own.

Owen groaned and lifted his head. His gaze locked with mine, and his hand clasped my fingers. I wanted to be with him tonight as much as he wanted me. Wordlessly, with my pulse pounding and my limbs shaking, I followed him upstairs.

Inside my room, we turned to each other. I nestled my face in his neck, his skin warm and his scent fresh like the outdoors, and he whispered my name. My gaze flitted to the hallway. "Cassie—"

"—will never know I'm here."

And he was here, with me.

His gray eyes, vibrant with flecks of blue, raised to meet my green ones. I pressed closer against him. "Kiss me."

Without taking his eyes from me, Owen closed and locked the door. Then his lips were on mine. We quickly shed our clothes, making our way across the room. He tossed a condom on the nightstand, then we tumbled into bed.

A dull glow from the bay window reflected off his cheekbones, deepening the angles. He braced his forearms by my head and kissed the tender spot where my jawline met my ear. His eyes, heated in the semidarkness, found mine. He smiled. "Hi."

I smiled back. "Hi." Despite his weight on me, I felt light, loved.

His fingertips traced the lines of my face, his hand trembling, and his expression turned serious. My heart pounded faster, and I rested a hand on his cheek. "What's wrong?"

"I'm just . . ." He hesitated, a note of vulnerability in his tone. He frowned slightly and laid a hand over my heart. "Are you feeling this? Us?"

I wanted to crawl inside him, and I didn't want the night to end. "Yes." I breathed the word, combed my fingers through his hair, and brought his face toward mine.

"Good, because this is us. It's always been like this for us."

And I'd missed the feeling of us, together, entwined.

Our hands flowed everywhere, lips following, as we relearned each angle and sensitive curve. Then he was moving over me—the tear of foil, a ripple of noise—and then he was moving in me.

His teeth skimmed my ear, and his fingers pressed into the soft flesh of my hip. "Together, Molly. This is us together, and we'll work on us together."

I held him to me and sent up a silent prayer. I wanted more time and I wanted to live past Friday. Because I wanted the same thing as Owen. Another chance to work on us.

It was eleven thirty when Owen went home to prep for the conference. He had to be up by four and on the road before five. Traffic would be heavy going into San Jose.

After locking the door behind him with the promise that I'd call Phoebe over first thing in the morning, I closed up the rest of the house, turning off lights and checking doors. I then looked in on Cassie again.

She shifted under her covers, mumbling, "Sit. Stay. Heel," dreaming about the dog commands Owen had shared with her earlier in the day.

I straightened the covers and kissed her forehead.

"Night-night, Mommy," she murmured in her sleep.

"Good night, Cassie," I whispered and left the room.

Rather than going to my bed, I slipped into Nana's room and stretched out alongside her like I'd done on many nights when I had been young. We'd talked about my class field trips to the aquarium or the glass I'd discovered that day at the beach. She'd always wanted to know what Phoebe and I had been up to, and somehow she'd convinced me to confess our latest antics, bribing me with a trip to the Ghirardelli Ice Cream & Chocolate Shop. Then she'd read to me.

But tonight was different. Nana was asleep, and she was dying. I wanted to be with her.

As I watched her sleep, I slipped my hand under hers. She stirred, and her fingers clutched mine. Before I lost the nerve, before she became aware I was with her, I reached for her mind. A light touch, like when I tapped Cassie's door, thinking she was asleep, and didn't want to disturb her.

But it didn't matter how lightly I treaded. Nana's walls were up again. They shoved me back into my head.

She opened her eyes, the whites bright in the dark room.

"I'm sorry." Invading another person's mind without their permission was worse than reading their diary, according to Mom.

She shook her head. "Don't be." Then she yawned.

"I'm so tired I can't sleep," Nana murmured. She rolled over and turned on the bedside lamp. Her movements were slow and measured, as if lifting her arm was an effort. She shifted to her back and dragged a book across her stomach. "Read to me."

I took the book, a compilation of spiritual poems and essays. A rainbow-yarn braid poked from the top. I opened the marked page and tentatively touched the wool, almost expecting it to fall apart under my fingers. The edges were frayed and unraveling. I made a small noise in the back of my throat. "You still have this." Mom used to make them from Nana's yarn scraps.

"I've kept them all." Nana lifted her arm, wincing as she pointed to her dresser. "Top drawer in the red shoe box. They're fun to look at." She sighed. "Will you read to me?"

I scooted into a sitting position. "Do you want water?" I asked before starting. "Any medicine?"

She shook her head. "Just read, please."

"All right." And so I began.

I must have drifted to sleep a few pages later, because the ceiling suddenly came into focus as if my eyes had popped open. I was instantly wide awake. The book I'd been reading was facedown on my chest. Beside me Nana dozed. The rain had stopped, and the wind had died.

I glanced at the clock and frowned. 3:01 a.m. Every cell in my body was on instant alert, fully charged like I'd drunk a dozen coffees and run a marathon. Why was I awake?

My heart pounded, and my leg, which hung over the bed edge, started bouncing. I felt anxious and edgy, like I'd get when I dropped Cassie off at school, watching the way she ducked her head to avoid the piercing stares and wary glances of her peers.

Thoughts of Cassie brought an overwhelming urge to look in on her. As I rose from the bed, the compulsion grew stronger. I had to check on my daughter.

Something wasn't right.

Chapter 27

Thursday, predawn

Cassie's room was eerily quiet and too dark. The bulb in her night-light had blown. A dull light stole through the slats in the window blinds from the streetlight outside, outlining Cassie's silhouette. She sat upright in the middle of her bed.

"Cass?" I whispered.

She didn't reply, but kicked her sheets.

I turned on the bedside lamp. "Why are you awake, honey . . . oh my God!"

Cassie clawed her throat, leaving thin red lines. Her mouth hung open, and her eyes bulged. They were glassy, unseeing, and she wasn't making a sound.

She looked like she was drowning. She *was* drowning!

"Cassidy!" I screamed. "Breathe!"

Her nails scratched her throat, and her legs pedaled under the sheets. I pulled her hands away and clutched her face. "It's a dream. Breathe, baby! *BREATHE!*" The compulsion shot from my lungs.

She blinked. Her pupils shrank to small black dots, and she focused on my mouth.

"You can breathe. It's just a dream. Please breathe."

She gripped my wrists and inhaled. Long and deep, the sound raspy and dry.

"*AGAIN!*" I ordered.

She dragged in another breath. Her back arched as she inhaled, and her shoulders bowed on the exhale. When she inhaled again, I watched her expression change as she became aware of her surroundings and what was happening to her. Her glassy eyes sheened, and her mouth twisted.

Without the tea, the nightmares had come back, and like her previous visions, an echo of the premonition had stayed behind after she woke. Only this one wasn't a migraine or a sore leg. Cassie had stopped breathing. She could have died, which was probably why Nana had given her the tea in the first place. No wonder it was dangerous for her not to drink the tea.

Guilt clawed inside me the way Cassie had been clawing her throat. How had I failed to consider this could happen?

She started shaking. Tears spilled down her cheeks, leaving wet splotches on her nightgown. Her lips trembled. "Mommy?" she cried. "I'm scared."

I was terrified. I pulled her from the bed and onto my lap. We rocked on the floor. "I'm so sorry," I murmured in her ear. "I'm so sorry."

Twenty minutes passed before Cassie's crying eased. I thought of the tea blend downstairs. It wouldn't do any good. The nightmares had already come tonight. Milk was better. I'd give her a glass, and then we could watch TV together until we fell asleep on the couch, like we'd done many nights these last months. Tomorrow night, which should be the last of the nightmares for her premonition about me, I'd give her the tea. The risk to Cassie was too great not to, as was the risk to not fulfill the premonition. I had no proof one way or the other whether avoiding water through Friday altered the outcome of the premonition or only delayed it from happening. If the latter, the longer I put it off, the more nights I'd have to give Cassie the tea. God forbid I forget to give it to her one night.

My eyes drifted closed, and I held Cassie tight as my mind absorbed what had to be done. Grace had survived her accident without extensive head injuries because of her new bike helmet, but the car had still hit her. Only after the accident happened had Cassie's nightmares of Grace ceased. It had been the same with Ethan and the swing. Nightmares about him had stopped once he broke his leg.

This meant one thing.

I had to drown. It was the only way I knew how to stop Cassie's nightmares of me.

I smoothed the hair from her face. "Look at me, honey. I'm going to say something very important, and I need you to listen."

She lifted her chin, sucked in a sob, and hiccupped.

"People survive drownings, so I need to figure out what will help me survive."

She inhaled hoarsely, her lower lip flapping, and turned in my lap. Rising to her knees, she hugged me hard. "I want to help. Will you let me help you?"

"Yes. We'll think of ideas together. Is that a good plan?"

Cassie nodded, and I crossed my fingers that I had my own version of a bike helmet and that I would come out on the other side of this intact. Or in my case, alive.

Cassie and I slept little through the remainder of the night. Curled in bed, we whispered about possible plans, from finding another life vest to locking all the doors and windows to keep me inside. I had no intention of going anywhere near the beach, though I did wonder how I would end up in the water. Various scenarios sifted through my mind like sand through fingers as I considered the plausibility of each one, from Nana sleepwalking out of the house to my car plunging over the side of the road.

As Cassie finally settled into sleep, a calm acceptance settled over me like a warm blanket. While I hoped there would be someone nearby who could rescue and resuscitate me, there was the chance that wherever and however my drowning occurred, I'd be alone.

A text message from Owen buzzed through at five a.m.

```
Message me when you get up. Need to know
you're OK.
```

Outside my window, I heard the low rumble of a car engine warming up. Owen was leaving.

My skin prickled along my arms. I wanted to cry with relief at his determination to get me through Friday unscathed, and I wanted to weep in sorrow. I couldn't let his plan work. There was too great a risk to Cassie for me not to drown.

Another text buzzed in.

```
We'll get through this, Lollipop.
Together. OK?
```

The corners of my mouth eased upward at seeing my nickname in type. But a weight quickly settled on my chest, directly over my heart. Owen might lose me again, and after all these years, I had to admit I didn't want to lose him either. Could we really work through my fears of his safety around me? Could I learn how to control my abilities, like Cassie was learning with hers? Or would the possibility always be there that I could lose control, like an alcoholic around liquor, and issue a compulsion that endangered Owen's life?

I may never have the chance to find out.

I sent a reply.

OK.

I could at least be hopeful.

And with that thought, I sent him another.

Definitely. Together.

Rolling onto my side, I spooned Cassie's petite frame. Owen revved his motor and then drove away, the motor fading off to nothing, taking my heart with him.

Several hours later, I went downstairs to fix breakfast. While the oatmeal cooked, I contacted Phoebe. She picked up after the first ring. Danica cried in the background. A kids' show blared from the other room, the voices high-pitched and cartoonish.

"Will you be home today?" I asked after she greeted me.

She snorted. "When am I not? I'm a slave to the minions who live here. Please tell me you're coming to save me from this madness."

"Actually, I was hoping you could come here. Nana's not feeling well and I'd love to see you. I have a quick errand to run this afternoon, but maybe we can go to the aquarium beforehand." The outing would keep Cassie's mind off tomorrow.

Phoebe yelled at Kurt and I pulled the phone from my ear until she came back on the line. She made a grunt of disapproval. "That boy . . . ," she bemoaned. "Yes, that sounds awesome. What time?"

The oatmeal bubbled over and I leaped for the pot. "Ten?" I suggested, turning off the stove. I moved the pot to another burner.

"Perfect. See you then," she agreed.

After our call, I arranged a tray with the oatmeal, juice, and tea, and took breakfast upstairs to Nana. She was returning from the bathroom when I entered the room. I set the tray on the dresser and hurried to assist her.

"Why are you out of bed?"

She batted my hands away. "Can't an old lady pee without you fussing?"

"All right, all right." I held up my hands and stepped aside.

She moved slowly to the bay window and eased into the rocking chair. I opened the curtains. The blush was back in her cheeks, her eyes rested and alert. "You look better this morning."

Her gaze danced over me. "I look better than you for sure. Long night?"

Thinking she'd heard Cassie's early-morning cries and that I looked like I hadn't slept, I patted my head, running fingers through my hair like a comb. I hadn't checked myself in a mirror yet. Then I noticed Nana's expression. Her eyes sparkled. Mine drifted to the wall our rooms shared, and my face heated.

Her shoulders shook with silent laughter. "Owen's a nice young man. I'm glad you found each other again."

We won't be together for long, though. My eyes drifted to the floor. I cleared my throat and retrieved the breakfast tray. "What's on your agenda today? Lots of bed rest?" I transferred the oatmeal and drinks to the table beside the rocker.

She leaned over and peered inside the bowl. She scrunched her nose. "I'm dying and you bring me oats?"

My shoulders dropped. "I'm sorry. Let me fix you something else. Eggs?"

"Och! I'm teasing, Molly dear." She moved her cereal out of reach when I tried to take the bowl. She ate a bite, smacking her tongue against the roof of her mouth. "It's a tad pasty."

I twisted my fingers. "Sorry. I think I overcooked it."

She grunted. "You're so serious this morning. Stop fidgeting. You should be relaxed. You got laid last night."

My jaw dropped. "Nana!"

"More than once, I might add." She brushed off my appalled look when I glanced at the thin wall between our rooms. "Stop apologizing and stop treating me like an invalid. I have cancer. I'm dying. It's not the end of the world."

But it is *the end for you. And me.*

Nana dropped her spoon. It clanged loudly on the floor.

I swore and apologized again.

"I sense your fears, Molly." Her hands shook. "Don't worry. You won't die. You're too stubborn."

"How do you know? Cassie saw me." I picked up the spoon and cleaned it with a napkin. "Her nightmares came back last night. I didn't give her the tea." Guilt burrowed deep in my chest. "Her reaction to the nightmare scared me to death. She couldn't breathe."

Nana inclined her head. She stirred the oatmeal. "It's not your fault. I should have mentioned something like that may occur, given what happened to her with the other premonitions. It's been so difficult to focus lately." She tapped her forehead, referring to the mass inside her head.

"Still, that should have occurred to me." I unfolded a blanket across her lap and pulled a clean set of pajamas from the dresser.

She pushed the blanket off. "Sun's out. I'm gardening. And you're not stopping me." She shook a finger at me.

I yanked off the bedsheets. "Fine, go ahead and garden." I shook a pillow from its case. "But promise you'll take it easy."

"Only if you stop dwelling on the ridiculous notion you're going to die. The only person dying around here is me."

I wished I had Nana's confidence, but I pasted on a stiff grin for her benefit.

"That's more like it. You have a beautiful daughter and a delicious-looking man."

She polished off her oatmeal as I finished making her bed, then I left the room at her insistence. She wanted to change in privacy, said I was hovering too much.

Cassie was climbing out of bed when I entered my room. She ran over to me and hugged my waist, pressing her ear to my rib cage.

I kissed her head. "Let's eat breakfast, then go let the dogs out. Auntie Phoebe is coming over. I think we might go to the aquarium. Would you like that?"

She tilted her head back and beamed. "Yes."

"Good, come on. We have lots to do today."

Chapter 28

Thursday, morning

It was after nine when Cassie and I made it over to Owen's to let out his dogs. Typically, Mudd and Dirt spent the days outside. There was a doggie door in the side garage door that gave them access to the water and beds Owen kept there. But with the faulty gate latch still in need of repair, Owen didn't want the dogs outside unattended.

Cassie and I made our way through the side gate, closing it hard to ensure the latch connected, and went into the garage. I found the spare key Owen kept inside a plastic container of bolts on his workbench. Hearing noise in the garage, Mudd and Dirt barked from the other side of the door into the house. Paws scratched at the base while I worked the lock. When I opened the door, the dogs fought for space to get out, greeting Cassie first. They squirmed around her legs, bouncing her back and forth between them like a Ping-Pong ball. She dropped to her knees in a fit of giggles, rubbing their bellies and kissing their snouts.

Mudd lifted his head and sniffed the air. His ears perked. He looked at me and let out a sharp bark. I rubbed his head, scratching behind the ears, then patted my thighs, encouraging him to follow me outside. He bounded over, gave my hand a wet-nosed swipe, and trotted into the backyard. Dirt dogged behind him.

Cassie came to stand beside me. I rested a hand on her shoulder. "What do you think of Mudd and Dirt?"

"They're filthy." Cassie giggled, pointing at Mudd, who pranced through a puddle along the back fence.

"Yes, they are." They definitely lived up to their names.

After the dogs did their duty and we played catch, I herded them into the garage to clean their feet and lock them back inside the house.

"We'll come back at six to feed them and let them out again," I told Cassie, slamming the gate behind us.

"Look!" She pointed at a minivan parking behind my car. "It's Aunt Pheebs!"

Phoebe stepped from the minivan, and Cassie ran to meet her. She squealed and raced into Phoebe's outstretched arms.

"Is it ten already?" I asked when I reached the sidewalk.

"Yes, it is." Phoebe clicked the key fob and the minivan's side door opened. Danica slept in her car seat, and Kurt waved from his booster. "I've got four hours before school pickup time," she explained. "If we're doing the aquarium and your little errand, we've got to go now."

Cassie swung her linked hand with Phoebe. "Will there be dolphins?"

Phoebe briefly looked skyward as if thinking. "Don't think so, but there will be sharks and manatees—"

"And jellyfish?"

"Loads."

"Awesome. Let's go." Cassie climbed into the minivan and settled on the rear bench. "Hi, Kurt."

"'Ello!" he replied around his binky.

Phoebe walked to the driver's side. "You coming?"

"Let me tell Mary we're leaving and get my purse."

Finished with her morning gardening, Nana sat before the fire-place knitting. Frankie lay curled at her feet. He opened an eye when I entered the room, and finding me uninteresting, stretched his limbs and rolled onto his side, exposing his belly to the fire's heat.

"Cassie and I are going with Phoebe and her kids to the aquarium. Will you be all right or should I call Sadie to come stay with you?"

She gave me a funny look. "I don't need a babysitter."

"Nana," I warned.

"Go, go. I'm fine." She set her knitting aside and sipped tea. The folds between her brows deepened.

"Your headache is back."

"Which is why I'm resting. Granddaughter's orders." She gave me a smile over the teacup rim.

I held her gaze for a long moment.

"Please, go," she encouraged.

"All right," I said, relenting. "We won't be gone long. I'll make din-ner tonight." I kissed her head and ran upstairs to collect the sea glass necklace I'd put aside for Phoebe, the one that matched the earrings I'd given her on Monday. I also selected a few other items I hadn't taken with me to Ocean's Artistry.

I moved through the Monterey Bay Aquarium without bothering to read the exhibit boards, and half listened to the presentations. The sea life didn't capture my attention, but Cassie's reaction to them did. I couldn't take my eyes from her, fascinated with every move she made. The way she frowned while she read the exhibit signs to Kurt, or how she stood on her toes to look at the fish even though her view was unobstructed. How she twisted the hair around her finger and chewed her bottom lip as she listened to the aquarium guide. Phoebe tried to engage me in conversation while the kids' attention was elsewhere, but

I didn't have the energy or interest. All my attention was focused on the daughter who might lose me tomorrow.

By the time we reached Ghirardelli and were seated at a table with our ice cream, Phoebe shoved her sundae aside and leaned over the table. "That's it," she whisper-yelled. She flapped her hands between us. "Give it up. What's going on with you?"

Danica nursed a bottle. Cassie and Kurt delved into their sundaes. I retrieved the sea glass necklace coiled inside a clear plastic bag from my purse and slid it across the table toward Phoebe.

"Oh! It's gorgeous," she exclaimed, momentarily distracted. She opened the bag and pulled out the necklace. The wire-wrapped key lime sea glass pendant spun on a thin silver chain. She slipped it over her head, where the matching earrings swung from her lobes.

I aligned several more pieces, each tucked inside its own plastic jewelry bag, on the table.

"What's this?" she asked.

"For you." I dropped my hands in my lap, my gaze fixed on the jewelry so she wouldn't see my pained expression.

Phoebe selected a foam-pink ring. "I can't take these. Why are you giving me these?"

Her voice had an edge to it, drawing my face upward. She stiffened when she saw my expression. Her eyes widened. "First all the stuff about your will, and now you're giving away all your shit. You're scaring me."

I motioned for Phoebe to scoot toward me. I leaned closer. "You remember my mom and those odd things she could do?"

"The fortune-telling things?"

I nodded slowly and Phoebe mimicked, bobbing her head. "What about it?"

My gaze swung to Cassie.

Phoebe sucked in a breath. "Cassie?"

"Is like my mom."

"When did this start?" Phoebe said in a loud whisper.

I motioned for her to lower her voice. "A few months ago. That's why she's on suspension. She had visions about a couple of her friends. One was pretty gruesome, and she really upset the girl when she told her."

Phoebe's mouth turned downward. "Poor Cassie."

"It hasn't been easy. But Monday . . ." I paused, watching my daughter as she gave Kurt a taste of her ice cream. My heart went out to her, longing for more time, for more moments like this I could witness. "On Monday she had a vision about me."

Phoebe's brows creased. "You? What did she see?"

"Me, dying. It's supposed to happen tomorrow."

Phoebe gawked at me. Danica dropped her bottle. She wailed. Phoebe blinked. She bent over and picked up the bottle, giving it back to Danica.

"How?"

"I drown."

"The beach?"

"I think so."

Phoebe tossed up her hands. "Well, that's a no-brainer. Stay away from the water."

"That was the plan." I closed my eyes and let out a tortured sigh. "Cassie's premonitions have a weird side effect, though, emotional and physical. She gets nightmares about them, and the nightmares recur until the premonition is fulfilled. During the nightmare, and for a few seconds after she wakes, she experiences the same physical pain as the people in her visions. She dreamed about me last night and she stopped breathing. If I hadn't checked on her . . . if I hadn't gone to her room in time . . ."

"Jesus, Molly."

I wiped my face. "I don't want to think what could have happened."

"Yeah, yeah, I get it." Phoebe pursed her lips and looked away. After a moment, her nostrils flared and she turned back. "So you're all right with this? You're going to let yourself drown." She flicked her hand in emphasis, the motion a sharp jerk.

"People survive drownings all the time. I'm hoping to be one of them. I don't want to die, Phoebe."

"Good. We can laugh about this next week and you can apologize for being a jerk and scaring the shit out of me." She stood. Chair legs scraped hard against the black-and-white-checkered tile floor. "But first, I'm not letting you from my sight tomorrow. We're going to make sure someone sticks close to revive you."

My brows arched. "You know CPR?"

She gave me a look. "I have four kids. Of course I know CPR. Someone's always choking on something." She glanced at her watch. "It's one. We've got to go if we're swinging by your attorney's office."

Cassie was showing Kurt the sea glass bracelet she'd been wearing since Monday when I tapped her shoulder. "Finish up, honey." I pointed at her sundae. "Time to go."

Except for the babbling and chatter behind us, the car ride to the attorney's office to sign my will, and then the ride home, was silent and tense. Phoebe didn't look at me. When she pulled in front of Nana's house, Cassie kissed everyone good-bye. "See ya later, Aunt Pheebs." She got out of the car and ran into Nana's front yard. I saw her yank a cat from the bushes. She cuddled and kissed the animal before letting it go.

Phoebe kept her gaze forward. She gripped the steering wheel with both hands.

"I put Owen down as primary guardian, since . . ." My voice trailed. I steepled my hands over my mouth. "This is hard," I murmured, and took a deep breath. "Owen will care for Cassie since Nana's sick, and you, well . . . he's going to need your help."

Phoebe's chest expanded. Sunlight reflected off her cheek, revealing a tear trail. My heart twisted. "Pheebs . . ."

She nodded. "Fine, okay. But I'm hoping this issue will be moot by tomorrow evening and we can all live happily ever after." She crossed her fingers. "I'll be here first thing in the morning."

I gripped the door latch and hesitated. My other hand sought hers on the steering wheel. "I'll see you in the morning."

She gave a short nod and released the parking brake. I left the car and watched her drive off.

Chapter 29

Thursday, afternoon

"The sharks were this long," Cassie described to Nana as I entered the house. Her voice danced down the hallway from the kitchen, where I found Nana before the fire, still knitting. "They swam around and around in this giant tank with all these little fish."

"Did they eat the little fish?" Nana asked. She nodded in my direction, greeting me with a knitting needle salute.

Cassie plopped into the chair beside Nana. "I thought they would. I mean, I kept looking to see if the sharks gobbled them up. Chomp, chomp." She mimed shark jaws with her fingers and released a big sigh, settling into the chair. "But they didn't."

"Sounds like you had fun."

Cassie folded her arms and yawned. "Sure did."

"How about you, Molly?"

I hummed a positive answer and peeked inside the Dutch oven on the stove. Stew simmered inside. Steam heated my face, leaving behind a moist mask on my skin after dissipating. Beef, onions, stock, and carrots, the scent hearty and earthy, filled the room. My stomach grumbled.

"I told you I'd cook dinner," I said, peeved she'd been cooking and not resting.

"It was no bother, dear. Come relax with me."

I glanced from the fireplace toward the staircase. I had preparations to make in the event tomorrow was my last day. I started moving toward the hallway when the house phone rang.

Nana pushed up from the chair. I motioned for her to sit back down. "I've got it."

"Is this Molly Brennan?"

"Yes, this is Molly," I replied, somewhat apprehensive.

"Hello, Molly. It's Jane. Jane Harrison."

I weaved my hand into my hair, and my gaze darted to the phone's cradle. I considered hanging up.

"I called your cell but you weren't answering my . . ." Her voice drifted, and I heard her take a deep breath. "There's no excuse for what I did."

I covered the receiver. "Excuse me for a sec," I told Nana and Cassie, then left the room. I moved to the front parlor and sat on the edge of the couch facing the front bay window.

"Will you give me the chance to explain?" she asked.

I didn't want to begin thinking how she'd riffled through Cassie's records to obtain Nana's address. Nor did I want to contemplate that she went out of her way, on a school day, to seek out my daughter for her own personal gain. What I should be doing right now was hanging up and contacting the school district.

But despite what Jane had done, I empathized with her. She was scared and, after witnessing the outcome of at least two of Cassie's premonitions, had sought out my daughter to look into her own future.

"My grandmother told me a bit about your situation," I said.

"Quinn and I have tried to have children for several years. Last Monday when I met with you, I'd found a lump in my breast that morning."

I leaned on my thighs and rubbed my forehead. Thinking about the meeting, I saw now why Jane had been distracted. "Is it cancerous?"

"I'm frightened it will be. I have a biopsy scheduled next week."

"I'm sorry."

"I thought my chances to have a child might be over. I thought my life might be over. But, Cassie . . ."

"She gave you hope."

"Yes," she said. "Initially Cassie scared me. But like I mentioned before, she's special. It's more than her extraordinary abilities. There's something magnetic about her. She emanates warmth and compassion. Of course, that's when she's not frustrated with her peers." A nervous chuckle came through the phone line, and for a long moment we were quiet.

I thought how Jane had come to accept Cassie's uniqueness. The same way Owen had always accepted mine. With only a little training, Cassie had shown remarkable improvement controlling her abilities. She'd brought on a premonition at will. It had been a positive vision. Imagine what she could do if she continued practicing the techniques Nana taught her. She could help so many people. *Like Mom,* I thought, recalling how she'd found the lost boy over two decades ago. Cassie was so similar to her. They both desired to help others.

Perhaps exercising her talent might diminish, and eventually eliminate, the grisly premonitions that came out of nowhere. Like an active child who exercised regularly, creating an outlet for all that extra energy. Cassie's talent needed an outlet. She should practice regularly.

As I sat there with a certain kind of wonderment, staring out the front window, the phone pressed to my ear, it occurred to me that with a little bit of training, I could do the same. My uniqueness needed an outlet. I needed to embrace it, not keep it locked up and out of sight.

Cassie's voice drifted from the other room, melodic and soothing. I lifted my eyes to the door, savoring the sound.

I thanked Jane and then ended the call. On my way back to the kitchen, my cell phone trilled with a text message. I retrieved the phone from my purse. The message was from Owen.

```
I have something for you. Getting home
late. Will leave on porch. Promise you'll
wear.
```

I texted back immediately, wondering how this fit into his don't-let-Molly-out-of-your-sight plan.

```
I promise.
```

∽

"Do I have to eat the stew?" Cassie complained to Nana as she set the dinner table.

"Eat your stew and we'll have hot cocoa and marshmallows," Nana suggested. She ladled stew into bowls. Her eyes met mine over the kitchen island, where I poured milk into glasses. The irony that I might end my time with Nana the same way we'd started together was not lost on me.

I felt a stitch in my chest. Nausea shifted in my stomach. This might be my last night alive.

"Owen loves this stew. We'll have to save some for him."

"He's not home tonight," I pointed out. I pressed my abdomen, trying to settle my stomach.

"Well, then, we'll have to bring it over tomorrow morning. He can have it for lunch." She pulled out a plastic container from under the counter and set it aside.

I closed the milk carton. "Does he ever do his own cooking?"

Nana chuckled. "I'm sure he does, but I enjoy feeding him. He's the only one who's been around for a while."

My stomach undulated with self-disgust. I shouldn't have stayed away.

Outside, a thin layer of clouds shielded the evening sky. Soft mist drizzled over the backyard. A new storm was moving in, the last of the season, according to news reports. The wind chime outside the kitchen window danced, the notes whimsical, the pitch evoking a sense of longing. A longing for more time. For Nana, and for me.

After dinner, Cassie and I went next door to feed the dogs. We played with them in the backyard until we were all tired.

It was dark when we returned home. Nana stood over the stove, brewing Cassie's tea. I made hot cocoa, and all three of us sat at the table. Like twenty-two years ago when my parents and I had moved in with Nana, I was unsure of my future. My abilities had recently surfaced, and my father had only started to blame us for everything that was wrong with his life.

Later, I took my time tucking Cassie into bed. Nana brought her tea, and Cassie drank it without any provocation. She put the cup aside and positioned Bunny beside her. "I'm reading to you tonight," she told me.

"All right," I agreed, and stretched alongside her. She tucked her head under my arm and opened the book. It was a children's book about moms kissing their children's boo-boos, but as Cassie read, she reversed the mom and daughter roles. The daughter kissed her mom's knee, held her as she cried, and hummed a lullaby.

When she finished the story, Cassie closed the book. "Don't cry, Mom."

My eyelids fluttered, and I was surprised to find them damp.

"We're going to resuscitate you." She held my hand and whispered, "We're all going to help."

I tugged her hand and crushed her to my chest.

Cassie fell asleep in my arms, and when her breathing evened and her face relaxed, I pulled myself away.

Nana had already fallen asleep with a book open on her chest. I marked the page with a braided yarn scrap and set the book aside, then turned off the bedside lamp. I kissed her good night and went outside to the studio.

For the first time all week, I used the equipment Owen had set up for me, and spent the next five hours crafting Cassie's mermaid pendant, wire-wrapped sea glass in teal and sky blue. I folded the sterling silver chain and pendant inside a gift box wrapped with a yellow bow and attached a small note.

To my beautiful mermaid. Happy Sweet 16. Love you always and forever, Mom.

In my mind's eye, I pictured a blonde woman, a younger version of me with blue eyes, smiling. She spun in a circle, her yellow sundress flaring around her calves. Then she waved good-bye and ran off, fading into the distance.

My heart ached for everything she'd experience without me there. Her first romance and her first heartbreak. Her driver's exam and her college entrance exams. Her first apartment and her first child. Who would she marry?

I couldn't imagine her life without me, but I prayed Owen would be the one who walked her down the aisle. He could be the father she'd never had. One who loved her in a way mine never could.

So many questions, and so many things I wondered.

Kissing the bow, I set the gift aside.

Rather than booting up the computer, I handwrote Cassie a letter. It was the hardest note I'd ever written. I admired her for the girl she was and the woman she'd become, so much more than I had ever been. I wrote a letter to Nana, hoping she understood why I wanted Owen to look after Cassie. Deep down I knew he'd love her as much as a father loved a daughter, and in the short span of a week, I knew he already cared for her a great deal.

Finally, I wrote a letter to Owen. Told him I loved him, and that had I been brave in my youth, I wouldn't be saying good-bye to him a second time.

As the sky lightened the studio on what might be my last day, I sealed the envelopes, leaving them on the worktable with my notarized will and Cassie's gift, and turned off the light.

Chapter 30

Friday, midmorning

"Mom."

I drifted somewhere on the edge of sleep.

"Mom."

My eyes fluttered open. Daylight filled the room, making every-thing look bright and fresh. I knew from the hue that it was already late morning. I'd crashed in bed at six thirty a.m., unable to keep my eyes open despite my resolve to stay awake.

Cassie stood over me. The edges of her hair dusted my shoulders, tickling my skin. "Morning, Mom," she said.

I scratched my shoulders, rubbed my face. "What time is it?"

She glanced at the clock. "Ten thirty-seven. This is for you." She held a canvas belt that looked like a fanny pack. "It was on the porch. It's from Mr. Torres."

I scooted into a sitting position and yawned. "What's that?"

"An inflatable belt pack. Mr. Torres says there's a life vest inside. It must be teeny-tiny." She frowned at the pack. "Now you don't have to walk around wearing that ugly life vest. You wear this." She shook the belt. "Nana thinks it'll make you look like a tourist, but I don't think you'll care."

I inspected the belt with the zippered pouch and reflective piping. A plastic handle I presumed inflated the vest when pulled dangled from the pouch's base. I thought about Owen's text message, and my promise to wear what he'd left on the porch. Cassie seemed to know a lot about the belt's workings. "Did you see Mr. Torres this morning?"

She nodded. "He came looking for you. I told him you were still asleep. He talked to Auntie Phoebe for a little while, then went home. Nana gave him more food."

Of course she did. "When did Phoebe get here?"

"Eight, I think. It was early." Cassie touched the belt. "Will you wear this? Pretty please?"

"Yes, I will." I'd made a promise to her should she find me something other than a life vest. I'd also promised Owen.

Again, the muscles in my chest twinged, and nausea rolled, pushing up into my throat, as I recalled what day it was. I swallowed the sour taste and forced a smile of reassurance. For Cassie's benefit.

"Yeah!" She clapped.

"Put it there." I pointed to the end of the bed. "I'll wear it as soon as I shower and change. Come here." I patted the space beside me.

She climbed up and lay beside me on her back, legs bent and crossed at the knees, hands folded on her chest.

"Is Nana up?" I asked.

"Yep." She jiggled a foot. The bed vibrated.

"Have you eaten?"

"Yep. Nana made pancakes."

I glanced at her naked wrist. "Where's the bracelet?" I asked, disappointed she'd taken it off.

Her mouth turned downward. "I lost it. I'm sorry, Mommy." She sounded sad. "I looked for it, and I couldn't find it anywhere."

"It's not your fault," I soothed. "The string was old and dried out."
I should have replaced it for her. There were so many things I should
have done for and with her this week. But there'd been so much on
my mind, so many preparations to make, that I hadn't even considered
repairing the bracelet.

My fingers clasped the pendant resting on my breastbone. At least
I still had this glass from Owen. I should leave it for Cassie.

Cassie sat up.

"Where are you going?" I grabbed her hand. I didn't want her to
leave. Not yet.

"My room." Cassie slid off the bed. Her eyes darted toward the
door. "I'm making a surprise."

"All right. Guess I'll shower. Give me one more hug before you go,
though. The biggest you've ever given me."

She squeezed me hard, and tears burned in the corners of my eyes.
I breathed her in, trying to imprint her scent on my brain. Lemon and
honey. My heart flooded with sorrow. I didn't want to let her go, but she
started squirming. Reluctantly, I opened my arms. She headed toward
the hallway.

Owen's dogs barked outside. "Hey, Cass, is Owen still home?"
Considering his don't-let-Molly-out-of-your-sight plan, I wondered
what time he intended to come back.

She stopped outside her bedroom door. "I think so," she yelled
back, and disappeared into her room.

My muscles ached from sleeping in one position. I didn't think I'd
moved once in the last four hours. I walked stiffly to the bathroom,
knees creaking, and cracked the window to let in fresh air. Mudd and
Dirt barked the entire time I showered. Something had them amped
this morning. Maybe Owen was finally working on the gate.

Other than momentary spurts of anxiety, I didn't feel any different
about the day than I had previous days. Just inklings of dread, and the
frequent tightening in my chest. The nausea was still there, too.

I dressed and, before leaving the room, clipped on the inflatable belt, adjusting the pack so it rested against my lower back.

Nana walked into the hallway the same time I did. "Frankie's got those dogs all riled up," she grumbled, and I imagined the orange tabby sitting on the fence, tail swishing. Nana mumbled good morning and ambled to the staircase.

"Where are you going?" I asked, moving to her side to assist.

"Getting that cat." She pushed away my hand and gripped the banister. "I'm fine, I'm fine," she said, taking each step slowly.

"Hey—"

She stopped at the bottom step and looked at me.

"I love you."

"I love you, too," she replied, then left the house through the front door.

One of the dogs started howling. I went to check on Cassie. She shoved items under her bed when I opened the door. "Don't look!"

I frowned. "What are you doing?"

"Stuff." She retreated toward the window.

"What kind of stuff?" My gaze darted toward the space under her bed.

"I'll show you later," she said. "Promise."

"All right," I relented, not wanting to upset her. I pointed at my waist. "Before I go downstairs to see Phoebe, I wanted to show you I was wearing the belt."

Cassie's face brightened. "Thank you, Mommy. It'll keep you safe."

I gave her a small smile. "I'll be downstairs should you need me."

"Okay," she said. She peeked out the window, distracted by the commotion.

I backed from the room and quietly closed the door.

Phoebe sat in the front parlor, flipping through a magazine. She looked up, then tossed the magazine aside as I landed on the bottom step. "Good morning, Sleeping Beauty." She stood and hugged me.

I glanced around the room. "Where are the kids?"

"School. I've got a neighbor watching Danica and Kurt today."

"Oh, nice. So, what's the plan? I assume you've got one and that it entails more than us staring at each other."

"Yes, we do have a plan." She sat down, rubbing her hands together. I settled on the couch opposite her. "I'm your babysitter until school pickup."

"Babysitter?" I scoffed.

She arced her hands back and forth with a flourish. "I'm kidding. Sort of." She chuckled, sounding a bit nervous. We both were. "Owen wanted to stay, but I told him I'd stick close to you. Besides, I wanted some girl time. So, what do you want to do with me? Bake? Watch movies? Order in?"

"Oh nooooo!" The wail came from upstairs. I frowned, my gaze drawn upward.

Feet bounded down the stairs and the front door flew open, then banged shut. Phoebe and I jolted, turning toward the foyer. My heart slammed in my chest, and my skin prickled everywhere. Tiny hairs on the back of my neck rose stiffly.

"Was that Cassie?" Phoebe started to rise.

I was already off the couch. "Yes." I threw open the front door and jogged to the sidewalk, my head swinging right, then left.

Cassie was sprinting toward the beach, chasing after Mudd and Dirt. My heart leaped into my throat as they flew across Ocean View Boulevard. Cars screeched to a halt, horns blaring. I'd never seen Cassie run so fast.

"Cassie," I screamed. Phoebe ran up behind me. "Get Owen," I yelled, then bolted after Cassie.

As I sprinted, I didn't stop to think what I was doing. I didn't stop to contemplate that all the events this week, every single second, had led up to this exact moment. All I cared about was Cassie and her safety.

I ran barefoot. My arms pumped, and my feet slapped the pavement. Pebbles and twigs bit into my soles. The scent of saltwater and seaweed was stronger than it had been in days. The odor stung my nose as I dragged air into my lungs in short, rapid breaths.

Water thundered like gigantic metal sheets. I heard the waves before I saw them. Ten-foot swells smashed the beach. The surf was rough and chaotic from recent storms. Dark gray clouds lined the horizon. A storm far off the coast was pushing the water inland.

Mudd paced the water's edge. He barked madly, the tone sharp and clipped, panicked. He bounded to the right, barked, and then turned, leaping back to the left. But he didn't go into the water.

Cassie moved into the foaming surf, and I screamed her name. She didn't hear me. She dodged a wave and cupped her hands around her mouth. I couldn't hear what she said. The waves drowned her voice. She yelled again.

I scanned the beach. Where was Dirt?

A large swell broke yards from Cassie. The wave moved fast and deep around her ankles, traveling up her calves, past her knees. I ran toward Cassie, circling my arms to get her attention.

Cassie inched deeper into the bay. She was screaming, hands still circling her mouth. Her words were muffled to me. Water retreated, moving back into the ocean faster than it spread along the beach. Her knees buckled. She fell forward on her hands. Her face dropped into the water.

My heart lurched, and a power stronger than I'd felt in twelve years exploded inside me.

"GET BACK!" The words ripped from my lungs. *"GET BACK!"* I yelled again.

Like a puppet on strings, Cassie straightened her legs. Her upper body jackknifed upward. She walked backward, legs stiff, kicking outward. Her arms flailed.

"Noooo!" She screamed when I reached her.

"I'm sorry, baby!" Her scream tore me up inside. I'd forced her to move against her will, but it was the only way I knew how to get her to a safe distance from the water until I reached her.

She gave me a panicked look. Her arms lifted in front of her as if she tried to walk forward.

"Don't, baby. Don't fight it."

Cassie continued to walk backward, fighting every step. *"STOP!"* I ordered when she'd reached the cement steps to Lovers Point. People gathered around her, gawking at our spectacle on the beach.

Mudd barked furiously. Tears cascaded down Cassie's cheeks. She pointed past me. "Diiiirrrt!"

I whipped around. My eyes searched the water. A wave crashed and then another. A large swell rose, expanding. I saw a shadow move below the surface, and then a head broke through. It was Dirt, about thirty yards offshore. He paddled to keep above water, his movements sluggish. His eyes rolled toward us before he sank back into the water. He'd only surfaced for an instant, but I'd seen enough. Dirt was struggling. He was going to die.

"Oh my God!"

Owen shot past me. "Get the fuck back!" he bellowed, eyes wild.

He plunged into the water, diving under a breaking wave, and came up on the other side. A wave swelled and he dipped below the surface again, going after his dog. He ducked through more breaking waves, surfacing, turning in circles, searching for Dirt.

Another swell pushed him up, giving him a height advantage. Dirt paddled below him. Another swell pushed Owen into Dirt. He grabbed the dog, who pawed Owen's chin, neck, and shoulders. Owen dipped below the water, surfaced, then dipped again. This happened a couple more times as he struggled with the dog, and each time I didn't see his mouth and nose rise above the water.

I gasped, my hands flying to cover my mouth. Owen was drowning.

"Owen!" I screamed his name again, moving into the surf. I was supposed to drown today, not him.

Someone grabbed my arm, hard.

"Molly!"

I jerked around.

"Don't you dare go in there." Phoebe gripped me tight, her finger-nails biting into my skin. "Cassie needs you."

"Owen's drowning!" I yanked my arm, but I couldn't shake her off.

I swung back around, my gaze darting left and right. The ocean was wild, and I couldn't find him.

A wave crested and there he was, dipping down the backside before disappearing again.

I started screaming.

A diver in a full wetsuit shot into the water, followed by another. They ducked and surfaced, wave after wave, powering toward Owen. A third man barreled into the surf, heading in the same direction.

I kept screaming, slowly becoming aware that I was issuing compulsion after compulsion.

"HELP HIM! HELP HIM!"

Heat scaled my spine. An electrical storm of power I never knew I possessed crackled inside my mouth.

Dirt surfed a wave to the shore, collapsing in the sand. Mudd bounded over, sniffing his exhausted mate.

The men reached Owen. He was alive, but all four were struggling as they fought the current.

"MOVE IT! SWIM! SWIM!" I yelled, over and over.

The surf broke, spilling the men onto the beach. They crawled-walked through the ebb and flow of the tide, collapsing on the cement steps.

Phoebe released me and I sprinted to Owen, kneeling before him. I touched him everywhere. His face, his shoulders, his chest. "You're alive," I cried, hysterical. "You're alive."

Owen folded his arms around me, shaking uncontrollably. "So-so are y-you." He tucked his head in the crook of my neck and held me tight. I barely registered the water from his soaked clothes seeping through mine.

An elderly couple wrapped a blanket across Owen's shoulders. They did the same with Cassie, who was tucked tight in Phoebe's arms a couple of steps behind us.

"Fu-fucking d-dogs," Owen mumbled against my skin.

I rubbed his back, his arms, trying to warm him.

"You-you p-put me under compulsion."

I stilled. Tears beaded, falling down my cheeks, and I nodded against his head. "I'm sorry. I had to, Owen. I was so scared."

He fell back against the steps, exhausted. "Weirdest . . . f-feeling . . . ever. It was like a shot of adrenaline right here." He thumped his heart with a fist. "I couldn't not swim."

I couldn't not touch him. My hands moved down his arms, across his thighs, rubbing vigorously to keep the blood flowing. I kissed his blue lips.

He grasped my face with a shaking hand. I clasped his wrist, pressing my cheek into his palm.

His eyes locked on mine, his lashes damp with saltwater. "You saved me."

"You saved *me*," I pointed out. He'd gone into the water in my place. He was my bike helmet.

"Do you think we did it?" His arm, muscles weak, fell into his lap. I held the blanket that was sliding off his shoulders. "Do you think we changed the future?" he asked.

My mouth worked, twisting into a smile contorted with emotion. "I think so." I hadn't avoided the water, which worried me that it would only prolong the premonition's cycle. Rather, I hadn't been allowed in it.

Cassie shook her head. Tears flowed like rivers down both cheeks.

"Cassie, baby, what's wrong? Mommy's safe. Come sit with me."

She shook her head harder. "It's my fault." She sobbed.

"What's your fault?"

"The dogs. I couldn't shut the gate."

I frowned, confused. "When? Last night?" I'd shut the gate after we fed the dogs.

"No, this morning," she cried, and held up her wrist. "I was looking for your bracelet."

My heart sank. "Cassie. It's—"

"Not your fault," Owen interrupted. "Cassie, look at me."

Cassie whisked her head in his direction, her lower lip trembling madly.

"What happened here is not your fault. It's mine. You understand? It's entirely my fault. I should have fixed that gate days ago."

"Come here, Mermaid." I beckoned her to my side. She scooted down the steps. I took a deep breath and hugged her tight. "I love you."

Her thin arms twined around my waist. "I love you, too, Mommy."

We returned to Owen's house, where he left the dogs in the garage to deal with later. He'd clean them off after he took the hottest shower known to man. Phoebe went to check on Nana, and to let her know where we were and that everyone was safe.

I elected to stay with Owen. He was still shivering, and I worried he had mild hypothermia. I didn't want to leave him alone.

While he showered, I drew a bath for Cassie in the guest bathroom, helping her out of her wet clothes. I'd text Phoebe to bring over dry ones.

"That was a lot of excitement this morning," I said, measuring the water's temperature as Cassie stepped into the tub. I turned off the faucet, and she eased into the water, hugging her calves and resting her chin on her knees. Slowly, she stopped shivering.

My own limbs started to shake as I came down from the adrenaline high. A giddy sort of happiness warmed inside me, spreading outward with each beat of my heart. I couldn't stop smiling. I was alive. I wouldn't miss my daughter's life. And I could have Owen back in my life.

I soaped a washcloth and washed her back. Saltwater and sand flowed into the tub. Tiny flecks floated to the bottom, where they sparkled and shifted inside the water. I took my time cleaning Cassie, relishing that I had it to take. And so much of it, too. Today was like a new beginning, and there was so much of the world I looked forward to showing her, including helping her hone her abilities. She could help me, too, pass on what Nana had taught her.

Her stomach growled. "I'm hungry," she murmured.

"I can hear that." I chuckled, handing her the washcloth. "Why don't you finish up?" I suggested, and grabbed a thick bath towel from the cabinet. I put it on the toilet. "I'll go downstairs and make us some lunch." Tea, too. We all needed to drink something warm.

In the kitchen, I texted Phoebe for clothes and set water to boil for tea in a kettle on the stove. I also poured four glasses of water and set them on the table. Opening the fridge, I found Nana's Tupperware of stew on the top shelf. Perfect.

I aligned four bowls on the counter and popped the lid. Beef stock, onion, and carrots. My stomach emitted a loud gurgle. I hadn't had breakfast, and after the adrenaline rush earlier, I was starving.

I portioned the stew, popped a bite of meat into my mouth, chewing the cold beef, and slid one of the bowls into the microwave. I set the temp to half power and the timer for three minutes, pushed "Start," and swallowed. My throat seized the meat.

Hands jerked to my collarbone. I swallowed again. My throat convulsed, stopping at the lump lodged in its way.

I inhaled, eyes bulging. Lungs convulsed, unable to pull in air. I tried again. Nothing.

My hands seized my throat, fingers biting into my neck. My gaze jumped wildly around the room. I couldn't call for help. I couldn't breathe. I couldn't move, even though I knew I should run upstairs to Owen. There was only one thing my body wanted. Oxygen. And it couldn't get it.

Instinct curled my hand into a fist. I drove it into and upward in my abdomen. I did it again. And again. The meat wouldn't dislodge.

Severe pain spread like a wildfire through my chest, expanding. Lungs straining, feeling like they were going to explode. Muscles burned.

Help. I needed help. I looked around, crazed, my gaze landing on the kitchen table. I stumbled over and dropped on the chair back, landing hard on my fist, which pressed into my abdomen. Nothing. I did it again.

And again.

And again.

Eyes watering, head spinning, my knees buckled. I slid to the floor, legs thrashing outward. They kicked the chair into the table. A water glass above toppled over, shattering on the floor by my head. Glass shards sprayed the side of my face, and water seeped into my hair.

With one arm outstretched in the direction of the stairs, my other hand tapped my stomach. The taps lightened and slowed. Easing until I no longer had the strength to move.

From a distance, I heard my name. Cassie, calling for me. The teakettle whistled and microwave beeped. Time was up.

Face turned toward the staircase, my vision darkened and the room faded. I felt cold.

And then I didn't feel anything at all.

Chapter 31

Friday, late morning

I breathed and smelled jasmine. Sweet and syrupy. I inhaled again and felt a rush in my lungs as if I'd floated upward, then rapidly descended. A giggle burst from me. I smiled. I felt happy.

My eyes fluttered open. They stung. I blinked over and over, adjusting to the sunlight. Everything around me was bright white and hazy, like I'd been swimming too long in a chlorinated pool.

I sat on a swing under an oak tree on a grassy knoll. The board under my thighs was rough, and the ropes I gripped, thick braided twine, reminded me of the kind old ships used. The ropes stretched skyward and coiled around a thick branch above me.

I swung back and forth, an easy sway on a lazy afternoon like the dozens of sea glass wind chimes overhead decorating the oak tree. They danced and played, their tune as delicate as glasses clinking together in a restaurant.

Back and forth I swung. I didn't remember pushing my feet against the ground, and I didn't remember how I happened to be here on this hill. I just was, with bare feet and toes polished bright coral. They looked so pretty, sparkling in the sunlight. I wore an eyelet dress in sunflower yellow. The skirt billowed around my legs as I floated upward, my toes pointing toward the beautiful azure sky. Fluffy white clouds floated like marshmallows in cocoa.

I smiled wider, my eyelids drifting low as my face absorbed the sun's warmth. It felt good, the temperature perfect, like the spring days when I'd stretch out on the sand to absorb the sun's heat chasing the chills that had set in during winter.

I didn't want to leave this place. I liked my perch on the hill, above my surroundings, where I could see for miles. It was round and high like the swell of a wave. I felt safe and loved, even though I was alone, which didn't seem right.

My legs lowered, toes touching the ground. I frowned. Why was I alone? Someone should be here with me. It was a happy place. Where was everyone?

I rubbed my forehead. My nose crinkled, and my brain felt foggy and heavy.

A young girl with long, blonde hair and sea glass–green eyes appeared from behind the tree trunk. She looked like me as a little girl. She laughed, the sound rich and lyrical. She waved and ran down the hill, a teddy bear clutched in her hand.

"Wait!" I jumped off the swing and started to chase after her. But I stopped. My chest constricted, and my heart raced. The chimes rattled and hummed, growing louder. There were more in the tree than before. Where'd they come from?

Don't go, they seemed to sing.

I retreated back to the swing and sat down. An unpleasant feeling came over me, and I knew if I'd gone after the girl I'd be unable to return to my hill.

I liked my hill, and I liked my swing.

My feet pushed against the ground. I kicked my legs and leaned back. I kicked again, flying higher, pretending my toes touched the floating marshmallows.

And I laughed. The chimes laughed with me. Such pretty music. Birds sang, and bees buzzed. Tiny, fluttery insects hovered above patches of daffodils in the grass.

Then all noise stopped like someone had unplugged the stereo. The only sound was the creak of the swing's taut ropes rubbing tree bark.

I listened for something, anything. Anticipation tightened my rib cage. I waited and waited.

Sea glass jingled. *It's your fault.*

A chill rippled through me, chasing the anticipation. I planted my feet and stilled.

Another chime joined the first. *It's your fault.*

My ears pricked. I straightened and looked across the small valley between my hill and the next. A figure of a man appeared on the rise, its shadow long and narrow, a bony finger pressing into the hillside.

The man approached, his shadow shortening. Chimes resonated in the valley, their warning incessant. *It's your fault. Your fault. Your fault.*

The fine hairs on the back of my neck fluttered. I stood and moved around the swing, putting it between me and the man coming toward me. I didn't like this man. I didn't want him on my hill.

"Go away," I whispered, then shouted. "Go away!"

He didn't turn around. He didn't stop.

Heat radiated along my spine. Electricity arced in my mouth. *"GO AWAY!"*

He pointed a finger at me.

Your fault. Your fault.

Sea glass swung violently above like thousands of beer bottles rattling on shelves during an earthquake. The noise was deafening.

Your fault. Your fault. Your fault.

I slammed my palms over my ears. It was no use. The noise was too loud. The chimes' racket oscillated in my chest. I felt the sound everywhere inside me as though I were in the front row of an acid rock concert. My organs vibrated, making my insides jittery.

The man came closer, his stride elongating, pace quickening. I made out his wrinkled tan pants and button-down shirt, stained as if he'd been rolling in the dirt, or in an accident. He fisted his hands, and the thin hair on his crown waved like a flag over his head.

The way he moved, his purposeful stride, his angry expression, it all seemed familiar and evoked old memories. Rotten, stale memories.

Sweat dampened my palms, the backs of my knees, my feet. I could see his bloodshot eyes, smell the stale beer on his breath.

I whimpered. "Dad?"

Your fault.

Wind chimes shattered. Glass rained around us, slicing my skin. I screamed.

His hands shot between the swing's ropes and latched onto my throat. My nails clawed his wrists, tugged his sleeves. His thumbs pressed into my larynx, collapsing my throat.

I inhaled. My lungs compressed and throat convulsed, but no air came in.

I trembled and tried to inhale again. Nothing.

My eyes bulged, the pressure behind them building. Blood roared in my ears, the noise thunderous, like hurricane force winds in a tunnel.

My knees buckled. I was falling, descending. Down and down, and there was no one to catch me. No one to break my fall. No hand to grasp.

I was alone and lost when a voice whispered inside my head. It was beautiful and magical.

And extremely demanding.

Breathe, Molly!

"Breathe!"

Chapter 32

Friday, late morning

I heard crying. The sobs tugged hard at my soul, and I wanted them to stop.

Something pressed against my lips like a hard kiss. My cheeks puffed, skin stretching, and pressure built in my chest. Then something flat pushed my sternum, again and again. It crushed me. Sharp points dug into my back like a bed of pine needles, but I couldn't feel my toes or fingers.

Someone was counting and then more crying. The crying grew louder, harsher. She sounded so sad.

Please don't cry.

"I heard her!" a child wailed. "In my head. I heard her. Mommy talked to me!"

Mommy.

An image shimmered before me. A little girl with blonde hair and sea glass–blue eyes. My little girl.

Mommy? A shy touch to my mind.

"Move back, Cass," a rough voice snapped.

Lips pressed my lips. Air pushed into my mouth and down my throat. Palms thumped my chest. "Breathe, Molly. Come on, baby. Breathe."

Yes, yes, I wanted to. But my body wasn't cooperating. It felt heavy, and I was trapped like a clam inside a shell.

Mommy!

A shrill ring inside my head. Cassie's voice. She sounded beautiful.

I'm here, Mermaid.

Cassie sobbed harder.

Pressure built in my chest. I couldn't stand it anymore. It burned. I felt my mouth fall open and lungs expand. Air rushed inside me. I inhaled again, a dry, hoarse gasp.

"Thank God."

I drank in several gulps of air. "Owen?" His name came out as a croak. My throat was raw. I started coughing.

"Don't talk."

No problem. It felt like a hot poker had been shoved down my throat. I started shivering instead.

"I'll get a blanket," Phoebe said. *When did she get here?*

Shoes walking on a hard surface clomped away, then came back. Warmth settled over me. I was still cold, but the trembling subsided.

"Are you okay, Mommy?"

My eyelids fluttered, and I squinted against the overhead lights. As my vision adjusted I realized it wasn't the LEDs, but Cassie's aura. Sunflower yellow and golden like her hair. Magical.

I stared up at her, awestruck. "You're so beautiful." My little mermaid.

Cassie collapsed on my chest, and I coughed.

"Careful, Cass. Here, let's have your mom sit up."

Hands pressed into my shoulders, lifting me. Through sheer force of will, I wrapped my arms around Cassie and held on. She buried her face in my chest. I kissed her head.

You saved me, I told her.

If I hadn't heard her voice, I might have drifted away. Forever lost to her and everyone I loved.

My tears dropped on her damp head. Her hair smelled of cucumber shampoo. *You saved me.* I sent the words into her mind. I didn't have the strength to speak. *You saved me,* I repeated, again and again.

"How are you feeling?" Phoebe asked after a moment.

"Wh-what . . . happened?" I forced the words through my thrashed throat.

She opened her palm, displaying a chunk of partially chewed meat. "You shot it clear across the kitchen."

My brows jumped into my hairline.

She chuckled, nervous. "Nah, kidding. I finger-swiped it." She hooked her index finger, twisting her wrist in a swiping motion. "You were unconscious, girl."

"Did you—" I stopped. My throat burned. It still felt like something was lodged there.

"Heimlich, baby, while you were flat on your back." Phoebe nodded, clamping her hands together and acting out the thrusting motion. "I have four kids, remember?" She tossed the chunk of meat into the sink.

Wow. Between the Heimlich and the death grip at the beach, Phoebe was the strongest woman I knew.

"Owen did the mouth-to-mouth stuff."

"Mouth-to-mouth?"

"I couldn't find a heartbeat." His chest rumbled against my back, his voice thick with emotion. His legs cradled my hips, and his arms wrapped around me, hugging me to his chest as I hugged Cassie to mine.

He dropped his forehead on my shoulder. Dampness chilled my skin. Owen was crying.

I felt behind me, finding his bare torso.

"Don't wander too far," he chuckled, the sound watery. "I'm wearing only a bath towel and it's slipping."

"I—I don't understand." I looked at Phoebe, but Owen answered.

"Cassie found you. She came running into my bathroom, yelling that you were dying. That you looked exactly like she saw it in her vision."

A chill that had nothing to do with Owen's damp body and my own body's near-death experience slid through me.

Dipping my chin, I looked down at Cassie's head and her messy part. Her face pressed against my chest, her little body cocooned in a bath towel. Because of my love of the ocean, and that I'd thought my sprinkler-drenched clothes and hair had triggered the premonition, I'd rashly assumed Cassie foresaw me drowning. That was the reason I couldn't breathe.

I thought back to Monday, us eating doughnuts, Cassie playing at the fountain, the whir of the sprinklers, me shoving a too-big bite of doughnut into my mouth, running across the lawn, juggling my purse and phone as I struggled to swallow, forcing the doughnut down. That was when I turned to Cassie, and that was what she'd seen. Not me wet, but me eating.

Oh my God. All this time, I'd assumed Cassie saw me drown. And through my questioning, I'd led her to believe that was what she'd seen.

Two things were for sure. One, Cassie had been right the other day. Staying in Pacific Grove was safer for me. Had Cassie and I been home alone in San Luis Obispo, there would have been no one there to do CPR. I would have died.

It hadn't happened, though, because I'd altered the outcome of Cassie's premonition almost immediately. I'd made the decision to visit Nana.

And second, Cassie had also been right about me being like everyone else when it came to her premonitions. I didn't listen. She'd said it right there, too, in front of the mission fountain. *You're just like everyone else. You don't listen to me. You don't believe.*

Owen shifted behind me. He kissed my shoulder. "Are we done saving each other today?"

I melted against his chest. "I sure hope so." I was exhausted.

⌒⊙

Phoebe took Cassie home with her while Owen took me to the hospital. Just to be sure everything was all right with my vitals, he informed me. I hadn't had a heartbeat for at least thirty seconds.

Owen believed Cassie had found me right after I collapsed. By the time he'd raced downstairs, barely getting a towel around his waist, Phoebe was already performing the Heimlich.

"I think my naked ass shocked her. That chunk of meat shot right out of you when she saw me." He grinned.

I snorted a laugh, which turned into a cough. My throat would be swollen and raw for several days, according to the doctor.

Owen came to my side, where I lay on a bed hooked up to various monitors. Wires were taped to my chest and forehead, and clamped to my fingers. He poured a tumbler of water and brought the straw to my lips. I drank greedily. The water soothed my throat.

"Thanks." I let my head flop on the pillow. He put the cup aside. "How much longer do we have?" We'd already been at the hospital for three hours.

"They said six hours, tops. Sooner if the tests come back earlier and everything looks normal."

Owen dragged a chair to the bedside.

"You look tired," I murmured.

He grunted and sat down. "It's been one hell of a day, Molly."

I searched for his hand and squeezed his fingers. His eyes were bloodshot from the salt water. Stubble coated his jaw. "Talk to me," I coaxed. I could tell something was on his mind.

He rubbed his brow with his fingertips, then sighed deeply. "I was terrified when I saw you on the beach ready to plunge into the water. Then seeing you lying on the kitchen floor, not moving. Jesus Christ, Molly." He cleared his throat and inclined his head. "You almost gave me a heart attack. Twice in one day. I don't want to lose you." His voice broke.

"Shhh." I soothed. I knew exactly how he felt. I'd almost lost him today, too.

My fingers skimmed through his hair. "Owen." I let his name carry the love I felt. "Look at me."

He shook his head. "I know you're afraid you might hurt me with your abilities. That you'll make me do something that could endanger me. It's why you broke up with me. You thought you were protecting me. It's also why you're planning to leave me again. But, Molly, I—"

"Owen." I tilted up his chin. "I love you."

He inhaled sharply. His eyes flared.

"I'm not going anywhere. I've come to realize that I need training like Cassie. I have to embrace that part of me rather than force it into hiding. And now I've seen the good I can do. I saved both you and Cassie today. I might have lost you if I hadn't issued that compulsion. And Cassie . . ." I paused, taking a moment to rest my taxed throat. "She would have ignored me. She would have gone after Dirt because she felt responsible.

"So, no, Owen, I'm not leaving."

Owen's mouth parted as my words sank in. "You're staying?" he gasped, rising quickly. I smiled as a myriad of expressions transformed his beautiful face. Surprise, hope, amazement, and love. He grinned from ear to ear. "You're staying." Then he leaned over the bed and kissed me. "I love you." He kissed me again.

"I love you, too."

The house seemed empty when we arrived home that evening, as though we'd been away on a long vacation. All lights were off, the doors and windows closed and locked, the air stale. Frankie meowed loudly upon us entering the kitchen. He rubbed my shins, back and forth, and then sat by the pantry door where his food was stored. He was hungry.

"Mary?" Owen tossed his keys and wallet on the counter. He called her name again. Frankie meowed, irritated by the loud noise.

Owen's gaze angled down to mine over Cassie's head. I picked up Frankie and handed him to Cassie. "Feed the cat. I'm going to check on Nana."

"Come on, Cass. I'll help you." Owen opened the pantry and picked up the cat-food canister.

Quickly, I went upstairs with clammy hands skimming the rail and fear in my heart. I lightly rapped my knuckles on Nana's door. The door inched open, hinges creaking.

"Nana?" I peered through the darkness. The heavy curtains were drawn, but a dull light from the hallway slanted across the room to reveal a slight figure on the bed.

"Nana?" I approached the bed. Floorboards creaked under my sneakers. The air smelled of medicine and sickness. Knowing she was dying and seeing her like this, still as death, made me want to compel her to fight the growth inside her. I thought of the years I'd had with her, and the years we'd missed. She would also miss all the things I'd been afraid of missing myself.

I turned on the bedside lamp. The thin skin around her eyes crinkled. Her chest rose and fell with shallow breaths.

As if she sensed me looking over her, she opened her eyes. She squinted against the light's glare. "Molly?" She sounded tired. Her face was pale, the muscles underneath her pleated skin taut.

"I'm here." I knelt beside the bed and clasped her hand. Her skin was cold.

She smiled, a tremble of the upper lip, but a smile nonetheless. "I hope you're not hungry. I didn't make dinner tonight."

She always wanted to tend to others, even on the brink of exhaustion. "Don't worry. I'll take care of dinner. We'll order in. How does that sound?"

Nana harrumphed as she tried sitting up. She struggled against the mattress, the sheets bunched around her legs.

I lifted her shoulders and stacked pillows behind her head. "Better?"

"Much." She moistened her lips.

"Does your head ache?" I asked, resting my hand over hers.

She hummed an acknowledgment. "I'm fine now. I came up here to rest a bit and fell asleep. What time is it?"

I glanced at the bedside clock. "Almost seven. Are you hungry?"

"Not really." She pulled her hand from underneath mine and patted my hand. "Phoebe told me there was a bit of excitement today. How is everyone?"

The right side of my mouth quirked. "We survived."

She smiled, close-lipped. "I suspected as much. Now tell me what's on your mind. I sense these things, you know." She chuckled, and a small smile peeked on my face.

I sighed, exhaling the long, weary day. "I didn't drown like Cassie had foreseen. Actually, Cassie never said I'd drown. I was the one who assumed so. What she really saw was me choking. I choked on some food after all that excitement on the beach you heard about." Dipping my chin, I looked at her hand resting over mine, the contrast of skin, thin and aged, so different from my own.

I took a deep breath. "Owen says my heart stopped. I think I died, I'm not sure, but whatever happened, I experienced something. I went somewhere, and I saw Dad."

Nana sucked in a breath, her chest rising steadily. I gave her hand a quick squeeze of reassurance and told her about my near-death experience. How Dad came after me, and how I kept hearing the words *your fault*, over and over.

"That's exactly what he told me, right after he killed Mom, and right before I expelled him from the house. He blamed me for Mom's death. And I've blamed myself for his death."

Nana rocked her head against the pillow. "Your father's death isn't your fault."

"I understand that now," I said, nodding. "I think that's why he's the one I saw, not Mom, wherever it was that I went. Years of pent-up guilt, I guess."

"Your mother's death isn't your fault either."

"I know. Dad blamed everyone but himself. He never took responsibility."

She tensed beside me. "No, dear. It's my fault."

Air lodged in my throat. My gaze lifted to hers. "What is? Mom's death?"

Her expression turned sadder than I'd ever seen. Her eyes sheened. "I'm the one who convinced her to leave your father. She was packing her suitcase when he came home earlier than we expected. She was already supposed to be gone by then."

"My mother was leaving? Where would she have gone?" My voice came out thin.

"To a women's shelter. I was hoping with some therapy she'd find the courage to file for domestic violence and eventually divorce him. You were already moving away and would be safe. That's why your mother insisted you go away to college." Nana's fingers twisted in the sheets. "Brad killed her because of me, because I convinced her to leave him."

"That's why you blocked me out," I reasoned. We'd both felt guilty about the roles we'd played that day.

"That's part of the reason, yes," Nana confessed. She lowered her gaze to her hands. "It hurt me too much to *feel* her pain. I was tired of *feeling* the way Brad treated her. She was weak and submissive and resigned to her circumstances. She tried, but she couldn't always block her emotions from me because he'd destroyed her confidence."

And that was why Nana's guilt ran deep, canyons of brown carving through her yellow aura. I sat back on my heels. As an empathic, Nana hadn't only seen the way my father had treated Mom; she'd felt it. And perhaps, over time, she'd started feeling the same as Mom. Worn down. Insignificant. Unworthy. A freak like Mom and me.

Nana's legs shifted under the covers, restless. "I blocked my thoughts from you because I didn't want you to know what I'd done. Your father would not have murdered Sheila had I not sent her away. I was afraid you'd hate me and then I'd lose you, too."

And she *had* lost me for a while. I had shut her out and left Pacific Grove for my own guilty reasons. I wanted to hate her and rage at her for the exact reasons she feared I would. I also wanted to cry for all the time we'd lost because we were both too damn stubborn and full of shame.

I sank to my knees and clasped both her hands. "Telling Mom to leave my father was the right thing to do. She wasn't strong enough to do it on her own. Remember how you told me I can't blame myself for my father's death? Well"—I angled my chin down and looked up at her—"you can't take the blame for your daughter's death."

The word choice was deliberate. As a mother, I understood Nana would have done whatever she could to protect her daughter.

"You didn't know my father would have reacted that way. He snapped, Nana, and that was his own doing. Neither of us could have predicted Mom's death"—I paused and frowned—"unless she'd foreseen it." The last statement came out sounding like a question.

Nana slowly shook her head. "Her premonitions were never of her, only those around her. The same with Cassie."

"See? That entire day was a series of unfortunate accidents." Much like my day had been today. This time, thankfully, we had all survived.

I kissed Nana's hands and met her gaze. "I forgive you, and I don't blame you either. But what you really need to do is forgive yourself." As I'd done about my father. I had no plans to take my guilt with me during my next brush with death. Knock on wood, that wouldn't be until I was way past my seventies.

Nana soon drifted to sleep. I left her room a few moments afterward.

Cassie and Owen ate downstairs. Owen pulled out a chair as I entered the kitchen and fixed me a bowl of split pea soup. It was canned, but I wasn't complaining. The soup slid down my damaged throat easily, and I didn't have to worry about chewing. I figured I'd be cutting my food into extra small bites and chewing twice as long for a long time to come. Choking was something I never wanted to experience again.

Nana had left the tea recipe on the counter along with a canister of what was left of the blend she'd made earlier in the week. But we didn't need it tonight. Cassie hadn't had another vision. Owen went home to check on the dogs and let them out back for a bit before locking them inside for the night. He returned a short time later, joining Cassie and me on the couch, remarking that he was going to the hardware store first thing in the morning. Time to repair that gate once and for all.

Soon Cassie drifted to sleep, leaning against Owen. It made me smile. He stretched his arm along the back of the couch and caressed my neck. His fingers were strong. I wanted this, the three of us together as a family. And for the first time since I'd returned to Pacific Grove and seen Owen, I believed it would be my reality.

We looked at each other for a long time. He smelled of the outdoors, driftwood and sea breeze. I had a lot to be thankful for. Him. My life. A new beginning.

"I love you," I whispered over Cassie's sleeping head.

Owen held my gaze and I felt tempted to jump inside and swim in the warm depths of those gray eyes. He stood and picked up Cassie. He carried her upstairs and tucked her into bed. I kissed her good night and turned off the light, knowing she would sleep peacefully. Owen followed me into my room. He wanted me to rest. I wanted him. I kissed his lips and jaw, skimmed my hands over the hard plain of his chest. He tugged off his shirt, and I fumbled with the fly on his jeans.

"Slow down," he murmured against my neck. "We have all night."

But I was desperate. After a brush with death I wanted to feel alive. I wanted to feel loved.

"I love you," I told him again.

He smiled against my mouth. "I have always loved you, Lollipop. Every side of you, the ordinary and the extraordinary."

Chapter 33

Nana passed away a month later. A massive stroke caused by the tumor. I found her when I brought up breakfast. She looked peaceful, the creases in her skin softened. Her eyes were open, staring at the ceiling. I wondered what she'd seen. Who she had reached out to in her last moment.

While the oncologist had informed Nana she didn't have much longer to live, her passing had happened sooner than he expected.

But Nana must have suspected her time was near.

At some point during the night, she'd written instructions about her will along with the combination of the safe where the document was stored. There was also a journal inside, passed down by generations of women from our Irish line. Nana advised that the journal could be used as a guide to help both Cassie and me with our extraordinary talent. Cassie and I had been reading it together, and already I felt more confidence in controlling my abilities.

Nana had purchased a plot at San Carlos Cemetery near my parents. Her burial was in a few days.

Owen draped his arm across my shoulders as we walked Carmel Beach. My feet skimmed the water line. White foam filled the imprints

Cassie's feet had left. She ran ahead, tossing sticks into the surf. Mudd bounded into the water, while Dirt barked impatiently by Cassie's side. Since the Beach Event, as we'd come to call it, Dirt had avoided the waves. And neither dog had escaped Owen's backyard since he'd repaired the gate.

Cassie bent over and scratched at the sand. She held an object to the sunlight, then ran back to us. The dogs tailed her.

"Look what I found." She opened her hand. On her palm rested a perfectly round, red piece of sea glass speckled with sand granules. Red was the rarest sea glass, and finding one was like discovering treasure.

"It's beautiful."

"Nana told me I could find glass like you if I looked closely."

I paused and considered her. "Nana Mary? When?"

Wind lifted Cassie's hair, twirling the sun-bleached strands across her face. She pushed it back, leaving a dusting of sand on her cheek. "The night she died."

I dropped to my knees. The wind blew her hair again, and I combed it aside. "Did she call to you?"

Cassie dusted the sand off the tiny glass orb. "I heard her in my head. She wanted to say good-bye."

My throat tightened. I wiped my eyes, blaming the tears on the sand in the wind. "Did you go to her?"

She nodded, flipping the glass end over end on her palm. "I want to be a sea glass artist like you."

"Really?" I asked, amazed. I'd have to start inviting her to spend time with me in the studio.

"Why didn't you tell me about Nana?"

Cassie inclined her head. "It was supposed to be our little secret."

"It's a good secret." I folded her fingers over the sea glass. "Guard your tears well, Mermaid. That's treasure in your hand."

Cassie rubbed her nose. "I miss her."

I pulled her against my chest and held on. "Me, too." Then I tapped the bracelet on her wrist, the one with Owen's sea glass, the one she'd lost. Owen had found it in his garage, under the workbench. I had immediately replaced the frayed twine with a sterling silver cuff that framed the glass. The bracelet shouldn't fall off again. "How about we make a matching bracelet?" I offered. "I'll teach you."

Cassie beamed. "I'd like that."

"Well, what do you know," Owen said above us. "Look at that."

I glanced over Cassie's shoulder. She turned in my arms toward the ocean. Mudd and Dirt frolicked in the waves. They played tug-o-war with the stick Owen had been tossing. Cassie squealed. She gave me her sea glass to hold and charged after the dogs.

I wrapped my arm around Owen's waist, and we started walking again. From habit, my fingers dug into my pocket, searching for the sea glass. I rolled the orb between my fingers, relishing the pitted texture. "Do you remember all those hours I dragged you to the beach to hunt glass?" I asked, watching Cassie, her eyes on the ground. She walked in circles, laughing when the dogs sniffed her toes. "You must have been so bored."

"I'll admit there were times I wished I was fishing."

I playfully punched him in the ribs. He grunted and pulled me closer into his side. I was thankful for every day to spend with him, even if he'd rather fish than hunt for glass.

Cassie had started at her new school several weeks ago and had made a few friends. But she missed Grace. They talked on the phone almost every day. We still had to move our belongings from San Luis Obispo, so Cassie would see her again soon.

As for me, I had taken the remainder of the school year off, and I was in the process of applying for a position at the local college. Hopefully I could start by the next term.

High above the horizon, the sun dipped into a blanket of gray. "What time is it?" I asked Owen.

He pulled his phone from his pocket and turned on the screen. "Four-thirty."

"We should head back." It was getting late, and the fog was rolling in.

Owen called over Cassie and whistled for the dogs.

"Ophelia's already sold the initial pieces I sold to her," I told Owen as we walked to the car.

He whistled. "That's great."

"She mentioned there's a gallery in Santa Cruz that's requested to display my work if I'm interested in producing more pieces for her."

"Are you?"

"I think I've got the time," I teased, giving his ribs a short tickle.

He grabbed my hand and kissed each fingertip.

"The curator's doing a beach exhibit and wants to try something new. She's introducing different mediums. Acrylics, jewelry, some textiles. Sculptures and driftwood, too."

"When's that?"

"This summer."

He hummed his approval. "You're going to be busy. New job, new exhibits. Think you'll have time for a wedding?"

"A what? Who's getting married?"

Owen chuckled, but he didn't answer me.

"Owen," I prodded right before it hit me. Blood drained from my face. I stopped and looked up at him. "Owen?"

"Don't look so scared."

"I—I'm not scared," I stammered. "Surprised. That's all."

"That's all?" He laughed, rich and genuine. He kissed me firmly on the mouth, and his face grew serious with a hint of hesitation. "Don't answer. Think about it. We've got time. But," he paused, and he rubbed the back of his neck, his expression turning vulnerable. "I really want to spend my life with you. And have more children with you. Because, if it's all right with you, and Cassie, of course, I'd love to be her dad."

He still wanted to adopt her.

Tears sheened my eyes, and love burned inside my heart.

"Yes." I didn't need to think. I didn't want to waste any more time. We'd already lost so much. And he had so much love to give me and my daughter. Standing on my toes, I grasped his shoulders and kissed him. "Yes."

Owen let out a shout. He lifted me and spun us around. Cassie ran over, laughing. "I wanna dance! I wanna dance, too!" The dogs barked and bounded around us.

"I love you," he murmured against my mouth before letting go. Then he picked up Cassie and potato-sack-carried her to the parking lot. She kicked and squealed. "This isn't dancing!"

I followed behind, my heart swelling at the sound of Cassie's laughter. For many months, Cassie hadn't laughed. She'd rarely cracked a smile. These days, I treasured every giggle.

After we showered and Owen took the dogs to his house and fed them, I cooked dinner. Nothing spectacular like Nana's roasts and breads. Spaghetti and sauce was about all my amateur cooking skills could manage.

Cassie set the table. When she was done, she ran upstairs to her room, mentioning she had something to show me.

Owen opened a bottle of wine.

"So," I began while he poured. "When we marry, which house will we live in?"

He handed me a glass and poured one for himself. "Do you have a preference?"

I traced the goblet rim. "You did put a lot of work into this house. I'd hate for it to go to waste and some stranger enjoy it rather than us."

He corked the bottle and swiveled against the counter, resting his hip on the ledge. He crossed his arms. "What about my house? I did grow up there."

"True. Though it is one house closer to the beach."

"Are you suggesting we sell my house?"

"Actually, I'm thinking it would make a great vacation rental."

"And we'd what? Live here?"

"Is that all right?" I set my wine on the counter and twined my arms around his waist. "It feels like home, especially when you're here."

He pressed his lips flat as though considering my request.

"What do you think?" I asked, waiting, breath held.

"I think"—he inhaled deeply—"I like it."

I grinned ear to ear.

He dipped his head, cradled my face, and kissed me. "But if I'm being honest, Molly, home to me is wherever you and Cassie are."

"Then I think it's settled. Welcome home, Owen," I murmured against his lips.

He kissed mine. "Welcome home, Molly."

We toasted with the wine; then Owen retrieved the plates from the cupboard. Cassie returned, carrying a photo album. She invited me to come sit by the fireplace.

"What's this?" I asked, settling into Nana's chair.

"I made it. It's for you."

Intrigued, I flipped through pages of pictures Nana had taken of Cassie and me during her short visits with us over the years. There were also pictures of me with my mom, and Mom with Nana when she was young. Four generations. Cassie had sketched drawings and written short poetic verses throughout the book. Stickers and glitter decorated the pages. "When did you make this?"

"I started before"—Cassie twisted her fingers—"before you died. Nana asked me to make it. She said it was to keep me occupied."

And not worrying about me.

"It took me a long time to finish."

A little over a month, assuming she'd started within a day or so of our arrival. The artistic detail and personal touches aroused the proud mom in me. Cassie definitely had a creative side. I pressed the album to my chest. "It's beautiful. I'll treasure it always." She hugged me around the neck. *You're the best mom in the world.*

She sent the words into my head, and I embraced each one.

We talked regularly in this manner, like Mom and I used to before moving to California. My bond with Cassie deepened with each conversation, and I found it helped me not only to really listen to what she had to say but also to truly understand her.

I kissed her head.

You're the best daughter in the world. I love you, Mermaid.

Acknowledgments

While I write, little bits of my own experiences and interests seem to find their way into a story's plot. I spent the summers of my youth scouring library shelves and typically found myself in a back corner devouring books about unsolved mysteries and unusual and unexplained events. Stories that allegedly were true but left you wondering exactly what was fact and what was just the trick of a camera lens or an embellished tale passed down through generations. Those little oddities found their way into *Everything We Keep* through the character of Lacy, the psychic who propelled Aimee on her journey. In *All the Breaking Waves*, while they take a bigger role in the shape of Molly's and Cassie's extraordinary abilities, they aren't the reason for the story. Molly represents every parent faced with difficult, and sometimes life-threatening, choices about a child's well-being. We all make sacrifices for our children, and that's the inspiration for *All the Breaking Waves*. For all of you parents out there working tirelessly to raise your children to be the best they can be, I admire you.

A big, heartfelt thanks goes out to my family—my husband, Henry; my son, Evan; and my daughter, Brenna—who put up with me when I stare off into space in the name of plotting or lock myself away for countless hours to type. Thanks for your understanding when dinner is delivered or comes from a box (not that I was much of a cook before I started writing with a deadline).

To the good folks of Monterey and Pacific Grove whom I met during my visits: Thank you for helping me understand life along the Peninsula—everything from weather to landmarks to the distinct scents of the bay. (Yes, I know dogs aren't allowed on Lover's Point Park Beach. Please forgive an author's transgression and the unruly behavior of Mudd and Dirt.) To the sea glass artisans at the Cayucos Sea Glass Festival, thanks for sharing your knowledge of the craft and folklore surrounding the origins of sea glass. I have developed a deep fascination with these bits of recycled treasure, thanks to you.

To my first readers: Elizabeth Allen, Vicky Gresham, Phyllis Hall, Orly Konig-Lopez, Kendra Niedziejko, Jamie Raintree, and Tasha Seegmiller. Thank you for your honest feedback. You helped this book find its way to readers and Molly her way home.

Hey, Tikis in the Tiki Lounge! You know who you are. Your enthusiasm, support, and encouragement when I share news about my books always amaze me. How lucky I am to have you by my side.

To my editor, Kelli Martin, who loves my characters as passionately as I do, thank you for guiding me through every round of edits with patience, wit, and keen insight. I am grateful for every day I get to work with you. Thanks also to my developmental editor, Tiffany Yates Martin, whom I have the pleasure of knowing through the Women's Fiction Writers Association. Such a joy to work with you in this capacity, as it has been conducting workshops through the association.

And to my agent, Gordon Warnock, who's always got my back, thank you, thank you, for all that you do!

All the Breaking Waves is being published on the tail of *Everything We Keep*, which launched in July 2016 as a Kindle First selection. Overnight, *Everything We Keep* became a bestselling novel and reviews poured in, some of them brutally honest in a not-so-generous way.

Most, though, were positive, and overwhelmingly so. *Everything We Keep* bridged genres—women's fiction, romance, mystery, and suspense—and there was something about that "secret sauce" that appealed to a wide audience. While the book has deeper themes woven into the plot, I wrote it to entertain. And from what I saw, it did just that: entertained. To all the readers who lost sleep, or were late for work, or forgot to cook dinner for their family because they couldn't put the book down, thank you for reading! I hope you stick with me throughout this journey.

Book Club
Discussion Questions

1. *All the Breaking Waves* starts with Molly contending with the aftermath of her daughter's latest premonition. What sort of tone did this set for the story?

2. Did you suspect Cassie would have a premonition about her mother? How did you think the book's events would unfold?

3. Molly clearly despises her extraordinary abilities. What do you make of her decision to not seek help for Cassie when her daughter's abilities first manifest? What do you make of her decision to not help Cassie when Nana Mary asks that Molly show her daughter what Molly can do? Is her reasoning justified given the circumstances?

4. Molly refers to sea glass as "trash turned into treasure." How can that outlook be applied in Molly's own life?

5. What do you think of Molly's confession about her father's death? Do you think she's to blame, or do you believe her father took matters into his own hands?

6. During her argument with Nana Mary, Molly accuses her grandmother of comparing her to her father. In what ways might her father have influenced her? How else had his treatment of her affected her life choices?

7. Whether it be impatience or miscommunication or simply the inability to "find the right words," parents often assume one thing when children are expressing something else entirely. Should Molly have been more patient and understanding with her daughter? Or is Molly's reaction to Cassie's abilities understandable given Molly's own turmoil and fears?

8. Had Molly's parents not died, how would Molly's life be different? Do you think she and Owen would have ended up together? Would Molly have ever come to appreciate her abilities?

9. When facing death, people choose to handle their impending demise differently. Nana Mary chooses to withhold the knowledge that she has cancer until she can no longer hide it. Do you think Nana Mary doesn't want to burden Molly with the knowledge, as Molly thinks? Or do you think there are other reasons Nana Mary feels unable to discuss her sickness with Molly?

10. Until the end, Molly never considers Cassie's premonition could have been about anything other than her drowning. Were you surprised by the outcome?

11. Owen was unable to save Enrique, the boy he wanted to adopt, but he does resuscitate Molly after she chokes. How do you think this will affect Owen's internal journey? Do you think he'll forgive himself for Enrique's death?

12. Throughout the story, Molly is faced with the decision to either embrace or shun her unique characteristics. How do Nana Mary and Cassie help or hinder Molly's decision making?

13. Many themes are presented in this story: acceptance, death, forgiveness, family, love, motherhood, and sacrifice. Which theme resonates the most with you? Which theme has the greatest impact on the story?

About the Author

Kerry Lonsdale believes life is more exciting with twists and turns, which may be why she enjoys dropping her characters into unexpected scenarios and foreign settings. She graduated from California Polytechnic State University, San Luis Obispo, and is a founder of the Women's Fiction Writers Association, an online community of authors located around the globe. She resides in Northern California with her husband, two children, and an aging golden retriever who's convinced she's still a puppy. Her debut novel, *Everything We Keep*, was published by Lake Union in 2016. Connect with her at www.kerrylonsdale.com.

Photo © 2013 Deene Souza Photography